BEGINNING

THE END

by VJ Dunn

TABLE OF CONTENTS

dedication

THESE things always read like an acceptance speech for an Oscar, don't they? I'll try not to do that but make it short and sweet.

First, and foremost always, thank You, Yeshua, for saving me, for accepting me, for choosing me. Help me to be more like You and a whole lot less like me.

Second, I want to thank my husband, Fred. He's my "soulmate," my one true love. I just wish we could have met sooner so we could have loved each other longer. You'll always be my "love of my life thingy." ;)

Third, I wish to thank my kids, Angelo, Natalie and Ava, for being smart, funny, goofy and for always telling me like it is. The truth hurts sometimes, but you always manage to put a bandage on the boo-boo. Kisses.

prologue

WHEN the end began, no one even noticed. At least, no one knew the end was approaching. Not for sure, anyway. And it was just an ordinary, everyday act that caused the end to begin—one that thousands of people in any given day performed.

In late autumn, Aleixo Comis went into his bank in Patras, Greece and closed his account. It wasn't a huge account, certainly not an amount that should have caused a financial avalanche. But the bank was already in trouble, as was the entire Greek economy. When Aleixo removed his small account from an already extremely troubled financial institution, it was the proverbial back-breaking straw.

Aleixo, of course, had no idea of what his one decision would cause. He only wanted to get his life's savings so that he could buy a sailboat. He and his wife, Zenia, wanted to see the world. The couple had never even been out of the country of Greece, and Aleixo had spent the past six months taking sailing lessons from a friend. They thought the time was now right for their adventure—the kids were grown with families of their own; Aleixo had recently retired from his job as a cabinet maker; Zenia's widowed mother had recently passed and Aleixo's parents had moved in with his sister. The couple was ready to leave; all they needed was the transportation.

The economical demise of the entire world was started over one man's desire for a holiday.

That account closure was the pebble in a pond that eventually caused a tsunami that wiped out first Greece, then Spain, then moved on to France and Italy. The whole of Europe quickly followed suit and soon the rest of the world was drowning under a tidal wave of economic ruin.

The only countries that weathered the storm were those that had always been considered "third world," the places that were already adapted to living in abject poverty. The world economic collapse was barely a hiccup for them.

In just weeks, food prices skyrocketed astronomically. Gasoline was so costly that most people simply abandoned their vehicles and walked wherever they needed to go. In a brief time, things we had always taken for granted—such as electricity and heating fuel for warm homes and hot showers and meat for our meals—became luxuries we could no longer afford.

As the economy continued to decline, the American dollar was literally no longer worth the paper it was printed on. Always proving to be resourceful, people once again took to the old-fashioned barter system and, in a sad testament to our culture, the commodities that were worth the most were cigarettes, booze and drugs. Regardless of the world's economic downfall, people still had addictions. It had just suddenly become even harder to satisfy them.

Those who were dependent and/or addicted could no longer easily acquire their fixes and became violent and almost inhumane in their quest for their drug of choice. The "Zombie Apocalypse" we

Americans had joked about for so long happened, but when it occurred the zombies weren't flesh-eating subhumans. Instead, the zombies were those desperate addicts bent on obtaining their next fix at any cost.

Shortly after the collapse, the U.S. president and all his cabinet mysteriously disappeared. No one could fathom what had happened to the entire leadership team, as most were had become well-respected and trusted.

And so it was a great surprise to those already struggling with surviving the troubled times to find themselves suddenly without a leader. Speculation was that the president and staff had been murdered, or at the very least kidnapped. Others wondered if they had left the country, knowing how bad things were going to get.

Unfortunately, the unpopular former president stepped up to take over once again. He had left his own presidency on a bitter note and had far fewer supporters when he left than when he had started. Americans were dumbfounded as to how the man could just come back and take over, but no one knew just what they could do about it. A political coup wasn't possible or feasible, not with it being so difficult just to find food and survive each day.

No one was safe, at least not those living in cities. Gone were the days when you could hide out in your home behind locked doors for safety. The home was where food and supplies might be, and the first place the zombies were going to look to burglarize, often thoughtlessly murdering innocents in their quest.

After months of this chaotic crime spree, the self-declared president instated martial law, enacting curfews and strict municipal boundaries. Without proper paperwork you couldn't even leave the city where you lived. Officials claimed it was for our safety, but those of us trying to survive in those cities without causing harm to others were the victims; we suffered the most. The criminals—the zombies—just went around the system, as was the usual way.

In a desperate attempt to survive, many people grabbed what they could and took to the woods, farmlands, mountains—anywhere they could to get away from the criminal cesspool the cities had become.

But most were especially anxious to get away from the heavily armed soldiers who were ordered to detain and imprison citizens for the smallest infractions—and they were given orders to terminate at will and without prejudice for more heinous crimes. The justice system had been reduced to a soldier with an automatic weapon who became judge, jury and executioner.

The new military law enforcement group was named the "Neo Geo Task Force," or just "Neos" for short, and had been built mainly from three former Federal agencies—the DEA, Homeland Security and the FBI, although the CIA and others also joined the group. Some former municipal police were also forced into service. The power given to them was unprecedented in the United States and indefensible, especially since the true military had all been disbanded and were actively hunted by the Neos, who claimed the former armed forces were "militants," and therefore, criminals.

The Neos' logo was imprinted on everything from their vehicles to their uniforms. It wasn't long before they required citizens to receive implanted microchips that also bore the logo; it was the only way a person could acquire food and supplies. Christians suspected and feared that this logo was the "mark of the Beast" the Bible spoke of in the Book of Revelation, and most chose to flee the cities to try to survive on their own.

Those believers who weren't able to escape the cities but who still refused to take the chip were sent to FEMA camps—those places that even long before the collapse we'd been warned were put in place for Christians. At the time we'd scoffed and cried paranoia, laughing at the doom sayers' assumptions. But we should have listened to them.

Not just Christians, but also Jews—anyone who didn't fall into the government's way of thinking—were subject to imprisonment and, considering that the government's way of thinking had become the antithesis of traditional Judeo-Christian values and morals, it turns out the doom sayers were right.

Those camps were originally designed to be used for detainment, a place to keep under the thumb those in society who might speak out against the wrong doings of the government. But the camps soon became no better than the Nazi death camps of WWII, and many were martyred there for their beliefs.

Most of mankind was totally unprepared for what happened, and how quickly it came about. But there were plenty of "preppers," those who fell into the doom sayers' category, who had been predicting the world's demise for years and had been making preparations for it. They stocked food, toiletries and ammo, came up with clever ways of storing and gathering water, read up on herbal medicine and edible plants, investigated solar power and wind generators. But those people were few and far between... and unfortunately, they were the only ones who were even close to being prepared for what was to come.

Then there were those we thought were the crazies, the guys who holed up in compounds, stockpiling firearms and ammo and shooting at anyone who approached their heavily fortified gates. They were the people who had instigated the anti-government campaigns, those who first warned us of what was coming, of what our government would turn in to.

For decades, we had laughed at them, calling them conspiracy theorists and militants. We argued that since the beginning of time, men had thought the world was going to end and time and again were proven wrong. What made *this* generation any different?

If only we'd listened, heeded their ramblings about the government, about the coming takeovers and unjust imprisonments... and later, the execution of the innocent. And if we'd paid attention to the doom sayers—mostly Christians who warned of the end times approaching and our need to accept the Savior—well, maybe then more people would have had a better time of it, been better prepared for what was coming.

We ourselves fell into the prepper group. Sort of. Only we were late comers, and we went through a heck of a time trying to meet the needs of our own family, much less all those who would eventually come to us for refuge, for sanctuary, from the chaotic mess the world became.

This is our story of the beginning of the end.

chapter 1

DANG, is he ever handsome.

Maybe not in a conventional way, but certainly in a way that made Nikki's heart beat just a bit faster. The man had all the attributes that she most admired—big strong shoulders, thick muscled arms, and a head of thick strawberry blonde hair, much lighter than her own auburn. His hair color didn't matter, but the fact that it was long, well past those oh-so-broad shoulders, was just the icing on the man's yummy appeal cake... and his Trace Adkins goatee was the cherry on top.

His voice was deep, and a shiver went down her spine at the sound. "Good afternoon. How can I help you?"

Hazel eyes that surprisingly matched her own stared at her from beneath a heavy brow. Her eyes traveled to his mouth, noticing that his lips were plump, the only soft-looking feature on a very masculine face.

Nikki suddenly felt a wave of embarrassment come over her as she felt her face heat and mentally kicked herself for acting like a teenager. She cleared her throat. "Hi. Um, I need, uh, a, uh..."

Oh no, what the Sam Hill is that thing called again? Oh geez—I'm such a dork! Now at least she had a reason for her face to be red.

Mr. Handsome Parts Guy grinned at her, as if he were used to women stumbling around him, stuttering and stammering, completely forgetting what they wanted to say. Well, she certainly wasn't one of *them.* She reminded herself that she was not interested in him—or in any man, ever. Not again. Lesson learned the hard way.

Her mental reminder helped. She cleared her throat again. "Uh, sorry. I need an ignition switch for an oh-five Chevy Suburban."

The man stared at her for a second longer than was necessary, his hazel eyes crinkling at the corners. Her eyes flickered to his beard and mustache, noticing a little gray amongst the dark red strands. She thought he was probably about her age, maybe a little younger.

Not that it matters how old he is… forget it!

His eyes finally shifted to his computer screen, and he punched at the keyboard. She glanced down at the name tag on his red shirt. "Reg" it said, along with "Manager." Well, the fact that he was in charge didn't surprise her at all; the man all but radiated authority. Just his powerful build alone was enough to proclaim that he was the big dog on the porch.

Her eyes moved to his fingers as he continued to enter info on the computer. She smiled slightly as he used just his forefingers to punch the keys. His hands, like the rest of the man, were large. Impressively so. She shuddered then, remembering how male hands that were much smaller had been the cause of so much pain for her in the past.

Stop. Just stop.

Nikki mentally shook herself, needing to get off the slippery slope she was in danger of sliding down. She didn't need to keep reminding herself of the poor choices she'd made in the past. It was over and done with.

He glanced back at her then. "Sorry, hon, we don't have it in stock here, but I can order it from our other store in Abilene and have it here by this afternoon."

The term of endearment caught her off-guard and she had to concentrate on the rest of what he'd said. She screwed her face up when she realized what he told her.

"Oh, shoot. Um, that doesn't really work for me, cuz I live forty miles away. I'd hate to have to make the trek back up here again."

Normally it wouldn't be such a big deal and she could just pick the part up the next day since she worked in San Angelo, but tomorrow was Sunday, which happened to be the only day her brother could work on the Suburban. She really needed to get that part today and wished she could have taken care of it sooner, but she'd had to wait on her paycheck that she didn't get until yesterday and by the time she'd gotten off work last night, the parts store had been closed.

Nikki thought about calling her dad and asking if she could keep his truck just a little longer and then find something to do in the city until the part arrived, maybe even go in to work and finish up a few loose ends. But she knew asking her dad was a lost cause, since she'd had to beg the man to let her use the truck in the first place. He had always been a bit difficult, but even more so in the years since her mom had passed.

She then considered driving to Abilene herself to get the part, but since her dad had written down the odometer reading before she'd borrowed the truck, he would know if she'd gone farther than she had told him she would. And then the stink would hit the fan. Her father certainly wasn't known for his charitable contributions to society and those contributions fell completely by the wayside when it came to his only daughter.

Nikki sighed and fought back tears. Life hadn't been too easy on her lately, not with the latest divorce and then having to quickly find a place to live when her soon-to-be-ex had thrown her out of the house—literally. "It's *my* house," he'd shouted in her face as he'd shoved her out the front door after a heated argument.

They'd bought the three-bedroom house in San Angelo just before they got married and while it was in his name only due to some credit issues she'd had thanks to her *other* divorce, she'd always held a job throughout their marriage and contributed to the bills. Since their money was pooled together, she'd obviously contributed to the house payment.

Nikki had only asked Matt to let her stay in the house until she could find her own place. She told him she wouldn't fight him over the equity in the house, but he didn't want to hear it—he wouldn't hear it. Nikki was frankly shocked at just how selfish the man truly was.

The only place she could find that would accept her pets and didn't cost more than she made was forty miles southeast of San Angelo. A widow owned the tiny ranchette and she wasn't asking very much at all for rent of the place. It was two bedrooms and sat on five acres of dry Texas land. And Mrs. Chalmers didn't mind her dog and cat at all, saying she was just thankful to have someone occupy the property for a change. Even though it was so far from her work in the city, Nikki still felt the little house was a blessing.

Another unexpected blessing came when Nikki had explained her situation to the kindly woman and told her how she didn't have enough money for both the first and last month's rent. Mrs. Chalmers had waived the fees and had even hugged Nikki and told her she'd be praying for her.

With the huge yard that her retriever, Zeke, loved to romp through chasing doves and the old farmhouse with the wrap-around porch complete with rocking chairs, Nikki had thought the place was a true godsend, despite the long commute she now had to work and the extra gas money she hadn't budgeted for. She'd had to reconcile herself to eating beans and rice until she could get some bills paid off.

At least her daughter, Anna, wouldn't visit often—the girl didn't like what she'd termed "ghetto hick living" and wanted to stay with her dad in San Angelo where there were such teenage necessities as Starbucks and shopping malls. At the time Nikki had been hurt by her youngest kid's abandonment, but she'd also realized that it was for the best—she really wouldn't have been able to afford to feed a growing teen on top of everything else. Thankfully, her other children were grown and living their own lives.

Forcing herself back to the issue at hand, Nikki tried a different tactic.

"Do you think any other parts stores would have it?"

He lifted his massive shoulders in a slight shrug.

"I can call around for you if you'd like, but if I remember right there was a recent recall on a Chevy OEM ignition switch on quite a few makes and models, so it's likely they'll be out of stock in most places. In fact, my Abilene store only had two on the shelf."

Nikki sighed, feeling defeated and helpless. She was caught in yet another situation that was out of her control yet affected her in such a profound way. Without a vehicle she wouldn't be able to make it to work come Monday. Being a contracted employee meant no time off, no sick leave, basically no money if she didn't show up. Her bills were paid for the month, but she still had to eat and buy fuel for her gas-guzzling Suburban.

The tears were gathering yet again, and she blinked furiously, desperately trying not to embarrass herself in front of the man. She cleared her throat before speaking.

"No, it's okay, don't bother calling around." She shrugged then.

"I'll see if maybe my brother can pick it up tomorrow on his way to my place. He's the one who's going to install it."

Nikki mentally groaned to herself then, wondering why she was giving the man so much information. He smiled sympathetically.

"Hate to say it, but we're closed on Sundays. Owner is a devout Christian." He grimaced over the last word.

Nikki felt her hackles rise a bit over that and hurried to defend the unknown owner.

"Hey, actually that's a great thing to hear, even if it is inconvenient for me. A Christian-owned business *should* be closed on the Sabbath. It shows a lot of integrity."

He snorted. "It shows a lack of business sense, if you ask me."

Nikki was somewhat relieved to know the man obviously wasn't a Christian, or at least not a practicing one. She thought of the Scripture that spoke of not unequally yoking yourself and reminded herself of the painful price she'd had to pay for ignoring that directive in the past. It was easier to ignore her ridiculous attraction to the man now. At least, that's what she kept telling herself every time her heart sped up just a bit when he looked at her.

She shook her head slightly. "Well, thanks anyway. I'm not sure what I'm going to do now. I guess I'll try begging my dad to let me keep his truck for the rest of the day…" She let her voice trail off, realizing she was once again divulging unnecessary information.

He got a speculative look then and cocked his head to one side.

"Um, where do you live? You said you were forty miles away, but where exactly?"

At her alarmed look, he held up his hands. "Now, don't be gettin' your feathers ruffled. I'm just asking cuz we have a delivery driver, and I could have him run it by to you this afternoon if you're near his route."

Nikki almost sagged in relief. When he'd asked where she lived, it felt like a massive invasion of privacy. Warning bells had even gone off in her head. It sometimes felt like she was in the Witness Protection Program with how secretive she had to be with everything, thanks to her ex and his penchant for causing trouble with her.

She swallowed before answering and knew her face was red, hoping the man didn't notice.

"Oh, um, well I live in Barnhart," she answered as she darted a glance at him.

He grinned at her. "Well, you're in luck. Turns out he's gotta go to Witco, so he can drop it off on his way there."

For the first time, Nikki smiled back. "Oh, that's great! That helps me so much!"

A sudden thought removed the smile from her face. "Uh, is there an extra charge for delivery?" She was going to barely be able to afford the part as it was, not to mention her hopes for possibly eating during the next two weeks until she got paid again.

He smiled sympathetically. Or at least that's what it seemed like to Nikki—but she also knew she tended to be a bit defensive lately, bouncing back and forth from thinking that everyone was either out to hurt her, or else feeling sorry for her. Either scenario didn't sit well with her pride.

"No, darlin', no extra charge. Like I said, it's on the driver's way."

Vastly relieved, Nikki paid for the part and gave the man her exact address, telling herself that it was okay—he *was* the manager of a store, after all. He couldn't be a weirdo who was just after her address, could he?

A Dodge truck pulled up to the ranchette just as Nikki had started boiling water for pasta. She knew it had to be the delivery truck from the parts store—no one else knew where she lived, not even her pastor. The secrecy was necessary for her safety. She just couldn't trust anyone to not tell Matt where she was.

Tossing the package of rotini into the pot, she hurried to the front door and opened it. Shock reverberated through her as she watched the manager of the parts store climb down from the tall truck.

What is HE doing here? Her previous thought of him being a weirdo came rushing back and she suddenly felt very vulnerable and defenseless. Heck, she didn't even own a gun, much less know how to shoot one and her little ranch house was by itself in the middle of five acres, too far away for neighbors to hear anything bad going on.

He waved at her as he sauntered up her walk, stopping to pet Zeke, who was doing an overly enthusiastic tornado spin around the man. The two shared a mutual admiration for a minute, then the man continued walking toward her, holding out a small box.

"I have a special delivery here for a Miss Nicole Jackson."

Shock that he knew her name shot through her before she remembered that she'd given him her name when she'd ordered the part. Nikki took the box and looked at him warily.

"Uh, thanks… but you said you had a delivery driver, so why are you bringing it?" She cringed at her rudeness, but she just couldn't help it. Her defenses were on alert.

He hooked his thumbs in his front jeans pockets and leaned his shoulder against the post on her front porch, grinning in that utterly charming way Texan men seemed to be born with.

"I lied," he admitted matter-of-factly without a trace of remorse, then shrugged.

"Well, we do have a driver, but he wasn't coming anywhere near here. I just thought you needed… you seemed so… well, you just seemed like you needed some help, honey. And I never mind playing the knight in shining armor to the pretty damsel in distress."

He grinned again and Nikki noticed he had twin dimples on each side of his dark reddish gold mustache. The thought that he really was a handsome devil ran through her mind again, but her conscience focused on the word "devil"—reminding her once again that the man seemed to be anti-Christian.

"'Sides," he drawled as he stared at her while absently scratching Zeke's head, who had parked himself on the man's boots, "I live in Witco, so this is on my way home."

The fact that the man was "just down the road a ways," as Texans say, was really disconcerting, not to mention the fact that he now knew where she lived. She once again reminded herself that she knew where he worked and shrugged her fears aside.

"Well, I do appreciate it, uh, Reg." She forced herself to smile at him.

He thrust his hand out and she automatically took it. "Albert Reginald Erskine the fourth. And yeah, just Reg."

Her grin got wider. "That's quite a mouthful. And you already know my name, although I go by Nikki."

Reg held her hand longer than was necessary and Nikki realized with a bit of a shock that she didn't feel intimidated by the man. Normally she would have been, though, just based on his size. He has tall, meeting her eye to eye even though she was standing on her porch step. He was also thick with muscle, but had a little middle-age paunch that she thought actually made him even more attractive. It somehow softened a body that would otherwise be overly intimidating.

The man no longer threatened her—on the contrary, she suddenly felt like being wrapped up in those big ol' arms. She cleared her throat against the confusing emotions roaring through her.

"Um, I was just starting dinner. You're, uh, welcome to stay if you'd like. Just spaghetti and salad. Uh, rotini and salad." *Ugh, you're rambling again, dork.*

His grin was back. "I'd love that, darlin'. I live by myself and don't cook, so dinner usually consists of whatever heat 'n eat I can find in the freezer, or whichever fast-food joint I stopped at on the way home."

Nikki turned and led the way into the house, trying to ignore the way her heart skipped a bit at his obviously deliberate inference that he was single.

Nicole Jeannette Jackson and Albert Reginald Erskine IV were married one month later by a woman judge in the county courthouse.

Nikki had fallen in love with the man that very first night when they'd had dinner—and Reg ended up staying almost the whole night. Not because things had gotten intimate, but because they talked. And talked. And talked some more. They just couldn't seem to get enough of each other, finding out each other's likes, dislikes, pasts, hopes for the future.

She'd told him about her previous marriages—and he wasn't even frightened off by how many there were. When she'd told him that she'd left each marriage knowing it had been wrong to divorce but just couldn't stay because the marriages were so bad, Reg had responded with "sometimes things just happen when we make the wrong decision, then make another wrong decision cuz it looked right at the time, and we were hoping to fix the first wrong decision. Then life just has a way of snowballing out of control."

Reg had also helped her feel even better about her past when he'd told her that she'd probably jumped from marriage to marriage because she was unconsciously hoping to somehow fix her parent's disaster of a marriage and her own difficult upbringing and probably even subconsciously was trying to find the love her parents hadn't given to her.

He'd proposed to her that first night, although in a joking way, when she'd promised to make him chicken fried steak and mashed potatoes the following evening, after she'd gone to church, and her brother had fixed the Suburban. After he jokingly proposed, Reg told her to call her brother and cancel, that he himself would put the part in for her while she made dinner. He'd even offered to take her to church the next morning, which she'd taken him up on, since it was a pretty far walk from her house.

"Just don't blame me if the roof caves in when I walk through the door," he'd teased.

Reg proposed in earnest a week later after they'd spent every single evening together. She'd laughed and told him "No." She tried to explain that there was just no way she could or would consider getting married again. She had too many failed relationships to even think about trying again. Her denial didn't stop him though and he persisted in trying to get Nikki to change her mind.

He'd also tried to get intimate with her, but she'd explained that she just couldn't "go there," not morally anyway. It was bad enough that she was a several-times-divorced woman; she didn't need to add adultery to her "record."

Nikki was honest with herself and admitted that it sure wasn't easy denying him sex. She wanted it too. She prayed to the Lord every night to help keep her strong, but she could feel herself losing the battle.

One night she was crying to Jesus about how hard it was to stay celibate at her age and with her past experiences. She admitted she didn't want to get married to a man who wasn't a Christian, but that Reg sure was an easy man to love.

"I don't know what to do, Lord," she'd cried.

The Lord had answered—audibly. Well, in her head, anyway.

"Marry him."

It wasn't often that He actually spoke to her—most often, she'd get her answers to prayer from Scripture, or from conversations with friends or even from messages on billboards along the highway. So, when she heard a voice in her head telling her to marry a man she would certainly be unequally yoked with, Nikki naturally assumed it was the enemy trying to lead her astray.

"Lord, I want to marry Reg. You know my heart and know that I do. But he's not a Christian and Your Word is clear that we're not to unequally yoke ourselves. I'm confused. Is that really Your voice I'm hearing, or the enemy's... or even my own wishful thinking?"

"Marry him."

"But he's not a Christian..."

"Trust Me."

So, Nikki finally broke down and married Reg, but she refused to have a church service, just in case she was wrong, and it wasn't the Lord who had told her to marry the man. She'd stupidly told herself that if she were making another mistake, it wouldn't be as bad if she didn't marry before God. But then she noticed the marriage license wording as she signed it—at the top in bold fanciful letters were the words "IN HOLY MATRIMONY," and she had halfheartedly laughed to Reg that she "was doomed."

Reg continued to go to church with her every Sunday and even accompanied her to Wednesday night Bible study when he could get away from the shop early enough. He seemed very interested in what the pastor had to say and when Nikki received a rebate check in the mail, she used the unexpected money to buy him a study Bible, which he read often.

Five months and three days after they were married, Reg shocked her by walking down the aisle during invitation and giving his heart to Jesus. As tears streamed down her face, Nikki was reminded of the Lord's words months before… *"Trust Me."*

She sure was glad she had.

Six months after they were married, Nikki found out exactly what kind of man she married. She was frankly a bit shocked.

One night the couple sat on the front porch and discussed life. In getting deeper into their respective pasts, Nikki discovered that Reg, who she thought was a San Angelo parts store manager, was actually a rancher. Or had been, in a former life. He knew everything and anything there was to know about livestock, farming, repairing tractors, et cetera. Before he'd moved to San Angelo, he'd had a several hundred-acre ranch in Colorado. After a mild stroke, he'd left everything behind—including a very bitter and angry soon-to-be-ex-wife and two nearly adult kids—and moved to Texas to start over.

The man also had a great interest in alternative energy—

everything from wind turbines to solar collectors. He'd studied and designed amazing systems for first collecting water and then heating it. He knew how and when to plant everything from sorghum to corn. He could take a John Deere apart and have it running as good as new in a few days. Reg even knew all about alternative fuels and how they were processed.

Until he'd left his wife and home, his cattle ranch had turned a profit every year. Reg knew how to pull a breech calf and then castrate and brand the same calf a few weeks later. He could vaccinate livestock, pregnancy test cows, and could even tell by an animal's eyes what minerals it was lacking. He knew how to shear sheep and shoe horses. The man could run a quarter mile of barb wire fence in a morning, then turn around and cut a field of alfalfa that afternoon.

In Nikki's eyes, her husband was nothing but amazing.

While she herself had no special skills or training, she and Reg both admitted that it felt like they'd been born "out of time." Nikki had always been interested in homesteading skills—everything from bread making to vegetable canning. She had even researched how to make soap, going so far as to find out just how lye was processed. A folder sat on her desk with printouts for using herbs for medicinal purposes, how to gather yeast for bread making, what wild plants were edible, how to smoke meats, and even how to make cheese.

She shared her interests with Reg that night and they both were a little stunned to find that they had in fact married a kindred spirit, both who were interested in surviving "off the grid." That realization just added to their growing marital bliss.

A few nights later, again after dinner, Nikki had tentatively broached a subject she'd been thinking a lot about: End time prepping. While they were curled up on the sofa together, she read Scripture from the Book of Revelation, emphasizing the parts that spoke of just how difficult things would be "in the end."

"Revelation chapter six, 'Two pounds of wheat for a days' wages, and six pounds of barley for a day's wages...' And here: 'They were given power over a fourth of the earth to kill by sword, famine and plague, and by the wild Beasts of the earth.' And also here: 'There was a great earthquake. The sun turned black like sackcloth made of goat hair, the whole moon turned blood red, and the stars in the sky fell to earth, as figs drop from a fig tree when shaken by a strong wind. The heavens receded like a scroll being rolled up, and every mountain and island was removed from its place.' It goes on to talk about how everyone, whether rich or poor, powerful or weak, will try to hide from God."

She sighed and closed her Bible and hugged it to her chest. "I always hoped we'd be spared from those hardships. All my life I was taught about The Rapture, but I discovered recently that what I always believed may not be exactly accurate."

"What's 'The Rapture'?"

Nikki smiled. Sometimes she forgot that Reg was still new to Christianity and its teachings, although he never failed to read his

Bible every chance he got, even at work during slow times.

"It's what most evangelical people believe—uh, evangelical are the Christians who are considered 'born again', like us. Anyway, it's the belief that Christians are going to be taken away—caught up in the air—by Jesus before the end times start."

Reg looked skeptical. "So, we're supposed to be spared from the end stuff, all that stuff you just read about, the famines, diseases and things?"

Nikki nodded. "Yeah, so they teach. But I started having a lot of doubts about that recently—"

"Why?"

She frowned. "Why what?"

Reg cocked his head to the side. "Why were you having doubts?"

She sighed. "Well, for one thing, I've been having a lot of dreams about preparing—storing food and getting things ready for housing strangers. Like I was going to be helping a lot of people survive the end or something. It didn't make sense according to what I'd always been taught, so I started researching The Rapture. I was shocked to find out that it's a fairly new teaching, recognized just a few hundred years ago. It's not something that's been around since Jesus' time, anyway."

He took a drink of his iced tea. "Then where did the idea come from?"

Nikki shrugged and took a drink from her glass as well before answering. "Well, there are some verses in the Bible that describe a changing or taking away."

She picked up her Bible again. "Here, I have them all marked."

Thumbing through her sticky notes, she continued. "First Thessalonians, chapter four, 'For the Lord Himself will come down from heaven, with a loud command, with the voice of the archangel and with the trumpet call of God, and the dead in Christ will rise first. After that, we who are still alive and are left will be caught up together with them in the clouds to meet the Lord in the air'."

She took another drink of her soda before continuing, flipping back in her Bible. "There are other verses that talk about the trumpet sounding, too. From First Corinthians chapter fifteen, 'We will not all sleep, but we will all be changed—in a flash, in the twinkling of an eye, at the last trumpet. For the trumpet will sound, the dead will be raised imperishable, and we will be changed'."

"Okay, so those verses aren't exactly saying 'God's going to quietly bail you out before things get scary, so don't worry, be happy'."

Nikki laughed. "Yeah, I know."

She tapped her Bible. "And these verses talk about the *last trumpet*. What I'm thinking is that, yes, The Rapture will happen because Scripture speaks of it, but it's not before the Tribulation, but just before Judgment Day. I always hoped for a pre-Trib Rapture, but it doesn't seem like that's the way it's going to go. And even if I'm wrong and it *does* occur pre-Trib, how bad are things going to get here on earth before we're raptured? That's really something to think about."

Reg nodded his head in agreement and Nikki stared at the coffee table. "I'm just starting to doubt that we'll be out of here beforehand. The Bible even talks about the last days being shortened for the sake of the elect—believers—or else we wouldn't survive it. So, how are 'the elect' still here if we're supposedly raptured?"

She shook her head at her own question. "I honestly think that we might very well be here for the end times."

Reg was quiet for a minute, then he cleared his throat before speaking. "I had wanted to tell you about a dream I had a few nights ago, but I figured you'd think I had blown a head gasket."

She chuckled over his expression. "Nah, wait 'til I tell you some of mine. Go ahead—you first."

He got a faraway look as he stared past her. "Well, I thought it was really weird, so I just kinda forgot about it, but now that you're talking about end times and stuff, maybe it's not so weird after all. I dreamed that we were living on a farm, or a ranch; somewhere it was really green. There was a lot of acreage, and I was working in a field. I think I was plowing, or planting, I'm not sure which. Anyway, I looked up and saw all these little kids walking toward me—young kids, the oldest being maybe ten or so. They ran up and started speaking in Spanish. I'm guessing they were all Mexican. For some reason I could understand them, even though I can barely order a taco plate without messing it up."

Nikki laughed. "Mexican kids, huh? Well, back before I walked away from God, I had felt kind of led to start an orphanage in Central or South America. Maybe your dream was confirmation from the Lord about that."

"No. Like I said, I could understand them, and they told me that they had crossed over the border and needed help, that their parents had all been killed. There were like twenty kids. You would think I would have been shocked or something over that, but in my dream it was like a normal occurrence or something. Anyway, all of a sudden you and some other women were there and took the kids to this big white house. And then I noticed there were kids all over the place— Mexican, White, Black, Natives. Some were running around playing and laughing and others were doing chores, like weeding a garden. But there were lots of adults too, more women than men."

He rubbed his forehead, trying to remember everything. "The dream was just so real, so detailed. It was like I was *there*, you know? Most dreams when you wake up you know you were dreaming, but this was more like... like..."

"A vision?"

Reg looked up at her, a surprised look on his face. He reluctantly nodded. "Yeah. A vision."

He seemed hesitant to admit to that, so Nikki hurried to reassure him. "The Lord often speaks to us in dreams, you know. Maybe He's trying to tell us something here."

Reg shrugged and took a drink of his iced tea. "Maybe. I'm just not sure what it is."

Nikki was quiet for a moment. "I think He's telling us to prepare."

He looked back at her. "Prepare? Like for the end times?"

He sounded so incredulous, Nikki laughed. "Yeah, exactly. He told us in His Word how hard things were going to get. He also told us that in those times young men would have visions and old men would dream dreams."

Reg snorted. "And which category do I fit in—young or old?"

Nikki grinned teasingly at him. "Both—you had a dream that was a vision."

He snorted and shook his head, obviously doubting what she was telling him, and Nikki hurried to reassure him before his doubts took root.

"Don't shake your head. The Lord's Word is truth, honey. He gave us lots of warnings of what's to come."

Reg frowned as he stared out the window past the front yard fence. "Oh, I don't doubt His Word. What I doubt is Him using someone like *me* to tell His secrets to. I mean, why didn't He tell you? You're way better than me."

He looked back at her then, eyebrows raised in question and Nikki rolled her eyes in response to his comment.

"Oh yeah, I'm *sooo* good," she replied, her voice dripping with sarcasm. "I was married *five times* before you, had a kid out of wedlock, used to party like there was no tomorrow. And this was all *after* I'd gotten saved at twelve!" She shook her head, as if in disbelief at her own actions.

Her voice softened as she continued. "But none of that matters to the Lord, not when we ask Him to forgive us. He can use whomever, whenever, for whatever. Look at all the examples we have in the Bible of the people we would have said weren't 'good enough' to serve Him, yet they were the ones HE chose. There were liars and cheats, adulterers, murderers, even a whore or two."

She smiled softly at her husband. "He knows we're not perfect and are never going to be, honey, but He just needs us to be willing to be used by Him."

Reg was quiet, mulling everything over. They both sat in silence for a long time and then he finally spoke. "Well, it's pretty danged humbling to think the Creator of the whole universe is speaking right to me, a nobody with a shady past and nothing to offer Him."

Nikki reached over and laid her hand on his arm. "I agree it's very humbling when He talks to us. But you, Albert Reginald Erskine the fourth, have a whole heck of a lot to offer Him… your heart. That's all He's ever wanted, all He ever asked for."

She lightly slapped his arm where she had laid her hand and sat back. "So, quit thinking you have to be worthy, or good enough, or whatever. God doesn't tell us to clean ourselves up to come to Him—*He* does the cleaning. We just have to be willing to let Him."

Reg nodded, but Nikki could tell he was going to take a lot more convincing. She decided to take her own advice and pray, asking the

Lord to do the convincing.

chapter 2

NIKKI? Hey, it's Don from the store. Uh, Reg hurt himself and I think you need to come get him."

"What? What did he do?"

Nikki fought back the panic rising up. If Don was calling her instead of Reg, then it must be really bad. She cradled her cell against her ear with her shoulder as she grabbed her purse and started walking to her boss's office to tell her she'd be leaving.

"Well, he slipped on some oil on the floor and slid into the counter. His knee is already swelling pretty bad, but the stubborn jerk won't let me take him to the hospital. I figured if anyone can get him to go, you can."

He laughed a little. "Just don't tell him I called you, okay?"

Nikki breathed a sigh of relief. While she still upset her husband had gotten hurt, a knee injury was certainly better than the coma she was envisioning just moments ago.

"I won't tell him," she reassured the man. "I'll make it seem like I was just stopping by to take him to an early lunch. Thanks for calling me, Don. I really appreciate it."

The auto parts store was clear across town from where Nikki worked as a bookkeeper for a CPA firm, but thankfully traffic was light, and it only took her fifteen minutes to get to her injured husband.

Once she was finally able to bully Reg enough to get him out of the store, she drove to the hospital and made him stay in the car while she got a nurse to bring a wheelchair out to him, with Reg grumbling the entire time that he "wasn't no invalid."

As the nurse pushed the wheelchair, Nikki walked alongside and informed her that Reg had had a prior injury to the same knee and had a knee replacement years earlier. She also told the nurse that he had high blood pressure. The nurse asked a few questions while she wheeled him into the ER and Nikki answered them as best she could.

"Uh, hey, ladies? I hurt my knee, not my head. I can hear you *and* answer the questions myself."

Nikki patted him. "Not on my watch. I know you, you stubborn ol' fart—you won't tell them everything they need to know."

The nurse laughed and said, "If I had a dollar for every time a wife had said the same thing…"

Reg was going to need a new knee replacement. That's what the orthopedic surgeon told him, but he'd also said they would have to wait six weeks for the swelling to go down before doing the surgery.

Reg dreaded going under the knife again, having had so many surgeries in the past after incurring injuries on his ranch and in a bad car accident. Another surgery was the last thing he wanted to endure.

Nikki was in agreement, having come to the conclusion that doctors were "cut happy" after her mother had three surgeries all while dying of emphysema. She'd asked one of the doctors at the time why in the world they'd operate on someone who only had a few months at most to live, and the man had tried to argue that it was for her "quality of life." Nikki told the man she didn't see how a colonoscopy and subsequent colorectal surgery to remove a tumor was going to improve her "quality of life" when the woman was lying flat on her back in a hospital bed with a breathing tube. But her dad had agreed to the procedure and surgery, along with the two bowel resections that followed when the first surgery caused her bowel to infarct.

The whole experience had left her with a very sour taste in her mouth for the medical profession and she was adamant that Reg try natural medicine—in particular, acupuncture.

He wasn't happy, and in fact was quite belligerent about the whole thing. He'd all but growled at her when she suggested it.

"I don't see how sticking needles in my body is going to help. It's all voodoo hocus-pocus, if you ask me," he had snarled at her. Her once gentle and loving teddy bear had turned into a grizzly.

Nikki had sighed at his attitude toward something he'd never even tried. Caring for the man wasn't an easy task, as Reg was in a lot of pain and certainly wasn't the best patient with his stubborn nature and persistent quick denial that anything was wrong. Nikki tried to be understanding but living with a grizzly bear twenty-four seven was starting to take its toll. Still, she was thankful that her boss let her work from home so she could care for her husband.

She tried to reason with him. "Well, it won't hurt to try. If it gives you any relief from the pain, it'll be worth it, won't it?"

She paused in her argument and smirked with a challenge in her voice. "Oh, unless you're afraid of needles."

Apparently teasing him wasn't the best thing she could have done, but he finally agreed when she informed him that they couldn't afford to pay for a knee replacement, not with the fairly worthless insurance they had. Nikki made an acupuncture appointment for him the next day.

Thankfully, Reg liked the acupuncturist and didn't give the woman a hard time, although he did continuously express his beliefs about it being a bunch of bunk. The doctor had just smiled at his comments while she continued to stick needles in his body. Nikki had joked that his prickly looking body now matched his personality.

After scheduling Reg for twice weekly appointments, Dr. Ally warned him that he would get worse before getting better, but not to give up on the treatments as she was sure acupuncture would help him.

In the meantime, Helena, the owner of the parts store and Reg's boss, called the house phone to tell Reg that he "*had* to get back to work." Being the gentleman and genuinely nice guy that he was, Reg had always let the woman bully him and Nikki was thankful she was the one to answer the phone this time.

After listening to Helena's tirade for a few minutes, Nikki tried to remind herself that the woman claimed to be a Christian. It sure was difficult to believe, judging from her attitude. Everything seemed to boil down to the almighty dollar with her.

She tried to modulate her voice into one of patient kindness. "No, Helena, he can't go back to work yet. His knee is still swollen to almost three times the normal size. The ortho doctor's orders said he had to stay off of it for six weeks. I dropped the paperwork off at the store; Don should have given it to you."

When she answered, the woman's voice dripped in disdain and Nikki felt her hackles rise. "Yes, I read that, *dear*, but I have a stool here he can sit on, so he'll still be staying off the knee, per *doctor's orders*. I need him here to run things."

"Well, that's not going to happen. *Per doctor's orders.*"

Helena sighed condescendingly, like she was talking to a small child. "Like I *said*, he can sit on a stool all day, so he *will* be staying off of the leg," she huffed into the phone. "I really don't see what the problem is."

Nikki had to close her eyes and say a quick prayer to keep her temper in check. "Sitting on a stool is not staying off the leg. He has to keep it elevated."

Helena's voice rose in pitch. "Then we can bring a box out for him to prop his leg on. See? Problems all solved."

When Nikki stayed silent, Helena changed tactics and growled, "Just let me talk to Reg."

That did it; Nikki had just reached the end of her patience with the woman.

"There isn't anything you can say to him that's going to change a darned thing, Helena. *I'm* his transportation right now, and I say *he isn't going into work!"* It was with no small amount of satisfaction that she slammed the phone down.

Nikki almost regretted—almost—losing her temper with the woman. It certainly wasn't very Christian-like. But then she reasoned that maybe even God thought Helena had it coming.

Reg was a little upset by what he heard from his position on the couch, but Nikki wouldn't let him dwell on it. "I'm calling Worker's Comp tomorrow to see what we need to do to file paperwork. That witch owes you and she's going to pay you!"

Getting paid for the work injury turned into a big battle that Nikki was sure was won only through the Lord's intervention. Helena had denied the claim, stating that Reg himself was negligent in not cleaning the oil spill in the first place. The hearing officer seemed to agree and for all intents and purposes, it seemed they were going to lose the claim. But Nikki had prayed through the whole hearing and knew that no matter what, God was in charge. The officer had surprisingly found in their favor.

Shortly after the hearing, a letter of termination came in the mail. Reg had wanted to hire a lawyer to fight it, but Nikki reminded him that he didn't need to be working for such a mean-spirited woman anyway and that he could do so much better.

"The Lord will take care of us, just have some faith," she'd urged him.

But it was hard for a man like Reg—one who'd had to scrape and scrap for every single penny he'd ever earned—to accept anyone's help, even the Lord's.

What changed his mind about trusting the Lord, though, was the healing he received. Every day, several times a day, Nikki would gently place her hands on his knee and pray for a miraculous healing, asking that the acupuncture take effect and that surgery wouldn't be needed. After a few days, Reg had hesitantly placed his hand over hers and they prayed together.

Just two weeks after starting acupuncture treatments, the swelling had gone down and the pain in his knee was much more bearable. He still stayed off the knee as much as possible, but he was sleeping through the night and could even negotiate the porch steps by himself. Reg was amazed and again humbled that the Lord had chosen to heal him as He did.

A few months later, Reg was completely healed and wasn't sure what to do for work. He mentioned talking to Helena about getting his job back, but Nikki had hit the ceiling.

"Over my dead and rotting stinking corpse are you going back to work for that she-devil!"

"But we need the money—"

"I don't care if we have to eat beans and rice for the next five years and live in a cardboard box under a bridge—you can*not* go back to work for her! All she cares about is the almighty dollar. You know that."

Reg had relented to appease his wife, knowing she only had his best interests in mind. Besides, he really didn't want to go back to work for Helena anyway. Despite claiming to be a Christian, she truly was mean-spirited and had always seemed bent on working Reg to death, taking advantage of his salary status by forcing him to work lots of "free" overtime hours.

But he had his truck payment and insurance, plus rent and utilities to think about. Not to mention groceries and fuel for their gas-guzzling trucks, which was a huge expense. They talked about getting smaller economy cars, but where they lived the only thing that would get them home when a Texas downpour turned the dusty dirt road into a red clay Slip-N-Slide was a heavy four-wheel drive. Of course, with Reg not working, at least they only needed to buy fuel for one vehicle, since Nikki's boss had insisted she wanted her back in the office.

The worker's comp payments were soon coming to an end, and they were still waiting for Reg's unemployment to be approved, which of course was being fought tooth and nail by Helena. Nikki's job alone just wasn't enough to pay their bills since she'd barely scraped by with her own bills before they'd gotten married.

Reg was starting to feel like a hindrance, not a help. He knew the situation was making him grumpy and needed to be remedied as soon as possible. The last thing he wanted to do was make his already overworked wife unhappy by forcing her to live with a grouchy old man. The woman seemed to take everything in stride, though, and reminded him often that they just had to trust God to handle whatever came their way.

Her trusting attitude lasted until the third day after the worker's comp ended. Nikki had come home in tears, sobbing to Reg that her boss had informed her that, thanks to the dismal economy, the firm could no longer afford bookkeepers and were being forced to let them all go. Since the bookkeepers were independent contractor employees, they couldn't even apply for unemployment insurance.

It was Reg's turn to be positive and encouraging, reminding his wife that they had to trust the Lord to provide, that He'd proven faithful already and His Word promised He'd take care of their needs. As the words were coming out of his mouth, Reg was trying to listen to his own advice. Panicking now would solve nothing. But it sure was hard.

The couple had a lesson in faith and trust a few days later when a check unexpectedly came in the mail from a "class action lawsuit" that Reg didn't even know he'd been a party to. It was for the exact amount they needed to make his truck payment and pay the insurance.

Then when Nikki went online to cancel an automatic payment coming out of their bank account, she was shocked to see the account balance was more than double what she thought—and knew—it should be. Reg had laughed at that, teasing her that it was a good thing she'd made a mistake to their good.

"But I didn't make a mistake! I'm a bookkeeper, for Pete's sake," she'd huffed. "I've always been precisely accurate! There's *no way* I made a mistake that big! And I've checked and rechecked my numbers. The numbers add up, but the balance is still off. I'm calling the bank, because as soon as we try to spend that money, they're going to yank it right back out again."

After arguing with an account manager for at least twenty minutes, Nikki finally gave up and admitted the balance in their account was accurate—at least, that's what she told the manager. What she told Reg was another story.

She couldn't stop the tears from flowing. "It's the Lord, Reg, it has to be. There's just no other explanation. I know for a fact we should have exactly eighty-four dollars and thirteen cents in the bank, but no matter how far I go back in the account, it's accurate until the day I got laid off. That's when the extra hundred dollars appeared."

Reg had hugged his wife and they both had a good humbling cry over their Father's provision.

Things had gotten tight, to be sure, but the couple was happy. Reg took the odd auto repair job here and there and Nikki did taxes for friends and family. The money always seemed to be just enough to get by.

They were learning to live simply, getting rid of non-necessities like satellite television and cell phones. Thankfully, the landlady had insisted on keeping a landline in her ranch house and paid the bill herself. At least they had some form of communication, other than email.

Nikki and Reg stopped going out to eat and cooked at home. When things got really tight, they made the decision to sell the Suburban and used the money to pay off the truck loan, with a little left over for groceries and pet food.

"At least we won't have to eat the dog," Reg had joked. "I'm pretty sure Retriever is gamey."

As soon as they would get used to living without something that others would say was a necessity—like the extra vehicle—then the belt would tighten further, and they'd have to give up yet another luxury. First to go was propane; there just wasn't enough money to buy more when they ran out. Since they had a gas stove and oven, Nikki improvised by cooking with the electric toaster oven and a turkey roaster. She heated water for washing dishes by using the coffee maker, and the couple learned to take very quick cold showers.

"There's no way I'm shaving in arctic ice water," she'd informed Reg. "So, you better get used to having your woman *au naturel.*"

"No problem," he'd quipped back. "We can just braid your leg hair. That way it would look like those fancy French stockings."

But then the electricity was cut off when they couldn't pay the past due bill. That seemed to be the final straw that might just do Reg in, but Nikki insisted on making an event out of it, saying that doing all the cooking with the barbecue grill or over a small fire in the backyard seemed just like camping and that she was learning a lot about how to "rough it."

She wouldn't let Reg wallow in self-pity for long, insisting he help her count the stars at night while lying on sleeping bags in the yard while trying to catch a cooling breeze. They would argue over whether a particular star was a satellite or an airplane, then would contemplate which constellation was which and made a game out of making up ridiculous names for those they didn't know until their sides ached from laughter. Then they would hold hands and stare at the Lord's amazing creation until they both fell asleep under the stars.

Life had gotten difficult, but not impossible. They still had food—oftentimes thanks to the church's food pantry when the side jobs were slow to come in—and they had each other.

Little miracles kept coming their way in the form of unexpected blessings. A friend of Reg's had given his dogs away when he found out he was being transferred to Hawaii for his job and had given them over a hundred pounds of quality dog food, which the cat surprisingly also had a liking for.

Then at the store, Nikki ran into one of the secretaries she had worked with before being laid off. Rosemarie told Nikki that her brother had a company and needed a temporary bookkeeper to get his tax information organized. On her second day at the company, the boss's car had broken down and Nikki recommended Reg as a mechanic. The pay from those jobs filled the pantry and paid what they owed to the electric company. But they stashed the rest for the future, deciding not to squander the extra money on propane or getting the power turned back on.

But the biggest blessing of all was the time they were spending with the Lord. They were praying more, studying Scripture more, and both felt closer to Him than they ever had.

The couple joked that they were learning to live without, so they'd be one step in front of the rest of the world when the end times happened. Little did they know, that was exactly what was happening.

chapter 3

D ID YOU put the ad in for the bedroom suite yet?"

Nikki glanced up from her laptop screen. They were sitting at a McDonald's in San Angelo, sipping small sodas and using the free wifi. Reg was looking for a job and she was on Craigslist. Whatever possessions weren't necessities, they were selling. The belt had just tightened another notch.

"No, I'm looking to see what similar sets are going for. I have no idea what to ask."

"How 'bout ten thousand?" Reg asked with a grin.

Nikki smiled back. "Yeah, maybe if the nightstands were gold plated."

She went back to her perusing, scrolling through the screens absently while she contemplated the past four months since Reg had gotten hurt. It was funny—even though they were now reduced to selling off their worldly possessions, she wasn't upset. She wasn't even angry or bitter. It almost felt good to do so, like they were freeing themselves of unnecessary burdens.

Nikki wasn't finding any bedroom suites similar to the solid pine set Reg had brought into the marriage. It was a great set—the headboard and footboard were made from huge, curved logs, unpainted and unfinished, with a definite rustic look. With matching nightstands, a dresser and even a bench, it was sure to sell. Nikki just had no idea how much to ask.

An employment ad suddenly caught her eye. It was out of place in the furniture section, obviously mis-categorized. Thinking to be nice and contact the ad's owner to alert them to the mistake, she clicked on the notice.

Ranch manager and wife needed. Middle aged preferred. Small ranch operation on the Mexican border. Email for more info.

That was it. "Well, that was simple and to the point," Nikki muttered under her breath as she clicked on the "email" link.

"What?" Reg glanced at her over his laptop screen. He was busy scrolling through the job listings on the Texas Workforce Commission's site.

"This ad… it's in the furniture section, but it's for a job. I only opened it cuz I was going to let them know they messed it up. But hey, you wanna be a ranch manager?" She asked with a tease in her voice.

Reg snorted, then took a sip of his soda and asked her to read the ad to him, which she did. He then shrugged.

"Send them an email; see what they say. Just make sure you tell them I've had over twenty years ranching experience."

"Okay." She typed a quick note, not really expecting anything to come from it, and went back to perusing furniture ads.

Within five minutes, the email notifier popped up stating she had a new email from "pickensranch" and assuming it was an autoreply, she ignored it. However, a second email came in right after it from the same sender, so she opened her email to look at them.

The first email was an autoresponder message, but the second was from a real person. *Hi Nicole! Thanks for your reply to our ad. It sounds like you and your husband are very qualified for our manager position! I'd like to speak with you as soon as possible. Please call…*

She was a little excited by the quick response but tried not to get her hopes up too high. She and Reg had both applied to over fifty jobs each, with no hope in sight of ever getting one. Even though they both had lots of experience, most companies either wanted college degrees or seemed to be looking for someone much younger. This was the first job they'd tried to get that had actually *specified* they were looking for someone their age.

She looked at her husband. "Hey hon, the people from that ranch ad already replied! They want us to call them as soon as possible."

Reg glanced up from his screen with a slightly startled look. "Huh. That was fast. Well, guess we'll have to give them a call when we get home. Tell them we'll call in about an hour."

When they got home, Nikki checked the chicken legs she'd put in the crockpot, then started some rice to boil. They were both getting real tired of chicken, but since it was the cheapest meat, it was what they mostly ate. Nikki was also tired of trying to come up with different ways to cook the bird and she had just about reached the bottom of her creativity pool. Tonight, it was chipotle chicken legs with beans, rice and homemade tortillas.

She then got the phone from the living room and told Reg she figured he should be the one to call, since he was the one with ranching experience and could answer ranch-related questions.

Nikki sat on the couch next to her husband and anxiously listened to Reg's end of the conversation, jumping up once to turn the rice down to simmer.

After he got off, he filled her in, and Nikki couldn't help but smile at the enthusiasm and hope in his voice. It was nice to finally hear that coming from him, since he'd been so discouraged about not getting a job.

"Well, it was a full working ranch at one time, but now it's just a really small operation, only kept alive because the owner doesn't want to let it go. Seems it's been in his family for generations, but his kids don't want the place and he and his wife are now in a nursing home. They want a couple to live on the property and keep the place up, take care of the animals and such."

It sounded so promising and right up their alley, that Nikki felt some hope too. "So, who's running the place now?"

Reg shook his head in disbelief. "They actually have the sheriff going out there every other day or so to feed and check on things."

She laughed. "Small town, huh? Sheriff Andy and Deputy Barney?"

Reg chuckled. "Yeah, sounds like. No town there, though, from what Gina said. It's about two hundred miles due south of here."

"And who is Gina?"

"She's the lady who oversees things for the owner, Mr. Pickens. She's sort of a secretary, I guess, since he and his wife moved off the ranch. Gina said Mr. Pickens still has it together mentally, but Mrs. Pickens has Old Timer's, and that's why they moved all the way to Lubbock. Guess they got an assisted living place up there that specializes in it."

"It's Alzheimer's, honey, not Old Timer's," Nikki corrected with a smile.

His dimples showed when he grinned back at her. "Well, Old Timer's fits better, don't you think?"

Nikki laughed and nodded. "Yeah, I guess it does at that. So, what kind of animals do they have on the ranch?"

"Sheep, goats, a few head of cattle, a handful of horses and donkeys. They have a lot of acreage to farm, but obviously haven't had anyone to work the place. Anyway, Gina wants us to meet her down at the ranch tomorrow around noon."

"Oh! Okay, well that was quick. Guess they're desperate."

Reg grinned at her again. "Yeah, she said we were the only ones who replied to the ad. I didn't offer the fact that they put it in the wrong section."

Pickens Ranch was owned by James Pickens, aka "Tiny." The Pickens family had owned the twelve-hundred-acre ranch since the early nineteenth century, passing it down from son to son each generation.

Tiny Pickens and April, his wife of fifty-seven years, had two daughters and one son who wanted nothing to do with the ranch, having gone to college and then scattering across the U.S. with busy lives of their own. Still, Tiny didn't want to sell the ranch, hoping that someday one of his grandchildren might want to take over and run the place.

Despite the distance, Tiny still tried to keep his hand on the ranch and called often with ideas, suggestions, or just to share a memory or two. When he and April moved to Lubbock just six months before, they had let the hundreds of acres of fields go fallow and sold off the bulls, rams, bucks and one stallion so that there wouldn't be any new mouths to feed, since they had to depend on the hospitality of Wally Garcia, the sheriff of Val Verde County, to take care of the critters until they could find someone to fill the position permanently.

Gina Thompson was the daughter of Wally and was a tiny little thing, even compared to Nikki's small stature. But the dark-haired, dark-eyed beauty who reminded Nikki of Eva Mendes was bubbly, smart and a comedienne—she had the couple in stitches a few times while they toured the ranch.

"Back here is where they used to park the animals who were about to give birth. Guess they just tied them to the post there and waited for something to fall out. Don't know about you," she said to Nikki with a gleam in her eye, "but I can't imagine being on my feet to pop out a baby. Nope, I was flat on my back, screaming for a morphine drip and a loaded gun to shoot my husband."

Nikki laughed. "And me, I was too afraid of what the pain drugs would do to the baby, so I just white-knuckled it. Never yelled or anything either, so my son's less-than-bright father decided then that women exaggerate childbirth pain to get sympathy. Unfortunately for him, he decided to share that opinion with the OB nurse. She informed him that the pain of childbirth would be the male equivalent of having his privates stretched up over his head and tied in a bow. She volunteered to demonstrate it for him."

The ladies laughed while Reg cleared his throat uncomfortably as he turned toward one of the animal pens where a few cows had wandered in. "So, if we want to start raising animals again, Mr. Pickens would be okay with that?"

The ladies laughed again at his sudden topic change and moved toward the pen next to him. Gina leaned her shoulder on the top rail and watched as Reg fed a handful of grass to a longhorn.

"Oh yeah, Tiny would love that, to know that it was a working ranch again. Go to auctions, sell beef, work the fields, sell the produce, he's good with all that. He did want to maybe open the ranch to the public, though, so like schools could come out on field trips and see how their food looks before it's packaged nice and neat at the grocery store."

Nikki laughed again. "I foretell a new generation of vegetarians coming up. Kinda hard to eat a hamburger when you know it came from something with big brown eyes and a velvety soft nose," she said as she reached out to tickle one of the cow's muzzles. She was surprised they were so friendly and mentioned that to Gina.

"Well, dad says he thinks it's cuz this group that's here now wasn't with the ones back when they would suddenly disappear off to the auction. These ladies are more trusting of people."

"Maybe it's because they aren't being bothered by a big ol' pushy bull any longer." Nikki looked at Reg as she made that statement, a twinkle in her eye.

He raised an eyebrow at her. "Most cows like to be bothered by their bull once in a while."

Gina snorted. "Yeah, but only when they want to be bothered and not after working all day, then coming home to cook and clean, and definitely not just cuz they just asked for a back rub," she added vehemently and the three of them laughed.

"I doubt poor cows get many back rubs," Nikki mused.

Reg rubbed his chin. "Well now actually when the bull gets frisky—"

"TMI," Nikki interrupted and turned to Gina. "So, can we see the house?"

Gina laughed as she turned to walk toward the large white brick home sitting on top of the hill. "Now who's changing the subject?"

By three o'clock that afternoon Reg and Nikki were the new managers of Pickens Ranch, and the couple shook their heads in disbelief all the way back to Barnhart.

Not only did the job pay a generous salary, but it also included a three-bedroom house with utilities paid—including satellite television and wifi—plus cell phones, ranch credit cards for expenses and even a two-year old ranch truck. Gina said the only thing they had to buy was groceries.

As Reg drove north toward their soon-to-be former home, Nikki thought about the incredible blessings the job brought—not only would all of their needs be met, but a lot of wants were added to the mix. The Lord had truly blessed them in their situation.

She thought about how life had been so difficult for the past several years, in both their cases. But since they'd married—*no*, she corrected herself; *since Reg got baptized*—things had really gone from bad to worse. Materially, at least. And physically for Reg, until the Lord had healed him.

Spiritually, though, the difficult time had grown them both closer to God and to each other. Maybe this job, this new life, was an "attaboy" from the Lord, a reward for staying in the race and not giving up and rolling themselves into a tangled ball of "whine."

But I'm so unworthy, so undeserving, of any blessing, she thought. She was the woman at the well, with so many husbands in her past that their faces blurred along with the memories of the marriages. She deserved only condemnation. Yes, she knew in her head that the Lord had forgiven her the minute she'd asked Him to. The problem was getting her heart to believe in that forgiveness.

She thought about all the sermons she'd heard over the years on the Lord's forgiveness and grace and tried once again to convince her heart to listen. She knew her doubts and fears were directly from the enemy, from his arsenal of arrows honed to a faith-piercing sharpness.

Nikki shook herself. *God's Word says He forgives… if I don't believe THAT, then I'm doubting everything else He said, right? Am I going to doubt my salvation too? If I doubt that, then I'm calling Jesus a liar!*

With the final nail hammered into the doubt coffin, she turned her thoughts toward the amazing way God had answered all their prayers. They had first asked Him for a place of their own, and then when the jobs went by the wayside, they had asked for steady employment. Then when they had started to sell everything but the bare necessities, they had simply asked God to take care of their needs.

But this opportunity was far and above anything they could have imagined. A home, job, necessities *and* luxuries… well, this much blessing all at once was truly overwhelming.

Tears filled her eyes and her throat constricted with emotion as she reached over to lay her hand on Reg's arm.

"Pull over, honey."

He looked at her in alarm. "Are you getting sick?"

She shook her head, unable to speak, and Reg pulled the car onto the grass beside the two-lane road. He unbuckled and turned toward her, his hand gently pushing her chestnut hair aside to rub the back of her neck.

"What's the matter, darlin'?"

A sob escaped her as she tried to answer. "I'm sorry. I'm just so overcome with what the Lord has done for us. He's blessed us tremendously with this job. It's really an answer to all our prayers."

Reg nodded in agreement. "And then some. I just can't wrap my head around it all."

He ran his hand down to her shoulder while he continued his comforting massage.

Nikki nodded, then searched through her purse for a tissue. She dabbed at her eyes while answering.

"Yes, exactly. It's overwhelming. I just think we need to take a minute and thank Him."

Reg smiled at her, then took her hand in his and they bowed their heads.

"Lord, we just want to say 'thank You' for what You've done here, and what You're going to continue to do in our lives. We thank You for the past several months, even though they were hard for us. But we know that it was all part of Your plan and that You were just working behind the scenes for us. We know You have a greater plan in all this too and just ask that You help us to do whatever it is You want us to do, to keep our faith, to always keep our eyes on You. Thanks for helping us learn to trust You for everything. Amen."

"Amen." Nikki smiled at her husband, fighting back new tears at the pride she felt in him, in how far he'd come in his Christian walk in such a short time. The new job and new home were huge blessings, but her husband's salvation was the biggest blessing of all. And it looked like things were only going to get better.

chapter 4

T INY gave the go-ahead to plant whatever we wanted."

Reg made that announcement as he stood at the back door wiping his boots on the rug while Zeke barged in next to him, his paws leaving muddy reminders on the hardwood floor that the two of them had just come from the pond. That was the only spot on the ranch where the cell phone managed to grab any signal and Reg had wanted to talk to their boss and give him an update on things.

The pond was a new addition to the ranch. Reg had spent a full week digging the fifteen-foot-deep hole with the backhoe, then decided it wasn't wide enough and spent another couple of weeks widening it. By the time he was done, it was nearly a full acre across. He then trenched a strip from the property's fast-flowing creek to the pond, and figured it was going to take a month or so to fill. Once it did, it would provide fresh water for the cattle and open up another field for planting where before the cattle had to cut across to access the creek. He had then called the Game and Fish Department and asked them to stock it with a variety of fish.

Nikki looked up from her sewing machine. She was working on making some skirts out of her old jeans. She'd told Reg a few days ago that while she was doing dishes she felt like the Lord had spoken to her, telling her to quit acting like a man and to quit dressing like one. Having always been a tom-boy, Nikki had had a bit of a shock over that, but she was obeying and was determined to wear skirts and dresses, even though it made working on the ranch a little more difficult. But she figured if her pioneer ancestors could do it, so could she. And those ladies wore even more cumbersome skirts in addition to a dreaded corset. Plus, they worked a lot harder, thanks to not having modern conveniences such as riding tractors, which had become her new favorite toy.

Reg had taught Nikki to drive the old John Deere that belonged to the ranch and now he could hardly keep her off of the thing. She had dragged and disked the fields, plowed and seeded, fertilized and mowed. Reg teased her that she was going to burn up all the diesel in the four-hundred-gallon storage tank behind the barn before autumn if she kept up the pace.

Now they were being given carte blanche from Tiny to plant what they wanted. Nikki had been feeling the pull to start preparing for whatever disaster or hard times might come and had wanted to start planting things that could be stored. She thought the go-ahead must be yet another blessing from the Lord.

She grinned up at her husband. "Awesome. Now I can get corn down in the south field and maybe wheat in the east pasture."

He shook his head. "Nah, I don't think we need to be planting wheat. It takes too much acreage to amount to anything, plus we don't have the thresher to harvest it."

Nikki frowned at that information. Flour was a staple item—one she didn't think they could do without—and since it had a short shelf-life for storage, she was hoping to grow wheat for grinding themselves. Now she would have to rethink that idea.

Flour was something they would obviously need for breads, but if wheat wasn't practical to grow, then what? Despite Reg's and her southern roots, the down-home staple of cornbread all the time would get old, fast. Besides, even cornbread required some flour. She was going to have to do some research on wheat alternatives.

Her desire to start "prepping" had now become almost an obsession… it was no longer a want, but a *need* that she felt led to pursue. Lately she'd been spending a lot of time on the internet pouring over backwoods blogs, prepping websites, and homesteading pages. She'd started a notebook for all the information she thought would be helpful when the "end times" hit, everything from soap and candle making to harvesting honey and the use of herbs for medicines.

Knowing that computers—and electricity, for that matter—may not be things that were available when the stinky stuff hit the fan, she'd printed page after page of the info she'd found, putting it in a big red binder she'd labeled "How To Survive Disasters." That way, if she and Reg didn't live to see the end times, maybe the notebook would help someone else down the road.

Reg's voice broke into her thoughts. "What about sugar? You know we can't plant sugar cane here, but have you thought of a substitute?" He sounded a bit concerned.

Nikki smiled. Her husband had a definite sweet tooth and the idea of possibly doing without brownies and peach cobbler was a real concern for him. In fact, he'd recently planted eight peach trees in a line next to the creek, which he'd named "Cobbler Row."

"Actually, I ordered some stevia seeds. Stevia is a little bitter, but it's super sweet, like four times sweeter than sugar. Easy to grow, too."

"And cocoa? We can't exactly plant cocoa either." He still sounded concerned, and Nikki laughed out loud.

"That's something we have to store, along with baking soda and cream of tartar. That's what makes up baking powder, which I need for most of the baked goods."

"Why not just store the baking powder then?"

Nikki was sipping her coffee and grimaced. *Yuck, cold.*

"Short shelf life when they're combined, but you can store the soda and tartar almost indefinitely separately and mix as needed."

She lifted her cup. "This is something we need to store, too—coffee beans. Green coffee beans will store longer, but then we have the problem of roasting. Oh, and we need to store tea, too."

Reg sighed and leaned against the back of the sofa while crossing his arms. "There's an awful lot to think about."

Nikki pointed across the room to where her thick binder sat on the coffee table. "Tell me about it. That thing is already two inches thick and I'm not even close to being done. I just make mental notes all day as I go along and think of things we need, like coffee."

Reg grunted and smiled. "Yeah, that's a definite must-have. You wouldn't like me without it."

"Oh, I'd love you no matter what, even if you are a big ol' grumpy bear in the morning. But I have been looking at growing chicory as a coffee additive, to stretch our coffee bean storage. It's supposed to be easy to grow."

She absentmindedly took another sip of her cold coffee. "Ugh, that's so gross when it's cold."

He laughed. "Yeah, either hot or iced, not in between. You know the Scripture that talks about the Lord saying since the church was neither hot nor cold, He was going to spit them out of His mouth? I always figured He was thinking of lukewarm coffee."

They shared a laugh, then Nikki sighed and propped her elbows on the sewing table and leaned her chin on her folded hands.

"This prepping thing is a lot to think about. What I'm gathering from my research, though, is that a lot of people are just storing food and supplies. They're not thinking long term. I guess that comes from being told all this time that the Tribulation period is going to be seven years long and most are thinking they'll be outta here at the three-and-a-half-year midpoint at the latest."

"Well, that's just the Christians, though. Why would the others—those who aren't Christians—only be thinking in the short-term?"

She sat back in her chair and shrugged. "Who knows. Most sites and blogs seem to be geared toward disaster prep, like for a tornado, or snowstorm or something. The Christians are the only ones I've come across that are thinking long-term. But then again, most are just thinking the three-and-a-half-year thing. I just wonder how many people planting are, like we plan to."

His shrug matched hers. "Probably not many. Not too many people have the acreage to plant like we do."

Nikki shook her head. "I know, which is why I keep thinking we need to prepare for not just us, but for a *lot* of people. I have a feeling that we're going to be hosting a whole slew of people who can't fend for themselves after their supplies run out."

He sighed again and rubbed his forehead. "Guess I better start clearing some trees to build some cabins."

Nikki laughed. "Okay, Daniel Boone, you get right on that. Seriously, though, you can't worry about who might come, or how many. If the Lord sends them, He'll provide the means to house them."

Reg looked up and raised an eyebrow. "Just remember you said that when we're tripping over a platoon of refugees camping out in the living room."

Tiny called one Wednesday evening. Nikki half-listened while Reg talked to their boss. She wasn't sure what they were talking about, but she suddenly became a little alarmed from Reg's end of the conversation and couldn't wait for the call to end so she could find out what it was about.

Her husband sighed heavily as he set the phone down on the

coffee table, then he looked at Nikki with an expression that said, "Don't ask. I don't want to tell you, cuz it ain't good." She raised her eyebrows at him.

Reluctantly, he answered her unspoken question. "Seems that Jerry—Tiny's son—and his wife and kids want to come down for a visit."

That was surprising. "Really? I thought that he had no interest in the ranch."

Reg smirked. "Yeah, he didn't until he got laid off from his job and hasn't been able to find another one. Tiny is pretty excited about the prospect of one of his kids actually taking an interest in the place."

Nikki felt her heart constrict. If Jerry wanted to move to the ranch, that meant that she and Reg would no longer be needed. Then what would they do? She could feel the panic rising in her throat along with the acid from the pepperoni and jalapeño pizza they'd had for dinner.

Immediately her mind spun off into the "what if" scenarios. What if Jerry and his family decided to move to the ranch? Then what—she and Reg are just kicked off without so much as a "sayonara, it's been nice?" And what about all the stuff they'd already started—the pond Reg had worked so hard on and all the fields she'd plowed and seeded and fertilized, plus all the seed they'd bought at their own expense once Tiny had given them the go-ahead to plant what they wanted.

Reg sensed that she was worrying herself through her imagination and took her hand in his.

"Honey, don't be getting all worked up just yet. We both felt like the Lord brought us out here and if He wants us to be here, then no force on earth will change that. Maybe He has something better down the road for us; we don't know and can't guess. We've both been feeling the lack of fellowship with a church out here in the middle of nowhere—maybe this is His way of leading us somewhere else where we can get back into a church home." He shrugged.

"But all we can do is trust—and remember, you're the one who's been reminding me to trust Him since day one."

Nikki smiled and laughed weakly, knowing her husband was right. It was just so much easier to talk about trusting the Lord than it was to actually do it.

Jerry and Amelia Pickens, along with their two bratty children, showed up at the ranch that very weekend. Thankfully, they were driving an RV, because Nikki really didn't want them staying in the ranch house with them. It might have been Jerry's childhood home, but until she and Reg got word otherwise, it was their home now.

Nikki took an instant liking to Amelia, despite her aversion to doing so. As un-Christian like as it was, she really just wanted to despise the couple because of what they represented—the end of what Nikki had thought was a new beginning for Reg and her.

Her plans for disliking them pretty much went out the window the minute the couple pulled up in their luxury RV and a plump little ball of blond bubbliness jumped out and rushed up to Nikki for a hug.

The pixie grinned, her perfectly straight white teeth almost blinding in the sunlight. "Hi, how y'all doin'? I'm Amelia, but y'all can just call me Amy, if ya like."

She turned to wave a hand toward the tall sandy-brown haired man stepping out of the RV, followed by a boy and girl with disgusted looks on their faces, as if their shoes had never touched dirt before.

Turning back to Nikki and Reg, she added, "This here is my husband Jer and kids Becky and Ronny. It's so nice to meet y'all!"

Nikki was fairly certain that Amy had been a cheerleader. Head cheerleader, most likely. She was cute, perky, and very likable. Her thick southern drawl alone would charm even the most ardent of Yankees. Amy reminded Nikki of Reese Witherspoon's character in "Sweet Home Alabama."

Jerry, on the other hand, was very standoffish and Nikki decided that Ronny and Becky unfortunately took after their father personality-wise. All three looked like they would rather be anywhere on the planet other than where they stood at that moment.

Reg also disliked the father and kids immediately and immensely, although he did his part to be pleasant and welcoming. He stuck out his hand, forcing Jerry to return the handshake.

"Reg Erskine, this is my wife, Nikki. Glad y'all made it safely."

Jerry snorted. "Not much danger on the way… unless you count narrowly missing a cow or two. Oh, and there was that tumbleweed that nearly took out the RV." He rolled his eyes then.

"Oh, the dangers of country roads." His voice dripped with sarcasm and Nikki wanted to punch him. Right in the throat.

Amy took over that task when she whacked her husband in the chest with the back of her hand. She turned back to Reg and rolled her own eyes.

"Don't you never mind Mr. Grumpy Butt. He didn't want to come down here to his daddy's ranch, but I insisted. I was thinkin' we'd better use the time the Lord gave us to see this here country and I wanted to start with the place where Jer grew up. Figured the kids could use a little fresh air and sunshine, too. Back in Dallas, they hole up in their rooms like scaredy-cat armadillos all the time and never get any fresh air. 'Course, if you go outside in Dallas, the air's so thick you can chew it, and so full of exhaust fumes you might just spit out a Honda."

Reg and Nikki laughed at Amy's comment, which even earned a slight smile from her husband. The kids, however, were a different story. Both rolled their eyes at their mother, as if she were the family pariah, embarrassing and barely tolerated. Nikki wanted to take both the brats out to the willow tree and cut down a good-sized limb to beat some respect into their behinds, despite the fact they were both young teens and the boy already towered over her own petite size.

Reg and Nikki took the couple on a tour of the ranch since Jerry didn't seem interested in showing his wife the place where he grew up. The kids complained the entire time, worrying over such things as getting animal poop on their expensive shoes, which insect might bite them, complaining that the sun was too hot or too bright or too yellow and the wind was too windy. By the end of the day, Reg was trying to figure out where the best place was to dig a hole to put them in.

Later that night, Nikki shared with Reg that she thought that Amy's comment about insisting the family visit the ranch when they obviously didn't want to meant that the couple wasn't planning on moving in after all.

After that, the weekend was much more pleasant and on Monday morning, they happily said their goodbyes and watched Jerry and Amy drive off down the dirt road.

Nikki's daughter, Anna, came for a visit in July, fell in love with the ranch and, to the shock of both Reg and Nikki, decided to stay. Of course, the fact that Reg was fun-loving and nothing at all like her ex-military toe-the-line-or-else father had a lot to do with that decision.

Nikki looked into schools and found that the closest high school was nearly fifty miles away. There was a bus that picked kids up from the ranches in the area, but the bus ride was almost three hours long each way. Neither Nikki nor Anna could see her doing that, so Nikki enrolled her daughter in online school.

While Nikki was happy to have her daughter move in with them, she was also a bit apprehensive. Anna had always been a sweet child—until she hit puberty. Then she became an eye-rolling drama queen that Nikki didn't even recognize. And to make things worse, from moment to moment the girl switched from being her old sweet self to becoming a raving and raging wicked witch of the west.

Reg took it all in stride, however, and seemed to have the patience of Job when dealing with Anna. Nikki was more than happy to let him take care of all the handling of the difficult teen.

Reg had very few rules, and one was if you want to eat, you work. Knowing that Anna wasn't used to doing much work by way of chores and had always lived in the city, he went easy on her and gave her simple chores to do. She only complained about the work to her mother, and then only when Reg wasn't around. The girl seemed bent on pleasing her new stepfather, which kind of annoyed Nikki, wishing the girl felt the desire to please her mother too.

"Ugh, he made me clean out the sheep stall today. It was sooo gross!" Anna whined while Nikki was making enchiladas for dinner.

"It wouldn't have been 'sooo gross' if you'd cleaned it out last week like you were supposed to," Nikki chided.

Eye-rolling ensued. "Whatever. You have no idea what it's like to have to shovel poop."

Nikki turned to her daughter with her eyebrows raised. "Oh really?" She quipped, her voice dripping sarcasm.

"Just who do you think was cleaning out the stalls before you got here? And besides that, you only have to clean one stall. There are still the goats and the horses to clean up after. Keep up your griping, and I'll make sure Reg adds those to your list. *And* the cow pasture."

More eye-rolling. "Yeah, like anyone cleans a cow pasture." Anna huffed and brushed her blue-streaked auburn hair out of her eyes before turning and stomping down the hall to her room.

Nikki felt like growling. A wave of guilt came over her when she thought that things were a lot easier when Anna had been living with her dad. *She's your daughter, for Pete's sake! And besides, this is just a phase... she'll outgrow this I-know-everything garbage soon. At least I hope so, for all our sakes.*

By the end of summer, Nikki and Reg had managed to grow and harvest a half-acre of corn and from the other half of the acre came stevia and quinoa, which Reg said he wasn't too sure of—he didn't want to eat something he couldn't even spell. But Nikki had assured him that it was a good grain and even though it wouldn't substitute for flour, it was at least a very healthy addition to the oats and sorghum they would grow instead of acreage-greedy wheat. Instead of growing wheat, they'd decided to store wheat berries which would keep longer than wheat itself, and also rice, which had a very long shelf-life and could be ground by hand into flour.

One morning after a very hard rain, the ranch house had sprung a leak and Reg had gone into the attic to find the source. Once there, he'd discovered that apparently Tiny—and his ancestors—had a penchant for hoarding and stockpiling. There were some useful items: Boxes of canned vegetables and fruits; a case of toilet paper, although it was so old that Nikki figured it would turn to confetti the second it touched skin; and crates of glass-bottled sodas. There also was a large amount of home repair items like window screening, roof shingles and ceramic bathroom tile. There were also a lot of things that weren't going to do anyone any good when the end times rolled around—like the seven-foot-high stack of National Geographic magazines and the giant collection of antique gas station signs.

But there was also a plethora of old pre-electricity tools and equipment, including flour mills, and Nikki had taken to trying her hand at grinding grain à la the eighteen hundreds. She'd joked with Reg that the muscles in her arms were soon going to look like his if she kept it up.

She had started experimenting with making potato flour but wasn't sure about the shelf life until Reg pointed out that she didn't have to store it—they could grow potatoes in barrels year round so they'd have a ready supply any time they wanted it and she could make the flour on an as-needed basis.

Yeast was something else that Nikki had been concerned about. It didn't store indefinitely, and in fact would only stay "alive" for two years *if* kept in a freezer. Considering that a freezer may not be something they would have in the future, Nikki had started looking at alternatives for dough rising. She was surprised to discover that you could gather wild yeast just by filling a mason jar halfway with unpeeled fruit—or better yet, peach tree leaves—topping off the jar with water, then capping it and leaving it in a warm area for a few days. When the water turned bubbly, the yeast water was ready to be used in a bread recipe.

Reg found an ad on Craigslist for a rancher who was liquidating and had twenty plastic rain barrels for sale. They bought them all, using half for the intended purpose, and the other ten Reg cut the tops off so they could be used for food storage. They then filled the barrels with corn meal, cocoa, wheat berries, rice and green coffee beans, then duct taped the lids back on.

Unfortunately, there wasn't a good place to store the barrels. The cellar under the ranch house was pretty small and the stairway was too narrow to tote the barrels down, so they were forced to stack them in their living room.

Nikki got tired of looking at the big blue barrels after about a month, so Reg laid a concrete foundation in the backyard and began chopping trees and splitting logs to use to build a shed. Reg decided to go "old school" for the roof in using thatch placed atop thin cross beams, saying that the shed would stay cooler that way. He plastered the interior to seal the cracks against bug invasion and put thick weather stripping around the door. He then built shelves along two walls and installed a solar-powered dehumidifier to guard against south Texas dampness.

By the time the cute little log cabin shed was done, Nikki joked that she wanted to move into it and use the ranch house for storage.

Nikki planted a garden and grew, as she put it, "salsa"—jalapenos, onions, garlic and tomatoes, and from her indoor herb garden cumin and cilantro. She also grew four different kinds of squash, cucumbers for the pickles that Anna was crazy about, and also okra, chicory, carrots, and three different types of lettuce.

The garden was both a blessing and a curse, because of course with the growing of the vegetables came the overabundance of weeds. Nikki had to enlist Anna's help to keep up with it, since Reg was so busy building and fixing everything else on the ranch.

Even though weeding was a cumbersome chore, Nikki found many object lessons in the process.

"You know," she said one day while she and Anna worked side by side pulling weeds from around the watermelon and cantaloupe, "this reminds me of something I read in the Bible." She could sense Anna's eyes rolling and smiled as she continued.

"Scripture talks about how weeds are like sin. They—the sin—rise up to choke the plant—that's us—and stops or slows the plant's growth. That's why we have to be so diligent to get rid of it. And that sin can be anything that takes our focus off of God—in my case, it's usually the books that I find myself so interested in... those romances that can get downright nasty sometimes." She shook her head, even though Anna probably didn't see it.

"In your case, it can be the Xbox—or the time you spend

playing games. The Lord doesn't want us to never have any fun or recreation, but He does want us to occupy ourselves with things that are good for us. Some of the books I've read and some of the games you play are not what we can call good, huh?" Anna didn't answer, but Nikki was pretty sure she was thinking about what she'd said.

They worked in silence for a minute before another revelation hit Nikki. She pulled up a weed that had a cantaloupe vine wrapped around it.

"Look at this," she said with disgust. "It's just like us. We cling to the sin, not wanting to let it go, even though it's blocking the light and robbing us of the good things. In the plant's case, it needs nutrients from the soil and water, but the weeds suck all that up. In our case, the sin consumes our lives and leaves no room for God and His Word—the good things."

chapter 5

B Y THE middle of fall, the family had quite a bit of food storage. Nikki had enlisted Anna's help—which was almost more of a trial than the help was worth—and the two had managed to can sliced apples, pears, peaches, tomatoes and had made enough jams and jellies to rot a whole set of teeth.

Since Reg had such a sweet tooth, they'd canned different pie and cobbler mixes from pumpkin pulp, yams and a large variety of fruits they'd bought at local farmer's markets. They then pickled everything from okra to jalapenos until Nikki said if she smelled vinegar ever again, she was going to puke, while Anna had sworn off her beloved pickles for life.

The sun dehydrator Reg had made from two old screen doors came in handy to dry banana slices, squash, onions, sweet and regular potatoes, jalapenos, and since they had such a bumper crop from their small orchards, more fruit. Nikki even made some jerky when she'd run out of freezer space to store all the meat from a steer Reg had butchered.

That lack of freezer space brought up a new problem that Nikki had no solution for: How to store a lot of meat—like a whole cow—if and when there was no electricity to power a freezer. Afraid to try canning meat for fear of botulism, she scoured the internet looking for a good answer, but most blogs and websites took the safe road and stated that it wasn't safe to store meats, even if dried, outside of a freezer.

Nikki didn't buy that answer since freezers had only been around for less than a century. But she didn't figure her family would appreciate a case of food poisoning in order to experiment with different methods. The best solution she came up with was drying the meat into jerky, then storing it in a bag using her suction sealer to remove all the air, and then for extra safety measures, stuffing the bagged meat into a jar and canning it. The only problem then was trying to get the meat to reconstitute well enough to avoid a shoe leather texture, which she hadn't quite solved. Reg like to tease her about her "boot stew."

Even in warm south Texas, things just don't grow in January and February, so Reg had decided to build a greenhouse next to the garden so they could have produce year round. But what started as a fifteen by twenty-foot space ended up covering nearly twelve hundred square feet. When Nikki asked her husband why he'd made the greenhouse so huge, he'd joked that it was Texas-sized, and, besides, his favorite motto was "go big or go home."

The gargantuan greenhouse drew the attention of Border Patrol, who were constantly on the lookout for drug runners. Nikki had warned Reg that it probably would cause them to look their way, since they would figure a plantation of marijuana was being grown in the huge enclosure, and so she was very nervous when she saw two agents approaching the house late one afternoon while she'd been making dumplings.

Nikki opened the front door and wiped her flour dusted hands on the towel she held, realizing she probably looked like the perfect stereotype of the country wife—long skirt, hair up on top of her head, and flour all over her apron. The agents probably thought she'd gotten stuck in a time warp or something.

"Hi, how y'all doing?" She smiled at the two stern-faced young men, hoping to make them relax a bit.

The smaller man spoke. "Good afternoon, ma'am." He nodded to his partner. "We're Agents Gonzales and Henderson from the U.S. Border Patrol."

She stuck out her hand. "I'm Nikki Erskine. Come on in." She opened the door wider and motioned for the men to come into the living room, but the two stayed right where they were, looking like she'd just asked them to some heinous act.

Gonzales spoke again, his voice very matter of fact. "We're here because of a report of a large structure in one of your fields that is suspicious for growing illegal substances."

Nikki couldn't help it when she gave them an eye-roll that even Anna the Drama Queen would have been proud of. "I told Reg— that's my husband—that y'all would think we were starting a pot farm with that monstrosity of his. But, no, it's just a greenhouse for growing vegetables."

The agents just stared mutely at her and so, sighing, she said, "Hold on a sec."

She took off her apron and hung it on the hat hook by the front door, then yelled for her daughter, who came around the corner with a disgusted "how dare you disturb my afternoon of 'Pretty Little Liars'" look. But then she saw the handsome young men standing on her front porch and her demeanor dramatically changed.

Anna smiled at the men and then turned to her mother and asked, "Yes, mama?" in such a sweet voice that Nikki was sure she'd just gotten a cavity from it.

"I need to go down to the south field. Watch the chicken I have boiling on the stove, please, and finish up the dumplings. You just have to cut them into inch sized squares and drop them into the chicken pot in about fifteen minutes."

"Yes, ma'am," her daughter replied, again in that sickeningly sweet voice.

Nikki couldn't help it—she just had to give the girl a hard time. Payback for all the snotty replies and disgusted sighing was going to be had. It was a mother's prerogative, after all.

She frowned at her daughter with a quizzical look. "Is something wrong with you?"

Anna glanced at the agents and blushed a little before looking back at her mother with overly huge eyes. Nikki wanted to roll her own eyes again.

The girl tilted her head to the side. "No, mama, nothing's wrong, why?"

Nikki didn't think it was possible, but her daughter's root beer-colored eyes got even wider.

She huffed. "Well, you're being nice, for one thing, and you're agreeing to what I'm asking without all the usual drama and hateful comebacks."

Nikki nodded to the two agents who were mutely watching the exchange. "If the behavior change is cuz of these two young men here, then I think I'll ask them to move in with us."

She was fairly certain the teen's face was going to melt right off the bones from the heat of her blush. She'd never seen anyone get that red. Anna's lip curled up and she snarled, "Whatever," and stomped off without a glance behind her.

Nikki laughed as she looked back toward the agents who both looked like they were having a hard time not busting a gut.

"And she's baaaccckkk," she joked in a high-pitched voice as she moved between the two men and closed the front door behind her.

Nikki waved at the agents as she stepped off the porch. "Anyway, come on, I'll show you the greenhouse. Reg is probably down there now. It's his new pet project. I swear, that man spends more time out there then he does in his own bed. Maybe it's a mid-life crisis thing, but instead of cuddling up to a new girlfriend, he's loving on some veggies."

She heard a snort from behind her as the agents trailed her down to the south field. Sure enough, Reg was inside the greenhouse, screwing some plywood to a couple of sawhorses.

Nikki turned to the agents and said in a low voice, "For

someone who hates working with wood, he sure spends a lot of time sucking up sawdust."

To her husband, she said, "Hey, hon, this is Agent Gonzales and Agent Henderson. They're here cuz they think you're giving the drug cartel competition. Told you so," she grinned at her husband.

Reg rolled his eyes and Nikki decided then that it must be contagious. Her husband put down his drill and moved forward while removing his work gloves so he could shake the agents' hands.

"Reg Erskine. Guess my wife told you she'd already warned me that I'd have you guys up in arms about this," he said as he motioned to the structure around them.

The agents looked around and actually looked quite impressed. "This is some greenhouse you got here," Henderson said.

Reg grinned at him. "Yeah, I might have gone a little overboard, but like I told the wife, this *is* Texas."

"And everything's bigger in Texas," Gonzales chimed in and they all shared a laugh.

"But as you can see, nothing suspicious here," Nikki offered.

Henderson frowned a little as he looked around. "But nothing is growing."

Reg stepped up to one of the shelves lined with neat rows of little peat pots and tapped the edge of the shelf where he had stapled a piece of paper he'd labeled "TOMATOES."

"Not yet, but we just got the greenhouse up and got the seeds planted. This here is the tomato row, and underneath that, different squashes, chiles and onions," he said as he pointed to the other labels on the shelves.

He turned and pointed to the opposite wall. "Over there are the lettuces, carrots, berries and beans."

"And peas," Nikki added.

Reg grimaced. "Don't remind me."

Nikki laughed. "Just like a little kid—hates peas."

"I'll second that," Henderson added with a grin.

Nikki laughed again. "So, anyway, we're not growing anything illegal, but y'all will have to come back in about a month or so after the plants get growing good so you can see for yourself."

She pursed her lips. "But now that we're on the subject, I actually have been wondering what the law is for growing marijuana. I mean, like just one plant. It would just be for medicinal purposes, for pain control," she hurriedly added.

Her husband was staring at her with a look that bordered on horror and complete and utter disbelief. She shrugged and gave him a "What?" look in return.

Agent Gonzales was rubbing his chin and Henderson looked like he was fighting back laughter once again.

Gonzales finally answered. "Well, the penalty for possession depends on how much you have. As long as you're not distributing, for smaller amounts it's up to one hundred eighty days in jail and two thousand dollars. For cultivation, it's the same—depends on what the crop weighs."

Nikki sighed. "I was afraid of that. I don't want to do anything illegal, but I'm also not big on using pharmaceuticals to treat the body. And marijuana is probably the best source of pain reliever there is."

She shrugged once more. "I believe that God gave us everything we need to heal ourselves and that the chemicals being prescribed are just making us dependent on the drug companies, the medical profession and the FDA."

Henderson nodded. "I actually agree with you one hundred percent. My mother is a naturopath doctor—an ND—and I've never had so much as a Tylenol. My sisters and I are all really healthy too."

Nikki's eyes lit up. "Oh, cool! I'm just now getting into learning about herbs and medicinal plants. It's really interesting. A lot to learn, though."

The agent agreed. "Yeah, it took mom a couple of years to get through school, and that was full time. My oldest sister had to run the household for her and take care of my other sister and me. She still resents us," he laughed.

"Does your mom practice near here?" Nikki asked.

Henderson shook his head. "No, my family lives in Utah." He grinned, although it was a little strained looking... with maybe a touch of sadness.

"I'm the black sheep of the family. They're all good Mormons, but I didn't want to go on missions and joined Border Patrol instead."

Gonzales frowned at his partner and Nikki assumed it was consternation. He was probably upset with the young man for giving out so much personal information. She wanted to tell the gruffer agent that that was commonplace with her—people just seemed to open up to her.

Gonzales pointed to the wine barrels with doors in the sides. "What's in those barrels over there?"

Reg walked over to one of the barrels and opened the little door he'd built into the side. "Most are regular potatoes and a couple are sweet potatoes. See?" He dug through the dirt and pulled out a small brown spud. "They're still small, but we just planted them a few months ago."

Gonzales took the potato from Reg. "Huh, I've never seen potatoes grown like that."

Reg stood and leaned his elbow on the barrel's top edge. "Nikki found the method on the internet. You plant the seed potatoes—or even just the eyes when they start sprouting—then add soil as the plant grows and keep doing that until you reach the top of whatever you're growing them in. The plant ends up with roots—and taters—several feet deep. You can have an unending supply of them year-round."

Nikki chimed in. "You can actually grow them right in a bag of peat moss too. Don't need a fancy barrel like Reg made. Same concept. Pour out most of the peat to start, then add it back in as the potatoes grow."

The agent snorted appreciatively. "That's pretty cool. I might have to try that at home. The wife uses a lot of potatoes."

Reg dug a small hole next to the plants that were already growing and buried the small potato he'd picked. "There. Hopefully, that'll grow into a new plant."

The group left the greenhouse just as Anna was coming down the hill toward them. Nikki noticed the girl had changed into one of her fancier pairs of jeans and had put some makeup on.

"I put the dumplings in like you said, mama," Anna said, again with those wide eyes and innocent expression. "Is there anything else you want me to do?"

Before Nikki could give the girl an answer, Reg piped in. "I have something for you—you never finished mucking the sheep stall. You left it half done with the shovel still in their pen." He then looked her up and down.

"Might want to change out of them fancy britches before you get started though."

The wide-eyed expression left in a hurry as Anna's cheeks pinkened, and she gave her stepfather a look, though she kept her comments to herself. "Fine," she said in a tone that could pierce steel and stomped off in the direction of the barn.

"I love that girl, but God save us from teenagers," Nikki muttered. Then she turned to the agents.

"Would y'all like to stay for dinner? Chicken and dumplings with green beans, fried okra and peach cobbler for dessert."

"Oh man, that sure does sound good," Henderson groaned. "But we're really not supposed to while we're on duty."

"Yeah," Gonzales agreed with a heavy sigh. "Besides, my wife would have my hide if she knew I'd eaten before I got home."

"That's just cuz you were always getting fast food on the way home before she put a stop to that," Henderson piped in.

"You've had my wife's cooking. Do you blame me?" Gonzales said as he looked at his partner.

"Nuff said," Henderson replied, and the men laughed.

Nikki smirked. "C'mon now, her cooking can't be *that* bad."

Gonzales shook his head. "She is getting better; I'll give her that. At least now her biscuits don't take an hour of gravy soaking to soften enough to chew. And to be fair, she never learned to cook, so I gotta give her credit for trying. I sure don't know the first thing about cooking either, so I ain't one to talk."

Nikki was liking the young agent more and more. Both men, in fact, had loosened up considerably in the past twenty minutes, a far cry from the stiff by-the-book attitude they had when they first showed up at the house.

"Well, you're welcome to join us any time," she replied as she gave them what she hoped was a welcoming smile.

Reg surprised her by adding to her invitation. "In fact, I was thinking about having a barbecue soon, inviting all the agents in the area who might be on duty. Thought we could do an all-day sort of thing, so the different shifts would get a chance to come by. Just not sure about the nightshift. I don't think I want to be up at two a.m. flipping burgers."

The men laughed and then Gonzales took his badge wallet out of a side pants pocket and pulled a business card out. He handed it to Reg.

"That's Tim Harger. He's the senior liaison agent for the ranches in the area. He's the one to talk to about setting up the barbecue. Might even be able to help with expenses."

"Awesome. Thanks. I'll give him a call," Reg answered as he handed the card to Nikki. "We just want to meet the agents, let them know we're friendlies, on your side."

The agents nodded and Henderson added, "That's nice to know. We don't get a lot of cooperation from the ranchers around here. Guess most are suspicious of the government."

Nikki looked at the card in her hand and tapped the logo in the lower left corner.

"I think it has more to do with Border Patrol being a division of Homeland Security. Not a good reputation with the American public, ya know?"

The men didn't answer but nodded in agreement, and Reg added, "Well, we're hoping to change that, at least around here. Maybe we could invite some of the other ranchers too."

The agents agreed that was a good idea, then said their goodbyes and headed out.

Reg turned back toward the table he was working on. Nikki

watched him for a minute, then asked, "Were you going to tell me about this barbecue idea of yours?"

He chuckled as he grabbed his drill. "Yeah, I wouldn't want you to be surprised when we had fifty guys show up wanting food."

"There are lady agents too," she added unnecessarily. "So, were you serious about the idea, or were you just making offers to see how they took it?"

He straightened from the board he was about to drill into. "No, I was serious. I think we need to do all we can to make sure the agents are on our side. I mean, out here, they're our first line of defense. They'd be who to call in any emergency, really."

She frowned. "But it's Homeland Security—you know, big government who watches our every move, listens to our phone conversations… the agency we're supposed to be keeping under the radar from?"

Reg snorted. "Yeah, I know. That's what you get if you read all that hype from the end times people. And they may very well be right. But the way I look at it, Scripture warns us of what's coming so I like to think it's better to keep my enemies close, and the enemy is going to be the government as far as I can tell. 'Sides, I'd rather treat the agents as individuals and not as a collective 'big brother' we gotta fear."

He turned back to his project and started drilling, then finished his thought loudly to be heard.

"And I figure when the end times come, the government is

going to collapse—well, at least it won't be like it is now. Figure it'll be more of a military organization. There won't be Homeland Security, or even the CIA, any longer." He didn't mention that he figured what would replace them would be much worse.

Nikki cringed. The idea of the government turning military, as in the case of martial law, was frightening. But then again, it was frightening as it was, with the over-the-top power it held and all the behind-the-scenes dealings that the general American public was so happy to remain ignorant about.

She was afraid that someday soon, Reg was right—a military takeover was likely. There was just no way things could continue the way they had been for much longer.

Late one Friday afternoon in the middle of November the power suddenly went out. Storms were raging in their area, and Reg figured a transformer got hit by lightning somewhere.

The couple took it in stride, having gone through the struggle of living without electricity once before, although Nikki did complain about the timing of the inconvenience, since she had been in the middle of doing dishes.

Anna, however, was freaking out.

"How long is it going to be off?" She whined to her mother in a panicky voice. "I was Skyping with Jacob and Tatiana!"

Nikki rolled her eyes at her daughter. "I have no clue how long it'll be out, since the electric company doesn't like for me to climb their poles. You'll just have to do without wifi for a bit. I'm more concerned with not having water, since the pump runs on electricity."

Her daughter's panic jumped ten-fold then. "No water? But I have to take a shower tonight!"

Her mother sighed. "It's not going to kill you to miss taking a shower for one night. It's not like you have to leave the house to go to school or anything. The chickens and sheep don't care what you smell like."

"Motherrr," Anna answered in a disgusted voice, dragging the word out. She then changed her complaining tactics.

"I have a paper due for English tomorrow!"

Nikki sighed again, wondering when the girl would figure out that the electricity being out wasn't within her mother's control.

Nikki's voice was clipped as she spoke through gritted teeth. "Then take your laptop out to the truck and plug it in to the converter. You don't need wifi to write a paper. Hopefully the power will be back on tomorrow, and you can upload it to your school then. Just make sure you start the truck and let it run a few minutes every half hour or so, so you don't kill the battery."

Anna huffed and stomped. Nikki started muttering under her breath as she continued scrubbing a pot, "It's not like we planned this, Anna. We didn't cut the electricity to ruin your life, you know? You should learn to be grateful for what you have."

Reg came in then and heard his wife. "You talking to yourself, hon? How's that conversation going for ya?" He teased.

Nikki flashed him a warning look over her shoulder. "Do *not* start, not unless you want to be added to my list too."

He grabbed an apple from the fruit basket on the counter and took a bite. "What list?" He asked around a mouthful.

"The 'Who I'm Going To Bury In The North Pasture' list. So, far only Anna's name is on it, but you could be next."

Her husband grinned at her. "You'd have to learn to use the backhoe first, and I'll be darned if I'm going to teach you just so you can hide my body."

Nikki laughed as she dipped the pot into the sink side full of rinse water. "Well, I think you should be a good husband and dig the hole for me. I might even promise not to put you in it."

She sobered then as she pulled a plate from the soapy side and started scrubbing it. "Did you find the generator Gina mentioned?"

They had called the bookkeeper to get the account number for the electric company so they could report the outage and Gina had mentioned a big generator that used to be on the ranch when Tiny and April had lived there.

"Yeah, it was way back in one of the old barns and thankfully on a trailer, but I need to run to town and get some fuel and an air filter for it. You wanna go?"

Nikki shook her head. "No, I have two sinks full of hot water and want to get the dishes done while I have a little daylight."

Reg shrugged. "A'ight. Need anything while I'm out?"

Nikki pursed her lips in thought. "I guess grab something for dinner. A couple of pizzas, or something that will give us leftovers."

"Running to town" for them meant a forty-five-minute trip one way. Since Anna was always wanting something from the store and they didn't give in to her too often, Reg asked the girl if she wanted to accompany him. Of course, she took him up on it and asked if they could "stop somewhere where they have wifi."

Nikki sighed once more, knowing it would be a good two to three hours before she saw her family again. Sitting in the dark waiting for them to return didn't sound like the most fun time, but she'd make the best of it by getting in some Bible study by candlelight. And praying.

She'd been feeling guilty lately for letting herself slip away from the Lord. When she and Reg were going through the tough times, they'd been so close to God, feeling His comfort, hearing His voice and seeing His answers to prayer. But since they'd gotten to the ranch and a busy life had consumed them, they'd both started slipping away from Him.

They weren't completely backslidden—not yet anyway—but just not fully relying on Him any longer for everything they needed. Once the blessings came, they just sort of slipped away from the One who'd provided the blessings in the first place.

There was something good about going through the hard times.

The electricity was out for two days, but thanks to the generator, they had water and a few lights, and the food stayed cold in the refrigerator and freezer. And Anna had her wifi, so she was content, as much as a usually disgruntled teen could be. But being without electricity once again had gotten Reg thinking.

"We need solar power," he said over dinner a few nights later. "I'm thinking a solar water pump for sure and some panels for the house."

Nikki frowned. "I don't think Tiny would appreciate us putting a bunch of ugly solar panels on top of his hundred-year-old ranch house."

Reg snorted. "No, not on the house, but in the back. I need to work out the details and the cost, but I really think it'll be something Tiny will go for. Hope so, anyway."

Her husband was right—Tiny did think it was a good idea and gave approval to Gina to fund the solar project. Thanks to Reg's designs and ingenuity, the total cost wasn't nearly what it would have been had they hired a solar company to come in, and since they'd saved so much money Tiny had insisted they get extra batteries and converters for back up.

Right after the solar pump and panels were installed, the fifteen-year-old hot water heater decided to die. It gave no warning whatsoever—one minute the water was scalding hot, then the next there wasn't even a drop of warm water. The plumber that came out said it was full of hard-water sediment, a bane of south Texas residents. Reg insisted on keeping the old unit "for parts," despite the plumber telling him it was no good.

After that was replaced, the stove decided to quit working and a few days later during a torrential downpour, the roof started leaking in the living room.

Nikki called Gina and said that she figured they were jinxing the place. Gina had laughed and said that everything was old and due to be replaced anyway.

"Just think, though—now you and Reg will have all brand-new stuff."

That got the couple to thinking. It was almost as if the Lord was taking care of things, making sure everything was in tip-top shape. They wondered just what it was that was coming that He was preparing them for.

chapter 6

I T'S STARTING."

Reg had just come back from town where he'd gone to get some lumber to build another storage shed. The first shed wasn't full yet, but the couple was hoping that with the next season's crop, both sheds would be full of stored food.

Nikki glanced up from the laptop where she'd been reading about how to make nixtamalized corn—ground into flour it was known as "masa" to those in-the-know about Mexican foods. She made a mental note to buy a bag of pickling lime the next time they were at the feed store, since she would have to boil and soak the corn in it to start the process to make the masa.

"Hi honey," she said in an overly bright, slightly sarcastic voice while puckering her lips. Usually when Reg came home—even if it was just from one of the fields—he greeted her and gave her a quick kiss. His abruptness was unusual.

"Sorry," he replied as he bent to kiss her.

"So, what's 'starting'?" Nikki asked as she looked back to her laptop, searching for recipes for corn tortillas, sopes and tamales that were made from masa. She knew how to make enchiladas, posole, et cetera, all the Mexican "staples," but tortillas and tamales were something she had always bought.

Reg went to the fridge and pulled out the jug of peach iced tea. "The end of the world," he announced in a matter-of-fact voice.

Nikki laughed. "Oh dear, did they quit making duct tape or WD-40?" She always teased her husband that he would never be able to fix anything unless he had those two items handy.

He poured the tea over his glass full of ice and grunted at her comment. "I'm serious. You know how Greece's economy collapsed last week and they were looking to Spain to bail them out? Well, on the way back from town I heard on the radio that now Spain's on the verge of collapsing too and the experts are figuring Italy is next. Looks like the entire European economy is flushing down the toilet."

Over that surprising news, Nikki sat back in her chair and crossed her arms over her chest. Reg was standing in the middle of the kitchen, glass in hand and frowning, looking like he had the weight of the world on his overly broad shoulders.

"And what aren't you telling me?" They hadn't been married long, but she knew her husband well enough to know that he was holding something back.

He came into the dining room and collapsed across from her at the table, the wood chair creaking in protest at the sudden heavy weight from her husband's large frame. Taking a long draw on his tea, he stared at the tabletop. It seemed he didn't want to get to the telling of it, and Nikki found herself suddenly feeling very anxious.

Finally, he answered as he continued to contemplate the table's wood grain. "The experts are saying that if Italy follows Spain, then it's certain all of Europe will collapse."

He took another long drink and finally looked at her when he continued. "And then it's just a matter of time before the rest of the world's economy collapses too."

Nikki made an "O" with her mouth, completely speechless. Suddenly her mind went spiraling into different "what if" scenarios, which she was prone to do when something was so blatantly out of her control.

She worried about their food storage, if they had enough for however long this crisis would last. Then she wondered if this was truly "the end," the final round before the Lord's judgment. Was she really ready to face Him on Judgment Day? No, she didn't think so. She knew she was forgiven of her sins once she'd asked Jesus to become her Lord, but she had to answer for all the things she'd done—and didn't do—after she'd made that commitment to Him. While she knew she would be spending eternity in heaven, standing before the Lord as she had to give an account of her sins was a scary thought.

Round and round her mind went, her heart rate and breathing shooting up to almost panic attack levels. She mentally forced herself to calm down, reminding herself that, according to Scripture, a lot of things still had to happen. The anti-Christ still had to appear and form the one-world currency and religion; the temple in Israel had to be rebuilt; the two witnesses had to testify for three and a half years. There was still time to get her act together, to confess and repent of everything she could think of. *Hopefully...*

Finally, she was able to form a coherent thought she could voice.

"So, what does that mean for us? What should we do?"

Reg nodded his head, as if he was answering a mental question of his own. "Means we need to get back to town and buy every supply we can think of with every penny we have, before our money ain't worth a dam—er, sorry, a dang."

Nikki blinked several times. For Reg to suggest spending money at all was a rarity—she swore the man could squeeze eleven cents' change out of a dime. But for him to say they should wipe out their accounts in order to buy supplies—well, now, that was something to worry about. It meant he was worried too.

Just then, Anna came strolling into the dining room and asked, "What's for dinner?"

They both looked at the girl and then at each other, neither saying a word.

Anna frowned. "What's wrong? What did I do now?"

Nikki sighed. "Nothing, sweetie. Reg and I were just discussing, uh... world events."

Her daughter scrunched up her face. "Eww. Okay, so does that mean it's 'yoyo' for dinner?"

"Yoyo" meant "you're on your own," a device Nikki employed whenever life got crazy, and she wasn't cooking.

Distractedly, Nikki answered, "Yeah, sounds like a good idea. I had thawed out hamburger, but I don't remember what I was planning to do with it now."

"Uh, the eighties coming back to get you, Mom?" Anna teased

as she headed in to raid the refrigerator.

Nikki halfheartedly laughed at her daughter's reminder that she had been a partier in her youth. Nikki had always believed in the philosophy of telling her kids all the bad things she'd done in her past in the hopes that they wouldn't repeat her mistakes.

The ploy had worked so far, except with her oldest, Alonzo, who struggled with addictions. He had gotten so bad that Nikki had lost touch with him and assumed he was homeless in the Dallas area. He and Reg had never even met.

She absently wondered what would become of him now if things were going to get as bad as they thought they might. *But then again if he's already homeless, he actually has an advantage, doesn't he? I mean, he would know how to survive with no money. And I did talk to him when we first got the job and told him how to get to the ranch, so maybe he might find his way down here...*

Her mind wandered to her middle child and oldest daughter, Leeann. She was in her third year of college in Austin, majoring in public relations. The girl would be totally lost with no idea of how to survive if things went south like Reg and the experts were predicting. She couldn't even survive camping. Leeann's idea of "roughing it" was a cheap hotel room with no room service.

And what about Reg's kids? They too were adults, but his daughter, Connie, was a product of "the system," taught well by her mother just how to abuse the American welfare and food stamp programs. Nikki doubted Connie would have any better idea of how to survive in a collapsed economy than Leeann would.

Reg's son, Nathaniel, would probably be okay, but with his temper and penchant for fighting, it wouldn't be long before he ended up in a situation over his head. Nikki shuddered as she ran through mental scenarios of Nathaniel having to fight off dozens of people desperate for food and supplies.

They needed to get word to the kids right away, tell them all to come to the ranch—especially Connie, who had a three-year-old son. At least here there was food and shelter. And safety. They were far enough away from civilization that it was highly unlikely that anyone would show up to rob and steal.

Nikki decided she needed to snail mail a map of the ranch to them all right away, something tangible they could hold in their hand just in case cells and emails were no longer available for whatever reason.

Anna was in the kitchen rummaging around for something to eat and Nikki looked at Reg, who appeared as deep in thought as she was.

"What are *you* thinking about?" She quietly asked him. There was just so much to consider.

He sighed and rubbed both hands over his face. "Anything and everything," he replied just as quietly. Neither one of them wanted to worry Anna—not until they had to.

"I just wish we had more time to prepare. There's so much left to do. I mean, the fields aren't ready, we maybe have enough food stored to last three months, *maybe*, but that's just for the three of us. I'm worried about the other kids, too."

Nikki felt tears stinging her eyes. "I know. I was just thinking about them. I'm going to mail all of them a map of how to get here."

Reg grimaced. "All of them, except Connie."

Nikki looked at him in surprise. "Connie? But why? Especially since she has Justin to worry about."

"Yeah, but she's also got her mama's apron strings tied in a noose around her neck and I don't want that witch knowing where we are. If Connie knows, she's sure to tell Brenda."

Nikki could understand her husband's reluctance to let his ex-wife know where he was. The woman had caused him nothing but pain all through their marriage with her countless affairs. She had even forced them into bankruptcy with her gambling and selfish pursuits.

But since Reg had left her, things had gotten even worse. Apparently feeling betrayed, the woman had tried everything from slander to filing false police reports in order to wreak havoc in her ex-husband's life. She'd even set his truck on fire and killed one of his dogs, heinous acts for which there was plenty of evidence, but she was never arrested.

Not long after Nikki and Reg had been married, Brenda had accused Reg of stalking—which carries a felony charge—claiming he was following her and watching her home. Nikki had had to go to the police station and give them proof that Reg had been with her at the times Brenda claimed he'd been stalking her—along with the doctor's reports of her husband's incapacitating knee injury at that time. He hadn't even been capable of driving then.

Nikki had wanted the police to press charges against Brenda for filing false reports, but they'd refused, saying that the woman was obviously just mistaken, that it wasn't her ex-husband following her after all.

After another similar situation arose when the police refused to do anything against Brenda, Nikki started to have suspicions that Brenda might have an "insider" in the San Angelo police department. They found out later that her suspicions were well-founded when Nathaniel let it slip that his mother had been having an affair with the married police chief—and had video-taped the liaisons, holding it over the man's head with threats of blackmail.

So, Nikki could well understand her husband's reluctance to tell his daughter where he was living, especially since Connie seemed to be turning into a clone of her mother. But she also felt a bit of a guilty conscience over it and voiced it to Reg.

"I understand what you're worried about, hon, but we have to let Connie know where we are, because she might need our help. You wouldn't want your grandson suffering, would you?" She knew that would get him.

He sighed again, heavily. "No, no, of course I don't. Can we just tell Nathaniel to kidnap Justin and bring him with him?"

Nikki laughed. "You know better than that." She sobered then and added, "Besides, Brenda might just need our help too. That's something you have to think about."

She could literally see her husband balk at that repulsive idea of helping his ex and hurried to add, "It's the right thing to do, honey. The Word tells us—Jesus *Himself* said it—that we have to love our enemies. No one is more of an enemy to you than Brenda, I know, but think about what a great opportunity it would be to witness to her if she came here."

Quietly she added, "Everyone is worth saving."

Reg scrunched up his face in disgust. "Yeah, I know. You're right. But let's just hope she gets saved somewhere else and doesn't darken our doorstep."

Nikki chuckled softly. "I'm thinking that we might just have a whole lot of people at our doorstep. Remember the dreams you've had of lots of people coming to the ranch and how we had to help them? I think your dreams are all going to come true."

He nodded in agreement. "Yep, you might be right about that. Only I'm afraid this dream might turn into a nightmare, one we ain't gonna be prepared for."

Nikki fingered the place mat in front of her. "A lot of people say, 'the Lord won't give you more than you can handle.' But nowhere in the Bible does it say that. The only thing close to that is in first Corinthians where it says we won't be *tempted* beyond what we could bear." She shook her head.

"Instead, Scripture speaks of many times when God's people

endured hardships that were so overwhelming there was no way they could have gotten through it on their own. I believe that the Lord *often* gives us more than we can handle, so that we have to rely on Him to provide the way."

They were quiet for a moment and then Nikki continued. "Whatever's coming, however bad things may get, it may very well be far more than we can handle. But remember that if God brings you to it, He'll take you through it."

Reg nodded again. "Yeah. I just want to make sure we're doing everything we can, and everything we're supposed to do, in the meantime. We have to prepare for the worst-case scenarios."

Nikki sighed, thinking that her husband just didn't get what she was trying to tell him, that the Lord would provide for whatever needs they might have. But then she thought about the times in Scripture when the Lord warned His people to prepare for what was to come—like in the case of Joseph, who was able to save not only Egypt, but other countries as well as his own family, from starvation, all because of a warning the Lord gave Pharaoh in a dream.

She realized then that while the Lord sometimes provided in miraculous ways, like the ravens feeding Elijah in the desert mountains, or sending manna from heaven to the wandering Israelites, at other times He showed the way for His people to provide for themselves.

Perhaps this was one of those times when He was leading his children to prepare, to provide for the future. She and Reg had both certainly felt the leading to prepare for *something,* some catastrophe coming their way, and had been trying their best to be ready for what may come.

Maybe the news of the financial collapse of Europe was the final warning… the "get ready, here it comes."

But there was another much more important way in which they needed to prepare, which she had reminded herself of when they started this conversation. She glanced at Reg, who looked like he too was deep in thought.

"Honey," she quietly said as she reached over to place her hand atop his, "we also need to prepare ourselves spiritually." She stroked the backs of his fingers.

"Since we moved here, we've been running around like headless chickens trying to fix a place to roost. But we've both stepped away from what's truly important… our relationship with Jesus. We need to make that priority numero uno. Especially in light of the fact that apparently our time here has just shortened."

Reg nodded without looking up from where he stared at her small hand resting on his. He shook his head as if trying to clear it and stared at her then, his eyes bleary-looking and red.

"Yeah, you're absolutely right. And I have a feeling that my dream of having dozens of people here at the ranch is soon going to come true."

Nikki nodded at him. "Yes, and they're going to need more than just food and shelter. Think about it—if things really get bad this time, if we get to the 'day's wages for a loaf of bread' situation, and the lines are blurred between government and military, then the people who come to us are going to be scared and desperate. They'll need to know about Jesus and what it takes to be saved. We need to be ready to answer questions they might have and that means that we need to know Scripture inside and out. It also means we need to strengthen our own relationship with God."

Her husband grimaced, the corner of his mouth lifting in a half-snarl, half-smile. "Been thinking the same thing, that we both need to get a lot stronger in our walk with the Lord. Seems like I'm sliding away from Him bit by bit."

She nodded again. "Exactly. Me too. It's that slippery slope we all find ourselves on at some point or another. We're close to the Father when we're in trouble, but when things start going good, off we go down that wide road and away from the straight and narrow path He wants us to stay on. And before long, we're tumbling off that road and rolling down that slope toward destruction."

Reg nodded. "I try to pray as I do chores and stuff throughout the day, but my mind wanders over every stinkin' thing that still needs to be done, or I'm being constantly reminded of all my failures."

Nikki sighed. "I know, me too. Honestly, I think that's the enemy trying to distract us. He's great at that—whispering in our ears all the things he knows will keep us focused on anything but God."

Reg turned his hand over and laced his fingers through Nikki's.

"So, love of my life, tell me what you think we ought to be doing to fix it."

Nikki laughed. "*You're* the spiritual leader of the house, remember?"

Reg returned the laughter. "Oh sure. Okay, fine. Play the submissive wife card whenever it's convenient—I see how it is."

Nikki widened her eyes in what she hoped was an innocent deer-in-the-headlights look, à la Anna.

"I'm *always* the obedient wife," she answered as she tried hard not to laugh. Then she smirked at him.

"At least I am when you're being logical and thinking my way."

They both laughed, but Reg became serious quickly as he rubbed his thumb over her palm. "Well, first things first is that we—and that includes Anna—need to start praying together. And doing a Bible study together. No more of this 'you do your study and I'll do mine.' We need to all be in the Word together and discuss it as a family."

"I agree completely. Just be prepared for a major episode of teenage groaning, moaning and eye-rolling."

chapter 7

I T HAD been three weeks since the overseas economy started collapsing and so far only Greece, Spain, Italy and France had been affected, although the experts were predicting an eminent German collapse.

In response to the upcoming worldwide economic demise, commodity prices in the U.S. had risen dramatically, which irked Reg to no end.

"There's no excuse for prices to have shot up like they have here already," he complained. "The only reason is because of the greed of the retailers."

He and Nikki had done exactly as Reg said—taken every penny in their account and bought supplies the day after they'd gotten the news of the problems in Greece. Since the only bills they had were their personal cell phones and truck insurance, they had quite a bit of money saved up and were able to fully stock the storage shed with canned goods, paper products, soaps and the like.

They then spent several hundred dollars on seed for the fields and Reg found a large fuel tank for sale that they'd had filled with diesel so there would be extra on hand to run the tractors. They'd also made sure their propane tank was full and had ordered an extra tank, which was backordered thanks to many others having the same idea. Reg had also insisted on buying several more solar converters "just in case."

Nikki worried, then chided herself for worrying and not trusting the Lord, then worried some more. *Do we have enough food stored until the crops start producing more? What about all the other essentials—toilet paper, toothpaste, soaps, shampoos, our monthly girl needs, razors. Some things we can make, but not paper products. And what about medicines? Do we have enough colloidal silver, aspirin, and all?*

The medicines worried her the most. While she had tried to steer her family away from the chemical end of the medical spectrum and moved toward more natural healing, she knew she was still very far from having the knowledge she needed to really help in the event of a true medical emergency.

And that thought got her worrying about injuries—for example, would she be able to stitch a wound if necessary? She seriously doubted it and shuddered just thinking about the prospect. She wasn't squeamish, but the thought of causing someone pain—as would be the case when piercing their skin with a needle—made her sick to her stomach. She decided she'd stock up on super glue for those cases.

But what about infection? She had gallons of hydrogen peroxide stored and maybe a gallon of colloidal silver—which would fight against bacteria, fungal infections and even viruses—but what about the future when that stock ran out? While she had the instructions for making a device that created colloidal silver, the homemade stuff wasn't something she wanted her family ingesting… but maybe they could use it for topical applications only.

And then there was hydrogen peroxide—it wasn't exactly something she could whip up in the kitchen. The best she would be able to come up with would be an alcohol or vinegar of some sort, something fermented, but would that be sterile? Would it be enough to kill germs?

That's when Nikki had what she thought was a bit of a crazy idea. When they had found all the antique tools and equipment in the attic, Reg had discovered an old rusty still hidden in the back behind some old furniture. They'd joked at the time about Tiny being a moonshiner, but now that she thought about it, corn liquor—or whatever kind they could brew—would make a great antiseptic for wounds, plus it had the added benefit of being somewhat of a pain killer. She thought of the countless old westerns she'd seen where the patient took a big slug of whiskey before the doctor yanked a bullet out of his body with a pair of pliers. She shuddered again. She hoped things would never get so bad that it would come down to that.

But since marijuana was currently illegal to grow, why not set up the still and make some alcohol? She and Reg weren't big drinkers themselves—just an occasional beer or glass of wine—but it seemed that a strong liquor might be a medical necessity if the road got as rough as it seemed to be heading toward. And it would be something they could also offer in trade. She hurriedly got on the laptop and started researching how to make whiskey.

When Reg came in from the workshop where he'd been making a solar hot water heater out of the old water heater they'd replaced, he found Nikki hunched over the laptop at the dining table, scribbling notes on the back of an envelope.

He smiled at the sight. "Now what are you working on?" He said with slight exasperation. Usually when his wife was this involved in something, it meant yet another project she was going to volunteer him for.

"Distilling whiskey," she answered distractedly.

That was a bit of a shock. "Whiskey? How'd you come up with that one, Jackie Daniels?" He teased.

Nikki rolled her eyes at him, reminding him of Anna. "It can be used for antiseptic and pain relief, plus we could also use it for trading purposes."

Reg pulled out the chair across from her and sat. "Wouldn't it be easier to just store a few cases of the stuff?"

She shrugged. "Well, yeah, but that stuff was expensive *before* prices shot up; I can only imagine what it's like now. Plus, we need to think long term. Who knows how long of a siege we're in for. We need to think about being self-sufficient for all things, not just food."

Reg nodded. "True."

He had a sudden thought then. "Hey, what about beer? You know I like a bottle once in a while. Can you make that too?"

Nikki sighed and gave her husband an "are you kidding me?" look.

"Now you're talking about growing hops and using some of our barley that we're growing *for food*. I'm not sure it's worth it for something that's just a pleasure drink."

Her husband had a dejected look at that answer, and she laughed. "Okay, okay, I'll look into it. Maybe we can store hops. And for the record, I wasn't looking to make whiskey for drinking, per se, but more for the medicinal side of it."

Reg snickered, the corner of his mouth lifting in a half-grin. "Yeah, sure. Just for your rheumatism, eh?"

Nikki laughed and answered in an "old lady" voice, "Now look here, ya whippersnapper, don't be giving me any of that lip, sonny, or else I'll be taking you out to the tool shed and giving you what for!"

Reg laughed at his wife's antics, happy that she could keep her sense of humor despite the overwhelming sense of waiting for the other shoe to drop that hovered over them. They were both trying to keep positive in the situation and doing their best to just do what needed to be done and not get bogged down with worry.

One good thing that had come from the impending crisis was that the family was now drawing nearer to God once again. Since they'd gotten word of the coming economic disaster, they had prayed more together—and not just at meals—and had begun an in-depth Bible study that they'd insisted Anna join in on.

At first the teen had grumbled about it, stating that she wanted to spend as much time playing Xbox and watching satellite television as she could before they didn't have the luxuries anymore, but then she'd suddenly become more and more interested in learning about

God's Word and had even asked several intriguing questions, which had all three of them digging through Scripture to find answers.

Through that closer relationship with the Lord, they'd all started having dreams, and strangely, sometimes very similar dreams. Reg had decided that it had to be the Lord speaking to them, warning and guiding them to prepare for what was to come.

In one of the dreams, Nikki had seen a multitude of women and children walking toward the ranch, leading horses pulling carts piled high with belongings. In another, she saw a caravan of RV's and travel trailers arriving at the ranch with families seeking refuge.

In one of Reg's dreams, he saw who he thought was Agent Henderson from Border Patrol up on the hill near the ranch house. He had a rifle and seemed to be watching the landscape. Reg had the sense that he was looking for people—those needing help—and not necessarily watching for "bad guys." Reg said he felt like in the dream the man he thought to be Henderson was with them, on their side.

Most surprising of the dreams, however, was Anna's. In it, she saw a long line of people alongside the pond. She saw Reg and another man she didn't recognize standing in the pond, baptizing all the people. That dream gave the family a lot of hope for the future.

The economic demise of the United States came a few months later, following Germany and the UK, then New Zealand and Australia. Soon Russia followed along with the rest of Asia, then the African continent and the Arab nations quickly succumbed.

The world had come crashing down.

The commodity prices, which were already through the roof in the U.S., climbed to such astronomical heights that people had taken to looting and robbing just to survive. A federal state of emergency and martial law were being discussed, but before the president could make an executive order to that effect, he and his entire cabinet vanished.

Almost overnight, the man the current president had replaced stepped up to take over, immediately instituting martial law, making himself the permanent leader of the United States. Americans were reeling and had no idea what had happened until it was already over and done with and soldiers were policing the country.

Reg and Nikki didn't leave the ranch after all the turmoil started. Anna wasn't too happy about the situation—being stuck at home with "the parentals" was never a teen's idea of a good time—but as Nikki pointed out to the young girl, at least she was safe.

Nikki and Reg continued to worry about their other children, who all stubbornly refused to come to the ranch to live, naively assuming that things would right themselves. Nikki still hadn't had any contact with her wayward son.

One evening the cell rang and Nikki jumped, grabbing the phone and noticing the display said "Unknown." They never got any calls, not since the U.S. collapsed, anyway. In fact, the family was somewhat surprised—and Anna was thankful—they still had reliable phone service, even though the internet and television were now a thing of the past. And of course, with the solar panels, they would always have at least limited electricity. So far, the collapse hadn't really affected them too much.

"Hello?"

"Hey. How are you guys holding up down there?" It was Gina. She sounded tired… and afraid.

"Good so far. In fact, we haven't really had any fallout from the collapse." She paused, realizing that her statement almost sounded like bragging.

"The Lord is taking care of us," she added, knowing full well *Who* was due the credit for their survival. "How are y'all doing?"

A heavy sigh followed by a moment of silence said quite a bit. "It's rough here. Really bad. We can't buy food and what I managed to stock up on when we first figured out what was coming is almost gone. My crazy husband has taken to sitting by the front window with a shotgun, waiting for looters. So, far he hasn't shot anyone but it's just a matter of time, especially with his temper. And then I'm afraid the soldiers are going to execute him if that happens. They seem to think they've been given license to kill. It's scary."

Nikki's heart started pounding. This was exactly what they'd feared the end times would be like, with citizens fearing for their lives from a corrupt government and literally having to fight for survival. The worry she felt for her own kids now turned to almost full-blown panic and she said a quick prayer that the Lord would get through to their stubborn hearts and send them to the ranch.

Speaking of. "Hey, you need to pack up and get down here where it's safe," she urged Gina, knowing that she didn't need to speak to Reg first. He'd be all for it.

"Seriously. Now. As soon as you can. Tonight."

Gina laughed, the sound half-hearted and dispirited. She sounded nothing at all like the vivacious girl Nikki knew.

"Actually, that's what I was calling about. Ben and I were talking about it and we have to get out of here, out of Odessa."

Her voice changed to an almost pleading tone. "Would you and Reg mind a little company? I mean, at least for a little while until we can figure out what to do."

She hurriedly added, "We have an RV, so you wouldn't have to put us up or anything—"

Nikki didn't hesitate. "Of course! We expect you to stay as long as you want. It's not our ranch, anyway," she added with a half laugh. "Speaking of—what about Tiny and April? Won't they want to come down too?"

Gina sighed again. "No. I talked to him the other day and strongly suggested it, but he said that they'd stay where they were. There's a nurse on staff at the nursing home who they're very fond of and apparently he told the couple that he'd take care of them, no matter what."

She paused and her voice sounded a bit watery as she continued. "I sure hope he *can* take care of them... no matter what. I sure do love that old man."

Nikki swallowed hard. She and Reg had never even met Tiny, had only spoken to him on the phone, but they'd both come to be very fond of him too. She said another quick prayer for the couple.

"Well, we'll be praying for their safety. But you don't waste any time and get your butts down here! Things are only going to get worse." Nikki paused as she had a sudden thought.

"Do you have gas for the RV?" Gas prices were at twenty-two dollars a gallon and rising quickly every day. The last visit they made to town—and the last one they would ever make, they were certain—gas stations had run out of fuel left and right. It had become nearly impossible to find a station that had any at all.

"Yeah, thankfully Ben had filled both tanks in the RV when we first got word of the economic crisis overseas, before prices shot up. And he also filled every gas can we had. We have enough to get down there and then some."

"That's good then." Nikki grimaced as another thought entered her head.

"Are you armed? I mean, you said Ben had a shotgun, but do you have plenty of weapons and ammo? For self-defense, I mean."

Gina chuckled. "I'm the daughter of a sheriff and wife of a police lieutenant who did two tours in Iraq. We're well-armed."

Nikki hated the thought, but with the way the world was going, you *had* to be armed for self-preservation these days. It had come down to kill or be killed. She and Reg had a few handguns, a rifle and a shotgun, and Reg had taken her and Anna out several times to teach them how to shoot.

"And what about your dad? Will he want to come to the ranch?" Nikki and Reg had only met the sheriff once, but he was a very likable man, just like his daughter. And being a widower, Nikki knew he was alone.

Another heavy sigh. "No. He's been press-ganged into the Neos."

"Neos? What's that?"

Gina chuckled again, although the sound wasn't humorous. "Yeah, I guess you wouldn't know, seeing as how you're away from *civilization*." The last part was said with such sarcasm her voice practically dripped with it.

"Neos is short for 'Neo Geo Task Force'... it's the new government, uh, police force, I guess. Thugs is more like it. Criminals with authority. They're who's in charge now, keeping us lowly citizens *safe*."

Nikki felt shock reverberate through her system at that. The government had formed its own brute squad? And they were also forcing people to join them...

"How is it even possible that they forced your dad to join them?"

Gina heaved another sigh. "Since the government isn't using the military to 'keep the peace' and instead using the Neos, they don't have enough personnel to cover all the rural areas—at least not here in Texas—so they forced the various county sheriffs and state police to join their evil forces."

"Wow. But not your husband?"

"No. Thankfully, they didn't recruit from the city police departments. That may be coming, though, which is another reason we need to get out of here. I'm not sure what I'd do if they come knocking at our door, insisting Ben join them."

Nikki shuddered. "Well, tell your dad he's more than welcome to come here, if he can get away from them."

"I'll try to contact him. But getting away from them is difficult, if not impossible. They're tracking everyone now, I hear. Even using our cells to do so. In fact, I'm ditching our phones before we come down there, so just expect us in about two to three days, okay?"

"Alright. Just be safe getting here. Low profile and all."

"Will do. See you soon."

When Reg came in, Nikki told him about the phone call and what Gina had said about her dad—and others—being forced into service.

He groaned. "Great. I bet that's not just in Texas, either, but all over the U.S. The Feds have taken over and I just bet the president ordered them to go after military personnel now."

"But why would he do that?" She asked, almost immediately answering her own question when she remembered how anti-military the man had been during his own presidency.

Reg shrugged. "Power has a funny way of changing a person.

Maybe he doesn't want anything to get in the way of his total control of the U.S. Or maybe he just doesn't want a wild card and wants to make sure his own people are running the show. Either way, it stands to reason that he'd want to be rid of the military."

Nikki's eyes widened at that. "By 'be rid of', you mean—"

Reg grimaced. "Execution."

"What? No way! He can't just order something like that…"

She let her voice trail off, knowing that what she was saying wasn't true at all—the man had proven his true nature many times before, and this was something he was entirely capable of ordering.

Reg sighed and looked very weary. "This is going to go south in a hand basket and fast. We need to step it up on getting ready."

He looked at Nikki pointedly. "Best be prepared for a whole slew of refugees to show up at our doorstep. Heck, we may end up with the entire military for all we know."

chapter 8

BY THE time the entire world fell apart, the south Texas spring rains had come and many of the crops Reg and Nikki had planted in the fall had started to grow.

And grow they did. The couple was amazed at the rapid growth and thickness and health of the plants. Reg said he'd never seen the like in all his time ranching and farming. Especially growing so well in the sandy south Texas soil. They again knew the Lord was blessing them and Nikki cited the "plenty before the famine" period Egypt had experienced in Joseph's time.

Nikki and Gina were busy grinding grains into flour and canning everything they could. Anna had taken a liking to dehydrating and had various foods sandwiched between screened flats Reg had made for her, on which she was drying everything from fruits and veggies to jerky made from marinated beef from a cow Reg had butchered.

Ben had turned out to be a huge help to Reg, having ranching experience as a teen when he spent four years on a ranch for wayward boys. He'd been in and out of trouble with the law since his father had left the family when Ben was twelve, and his mother, a struggling single mom with two other children, had enrolled him in the program when her son had gotten caught stealing change out of vending machines. The program was normally only for six months, but Ben had loved the place so much he'd decided to stay through high school and upon graduating had gotten a job working at the boy's ranch until he was old enough to enter the police academy.

The only thing he didn't know how to do relating to farming and ranching was butchering—a task the boy's ranch had deemed too gruesome for young boys, so they'd sent their livestock to a packing plant for butchering. And even though Ben had been a police officer, the sight of blood made him sick, which Reg found infinitely funny and had good-naturedly teased him about as often as he could, despite Ben's bad temper and penchant for flying off the handle.

Gina worried for Reg, knowing what her husband was capable of if he got riled enough at another man. "Thankfully," she'd told Nikki, "he's too chivalrous—you can read that as alpha male—to hurt a woman."

But she'd told Nikki that since the collapse, and with Ben subsequently losing his job after martial law was put in place, he'd been even more antagonistic than usual, blowing up at the slightest incidents. Nikki had reminded Gina that Reg was big enough to get away with teasing a grizzly bear and not to worry.

Despite his gruffness, it wasn't long before Ben halfheartedly laughed whenever Reg teased him and soon that teasing forced him to stifle his vomiting urges when confronted with a carcass. And true to his A-type personality, Ben wouldn't let up until he was even better than Reg at butchering. Eventually, much to Reg's relief, Ben took over the task. Butchering wasn't something Reg ever liked doing himself.

Gina and Ben's kids, Garrett and Britney, were sixteen and

twelve respectively, and had done the typical spoiled *"Me Generation"* eye rolling when they had arrived at the ranch and were assigned chores by Reg. It was hilarious to Reg and Nikki that Anna—the queen of complaining about having to do chores—had gotten after the two kids for being lazy. The kids had then reluctantly started doing what they were asked to do.

From the moment they first laid eyes on each other, Garrett and Anna had fallen into instant hate. For the life of them, the two mothers couldn't figure out what the problem was, since both teens had a lot in common and were both very attractive kids. Anna with her pale skin and pixie-cut dark auburn hair and big brown doe eyes and Garrett was the Mini-Me of his father with thick dark brown hair and grayish-blue eyes. Being teens, one would think it would have taken all four adults to keep them apart.

But no, they fought constantly, and about the dumbest things. One day, they were arguing over which dog was smarter—Zeke, the Golden Retriever, or the Thompson's Chow, Frannie. Reg had taken over the argument and told the teens that since both dogs had a penchant for eating horse turds, in his estimation they were both dumb as toads.

Ben solved the puzzle of the teens' animosity one evening after dinner when the couples sat around the table while the kids went off to their respective corners to entertain themselves. Of course, internet was now a thing of the past, as was the television, but with the solar electricity available, they were still able to play video games after a sunny day.

"They like each other. Or at least one of them likes the other and is covering it up by acting like a jerk," Ben had explained in a quiet voice so the kids wouldn't overhear after Nikki had lamented over the snarl Anna had given to Garrett when he'd offered to give her pointers for the game she was playing.

"But why would they act so snotty if they like each other?" Gina asked her husband.

Ben shrugged. "I think it's because they're both introverted and kinda socially awkward. Maybe they're also afraid the other one doesn't share the feeling."

"So, it's a protective thing," Nikki added.

"Yeah," Ben replied. "A sort of 'I'll attack first so you can't hurt me as bad' thing."

"That's dumb," Gina said.

"That's teens," Reg added, and the couples laughed.

The families had started out sharing meals together in the ranch house from day one, and it wasn't long before all spare time was spent there, since the RV was pretty small for a family of four. The Thompsons only returned to the RV for sleep, since the ranch house only had three bedrooms.

So, far, everything was going very well. In spite of Ben's surliness, the couples got along well, and, with the exception of the teens, the kids did too. Britney, who took after her mother in size, looks and personality, idolized Anna and followed her everywhere. Being the baby in her own family, Anna suddenly felt like a big sister and took Britney under her wing to show her the ropes around the ranch. It was an unending source of amusement for Reg, since before it took every bit of cajoling and threatening to get the girl to lift a rake or shovel. Now she was strutting around like she was the one in charge as she showed Britney how to feed and water the animals, muck the stalls, and groom the horses.

Reg and Ben decided that a cellar under the ranch house would be a good idea and one afternoon started tearing up the wood floor where the dining room table had been.

Nikki and Gina had come in the back door, their arms burdened with heavy baskets loaded with yet another ample haul from the garden and stared at each other worriedly when they heard the distinctive sound of wood planking being pried up.

Hurrying into the dining room, they stopped and stared in horror at the carnage. The large dining table had been shoved to one side and her husband and Ben were busy ripping up the floorboards with pry bars.

"What the heck are you doing?" Nikki exclaimed as she set her basket on the floor.

Reg barely glanced up at her as he continued working. "Tearing up the floor."

Nikki rolled her eyes, although her husband didn't see it. "I can see that," she drawled as she crossed her arms over her chest. "Mind telling me why?"

Reg waited while Ben used a saw to cut through a board before answering. The hole in the floor was now about three feet across and four feet long.

"That's good," he told Ben, before turning to his wife.

"We're gonna dig a cellar," he said as he handed a shovel to Ben that had been leaning against the wall. Ben started digging with a suspicious grin on his face.

Thank goodness this old house doesn't have a concrete foundation and they're at least putting the dirt in a wheelbarrow, Nikki thought to herself as she watched him dig.

"We *have* a cellar," Nikki reminded him. "Remember? Just outside the back door to the right." She made sure her voice dripped with sarcasm to make the point that she was sure her husband had lost his cotton-pickin' mind and had taken Ben with him for a stroll down Loony Lane.

Reg graced her with that crooked grin she loved so much, but at the moment she wanted to smack it off his face.

"Yeah, I know, but this one is going to be a *hidden* cellar. The door will be here, under the dining table. With the throw rug on top of it and then the table, you won't even know it's there."

It was Gina's turn. "Why do you need a hidden cellar?"

Ben answered his wife. "For hiding," he said, in a tone of voice that had an unspoken "duhhh" at the end.

"Hiding what?" The ladies asked in unison, then laughed at each other.

"Jinx," Gina said under her breath. Nikki lightly nudged her in the side with her elbow.

Reg sobered then. "Us. People. Whoever needs hiding."

The women made an "O" shape with their mouths. The realization that such a thing might become necessary someday filled them with a whole lot of trepidation.

Late one March afternoon, an old truck came down the two-mile driveway to the ranch, its bed filled with so much furniture and boxes that it looked like it was about to topple over. Reg grabbed the rifle and headed out to meet them, Ben following close behind while muttering expletives and unholstering his Beretta.

"Now Reg, don't be scaring off some poor people just looking for a safe place to stay!" Nikki yelled out the door, with Gina giving a similar directive to her own husband over her friend's shoulder.

The ladies called to the kids to stay in the house and rushed out to follow their husbands to hopefully keep them from causing trouble. Nikki knew that Reg would be kind to anyone who was looking for help, since they both felt that was the ministry the Lord was calling them to. But Ben and Gina weren't Christians, and she was worried what Ben might do, especially considering the fact that he was a former police officer and was a bit distrustful of people in general.

As they approached the truck, the passenger door opened and a blonde jumped out and ran toward Nikki, who gasped. It was her oldest daughter, Leeann. Nikki immediately started crying as she ran to embrace her daughter.

"You found us! I'm so glad you're here! I've been so worried about you," Nikki said between sobs.

Leeann was just as bad and was barely able to speak through her tears. "Me too, Mom. I'm so sorry I didn't listen to you and come sooner. Things got... really bad." Her voice broke at that admission.

Nikki hugged her daughter tighter, hearing the pain in her voice. They'd have time to talk later, but now was not the place for such a discussion. Over her daughter's shoulder, she watched as a middle-aged man exited the driver's side of the truck and stood talking to Reg while Ben stood watching suspiciously. Thankfully, he'd at least holstered his gun once more.

The dark-haired man was extremely thin, haggard looking and a bit scary; certainly not the sort of person she would have chosen to drive her daughter around.

"Who's the scruffy-looking guy?" She asked Leeann in a whisper as her daughter moved from the embrace to wipe her eyes.

Leeann half-laughed and half-hiccupped as she answered. "That's your son, Mom."

"What?" Nikki stood rooted in place, in total shock.

To say that Alonzo had changed in the eighteen or so months since she'd last seen him would be a gross understatement. Her once handsome and robust son was now a shell of his former self. His normally ruddy olive-toned skin looked ashen and clung to his bones. The young man slumping against the driver's door of the truck looked old, defeated, and at least twenty years older than what he truly was.

Cautiously she stepped toward him. "Alonzo?" She asked in an unsure voice.

All three men looked up at her at the same time. Reg looked surprised that she knew the man and Ben looked like he wasn't sure if he should cuff the guy or shoot him. But her son looked like he was fighting back tears.

"Hey Mom," he answered in a sad-sounding voice as he pushed away from the truck and turned toward her. He looked like he was ashamed and unsure of his welcome, the prodigal son returning to beg for forgiveness. She noticed the way Reg's head whipped back toward Alonzo and she knew he was shocked that this worn-out, old-looking man was her son.

Nikki's heart went out to her first-born, who had gotten so steeped in sin—in addictions and who knew what else—that he'd not only lost himself to his family, he'd been lost to himself. But worst of all, he had lost sight of God. But now her prodigal son had returned.

She rushed to embrace him. "Thank God. Thank God," she kept repeating as she cried against his chest. Despite his gauntness, he was a large man, almost as tall as her husband, and had to bend his head to hers.

"It's been so long since I saw you and I was afraid I'd *never* see you again," Nikki sobbed.

Alonzo was shaking against her, and Nikki knew he, too, was overcome with emotion.

"It's better you didn't see me, Mom. I was… I wasn't in my right mind for the longest time." He paused for a minute and shook harder.

"I'm still kinda screwed up," he admitted with a choked voice.

"It's okay, it's okay," Nikki whispered as she rubbed his back like she had when he was a child and she'd been soothing a boo-boo.

"You're here now, and safe. That's all that matters."

They held each other for a long time until Reg said with some humor in his voice, "Ya gonna introduce us?"

The pair laughed and stepped out of the embrace. Nikki wiped her face and turned to the rest of the group. "This is my son, Alonzo Martino. He's half-Italian," she added with a laugh, like the name wasn't enough of a clue.

The men shook his hand and Gina insisted on giving him a hug. Nikki then turned to Leeann and introduced her to Ben and Gina. Reg had met her once before when they'd gone to Austin for Leeann's birthday.

"And this is my oldest daughter, Leeann Pritchard."

Nikki laughed self-deprecatingly. "My kids all have different fathers. I truly am the woman at the well."

Ben and Gina looked quizzically at her while they shook hands with the kids, so Nikki elaborated, "The woman at the well is from the Bible."

She waved her hand. "I'll tell you the story later," she added with a laugh.

Just then, Anna came flying out of the house toward her siblings, followed quickly by Garrett, Britney and the barking dogs.

"I tried keeping her in the house like you said," Garrett yelled, his handsome young face red and angry as he charged down the steps on Anna's heels, "but the stubborn butt wouldn't listen."

Gina got after her son for calling Anna a "butt" and then reassured him that it was okay for her to come out, that the family was having a reunion, and then laughed when Anna turned in her sister's embrace to give Garrett a "nyeh" face.

Garrett and Anna had finally—and reluctantly—called a truce after the night Ben had blown up at the two of them when they were fighting over whether Call of Duty or Call of Duty Black Ops was the better game.

After calling the truce, the two teens had started getting along better, to the point that their parents now had to keep an eye on them and not let them be alone together for too long. Gina and Nikki had lamented the fact that, while glad that their kids were no longer fighting, the teens now needed babysitting.

"Well, now we're finally back together," Nikki happily announced as she grinned at her husband but noticed the slightly painful grimace on his handsome face before he smiled back at her.

"Once we get Reg's kids here," she amended, "the family will be complete."

Reg grumbled, "They're not coming, you know that." He shrugged, as if the fact that his kids had all but abandoned him didn't hurt, even though Nikki knew better. He'd been tormented by their abandonment for years and of course felt betrayed.

He snorted. "Heck, they wouldn't even know how to get to the ranch even if they did want to come."

Nikki frowned and laid her hand on his arm, aware that, despite his grumbling, he was worried about them.

"They'll get here, honey, I'm sure of it. And they know how, since I sent them a map to the ranch. Remember we talked about that? I sent it to all the kids—well, except Alonzo, since I didn't know where he was." She smiled sadly at her son over her shoulder.

He smiled back at his mother just as sadly. "Most of the time, Mom, I didn't know where I was myself."

She turned toward him and waved toward Leeann. "So, how did you two hook up?"

Leeann gasped and immediately protested her mother's word choice. "Mom! You don't say 'hook up' when you're talking about brothers and sisters. That's just... just so... eww!"

Nikki didn't know what in the world her daughter was complaining about, but noticed the other kids were laughing. Alonzo's face was beet red as he laughed and shook his head either in denial or disbelief. She reminded herself to ask Leeann later what "hook up" meant.

"Okay, okay, so how did you manage to *find* each other?"

Leeann answered after punching Alonzo in the arm for continuing to laugh. "Al had my number and called me about three weeks ago. He told me he was coming to get me and to not argue. By then, things were getting bad…"

Leeann's face paled as she made that confession and Nikki patted her arm, giving the only comfort she could without knowing what exactly "bad" entailed. Despite wanting to comfort and care for her daughter, she realized that she probably really didn't want to know the specifics of what she'd gone through.

Leeann blinked back at the tears that had suddenly gathered in her eyes and Nikki's heart clenched in sympathy as her own eyes misted.

"And so I agreed and he came to my apartment and loaded up my stuff and here we are." She shrugged as if to say, *No big deal. Just survived getting out of a city under siege by the out-of-control government, rescued by my drug addict brother, drove back roads for hundreds of miles to a place I'd never been, with the hopes that my mom was still here, and we'd be welcome…*

Nikki almost laughed. That was Leeann—the resilient one. Nothing had ever really fazed her, unlike Al who wore his heart on his sleeve. And, of course, Anna was the official the Drama Mama.

Leeann was certainly the strongest of the three, at least outwardly, but Nikki always wondered—and worried—about the day that was sure to come when her oldest daughter's Super Girl façade cracked, because she knew the girl was going to shatter into a million pieces.

She turned to her son. "But why didn't you call *me*? I called you with the new cell numbers back when we first came to the ranch."

He looked sheepish and turned his eyes to the ground. "Well, one night when Leeann had called me I was pretty, uh, high, and she told me that I needed to write her number down in case I didn't have my phone any longer."

Casting a glance at his sister standing next to him, he continued. "I didn't have anything to write with, so I, uh, used my knife and carved it into my arm." He pulled his sleeve up and showed them the scar.

Both women gasped and Nikki cringed at the sight of the ugly four-inch scar on his forearm.

"Ugh, Alonzo! That's horrible! How could you have done that to yourself?"

"Like I said, I was high and didn't even feel it 'til the next day." He shrugged. "Turned out to be a good thing I did that, though, 'else I never woulda found her. Lost my phone service a couple weeks later when I couldn't pay, then sold my phone and lost all the contacts."

Reg interrupted then, turning to Leeann. "Hey, do you still have your phone?"

She nodded and pulled it out of her pocket. "I don't have service anymore, but I kept it for the games I had downloaded."

Reg put his hand out and Leeann automatically handed it to him. Nikki watched, laughing to herself at the way people reacted unquestioningly to Reg's innate authority. They did the same with Ben. She shivered as she thought about the fact that that reaction was most likely going to come in handy in the months to come.

He turned the phone over and pulled the battery out. Leeann started to protest, but Reg answered before she could say anything. "Sorry, hon, it's mandatory. We can't have the government tracking anyone here."

Leeann frowned. "But I have my GPS and location services turned off. And besides, the internet doesn't exist anymore."

Reg shook his head. "The internet may not exist for *us,* but that don't mean the government don't still got it. Don't matter, though. Homeland Security has been able to track cell phones for years and you can be sure the technology is even better now. We just can't take any chances."

Anna stepped up then and slid her hand under her sister's arm, laying her head upon her shoulder. "Don't worry, sissy. If you want to play games, we still have PS4 and Xbox."

Garrett laughed then and added, "Yeah, we could use another player to make teams for Black Ops. Britney's kill ratio sucks though, just a warning." He mock cringed when his sister punched his arm.

He turned to Alonzo then. "In fact, if you want to make a team with your sister, Britney can take turns with Anna on my team."

Anna rolled her eyes at Garrett's obvious attempt at male

domination. Nikki had to bite her tongue to keep from laughing and commenting on the fact that Anna in fact, often beat the pants off of Garrett in whatever game they were playing. Gina didn't have any filter on *her* mouth, though, and uncannily voiced Nikki's thoughts. Garrett turned a lovely shade of crimson at his mother's teasing.

Alonzo laughed along with the group, but looked lost, like a foreigner trying to understand a new language. But even she knew what the kids were talking about, since video games seemed to be every teen's passion.

Nikki wondered if Alonzo had ever even played a video game or done any of the "normal" things his generation did since he'd moved out of her house at eighteen, or if he spent all his time seeking and doing drugs. Looking at the sad state her once healthy and beautiful baby boy had gotten himself into, Nikki figured that was exactly what had consumed him for the past several years.

She wondered what all he'd gone through, what all he'd put himself through. From his gauntness, it looked like he'd been near to starving and judging by the smell emanating from him, he hadn't used soap and water in quite a while. He was twitchy too, constantly shrugging his left shoulder and cocking his head, like a nervous tic. His bad choices had most certainly taken their toll on her only son.

The teens started arguing about the teams and turned away from the rest of the group. Nikki had a start when Leeann leaned over and in a quiet tone, voiced her mother's thoughts. *Can everyone read my danged mind?* Nikki thought with some exasperation.

"I knew he was in bad shape—I guess we all knew, huh?"

Leeann slid her hand under her brother's arm and leaned into his side. "So, anyway, back to the story: I figured it was only a matter of time until he didn't have a phone anymore, but I wanted him to be able to reach me. I was going to give him your number too, Mom. Guess it's a good thing I didn't," she said with a grimace as they both looked at Alonzo's arm once again.

Ben was still staring at Alonzo with narrowed eyes and a frown. Nikki wondered if he thought her son might be up to no good. She didn't think so; the young man in front of her resting his cheek atop his sister's head looked beaten down and ashamed. He just needed some comfort, food and shelter and some reassurance that he was now safe.

Reg encouraged the group to head inside where Leeann and Alonzo could get something to eat and drink, while he and Ben unloaded the truck.

Watching the group head into the house, laughing at the fact that Anna and Garrett were still arguing, Reg turned to Ben and asked, "What do you think?"

He didn't have to explain what—or who—he was talking about. Ben shook his head. His voice was grim, as was his expression. "The kid's still doing drugs, probably meth. Did you notice the tic? That's a classic meth symptom."

Reg sighed as he turned toward the truck and started untying the ropes holding the mass of furniture and belongings. "Yeah, that's what I thought too. I doubt Nikki even noticed; she was just so happy that he's here. She's been praying for that boy for a long time."

Ben snorted and curled his lip in disdain while muttering an expletive as he tossed a loosened rope over the pile.

"He's gonna need a lot more than prayer. If he's staying here, then he's not gonna have access to the drugs and he's gonna go through one helluva crash."

Reg regarded the man who had become a close friend since arriving at the ranch just a few short weeks ago, despite the man's atheistic views and proficiency in profanity. Reg had heard the near animosity in his voice when he said the word "prayer." It wasn't the first time that Ben had been somewhat antagonistic whenever Reg or Nikki had talked about God and faith. When they shared meals, Reg always prayed beforehand, and he'd noticed that Ben never even bowed his head during those times.

As they unloaded the furniture, he thought about the many times he'd wondered just how to bring up his faith to Ben, tell him about Jesus, about how to get saved. But he'd always been afraid of antagonizing Ben and alienating him, especially when their relationship was so new.

A quiet voice spoke in his mind just then. *He can't argue with your story. Tell him.*

Reg almost dropped the end table he was lifting out of the truck at the shock of hearing a voice in his head. But he knew it had to be the Lord and he felt a compulsion to obey.

He cleared his throat and said a quick prayer, asking the Lord to guide his words. "You know, back before I met Nikki, I felt like you did, that prayer didn't do no good. In fact, I wasn't sure if I even believed in God." He almost smiled at the way Ben's head snapped up at that comment.

"One thing I was sure of, though, was that if there was a God, there was no way He would forgive me for all the stuff I'd done."

Ben nodded as if in agreement and Reg snorted as he helped him lift a large box over the truck bed's side.

"And honestly, back then you and I wouldn't have been friends, cuz you'd likely be arresting me for something, and I woulda been resisting."

Ben chuckled as they set the box down. Reg continued. "I never did nuthin too bad, just fighting mostly. Had a bad temper. Had trouble obeying traffic laws too," he added as he grinned at Ben.

He leaned his forearm along the rail of the truck bed and stared off into the distance, remembering. Ben stopped and wiped sweat from his brow on his t-shirt, waiting to hear the rest of the story.

"But then I met Nikki and you know how it is—you wanna do whatever you can to impress that new lady. So, to please her I started taking her to church. I swear, that first time I walked into that little white church back in Barnhart, I was sure the roof was gonna come crashing down on this old sinner. I was sweatin' like a whore in church. Kinda literally."

He chuckled. "But not only did the place stay intact, everyone there was real friendly, accepting. They welcomed me like I was a friend."

He shook his head with a bit of wonder. "That was something I sure wasn't expecting. Figured all them Christian folk would be able to take one look at me and see all that bad stuff—all that sin—and they'd either run screaming, or look for a rope to string me up from the big ol' oak out front."

Ben shared a laugh with him as they lifted the last of the boxes out of the bed.

"So, I kept taking Nikki to church. At first it was just so's I'd have an excuse to spend more time with the little gal I'd fallen in love with, but pretty soon I was looking forward to going there and seeing all the people and having lunch after service with some of them. I even started looking forward to the sermons. After a few weeks, I started going to the Wednesday night Bible study and then the Saturday morning men's breakfast. Even went out to coffee a time or two with the preacher."

The men sat on the tailgate and wiped their faces. It was only March, but south Texas had a way of making a man sweat no matter what the temperature was. Reg sighed as he watched the dogs rooting around in the horse stalls, obviously looking for a turd. Thankfully, Anna and Britney had just cleaned them.

Reg leaned forward and laid his elbows on his thighs and propped his chin on his hands. "So, one Sunday the preacher gave an altar call at the end of service like he always did." He turned his head to glance at Ben.

At the man's quizzical look, Reg explained, "An altar call is where they invite anyone who wants to accept Jesus to come down to the front of the church and pray with the preacher. Well for some reason I felt this pull."

He shook his head, still in disbelief at the memory. "Hard to explain, but it was like everything in me was trying to get me to step out into that aisle and head down there to Pastor Lawrence."

Reg laughed at himself, grinning at Ben. "I was fighting the feeling, let me tell you. Going down there in front of all those people, all the people I'd befriended over the past several months, exposing myself like that, well, that sure wasn't nuthin I wanted to be doing. But it was like a… a force, I guess, was pushing me—"

"Okay, Skywalker, I think you've spent too much time in space," Ben interrupted with a half grin to go with his sarcasm.

Reg laughed good-naturedly. "Yeah, I know what it sounds like, but that's the only way to describe it—a force, one that I couldn't fight, and it was pushing me out into aisle. I even looked at Nikki to see if it was her, if she was shoving on me. But she was just standing there with her eyes closed, singing the altar call song with such a look of peace and joy on her face that I knew right then I had to have what she had—what a lot of the people in that little church had. So, before I knew what was really happening, I was standing there with Pastor Lawrence, giving my life to Jesus."

Reg grinned at Ben. "I stupidly thought my life would be smooth sailing from then on, ya know? Christians are happy, nuthin' bad ever happens to them." He laughed out loud at that.

"Boy, was I ever wrong. Not too long after that I got hurt at work, lost my job, then the work comp ran out right when Nikki lost her job. She didn't qualify for unemployment and my ex-boss was fighting the claim for mine. We were soon eating food from the church pantry and living without electricity or gas, down to one vehicle and selling everything we could just to stay afloat. But the Lord always provided just what we needed, when we needed it. Never went hungry and we were never without a roof over our heads."

He sobered then. "And we were happy. We were praying together, studying God's Word, and talking to God like He was a friend—which I discovered He actually is. None of the other stuff— the stuff we'd lost, which at one time seemed so darned important— none of it seemed to matter much anymore. In fact, the more stuff we had to let go of, the happier we got. Then Nikki found the job here at the ranch and now we know we have a purpose down here on this ol' rock that's circlin' the sun."

For the first time since Reg started telling his story, Ben actually showed genuine interest. "What's that... what's your purpose?"

Reg smiled and looked up at the blue sky, closing his eyes and enjoying the warmth of the sun on his face. "Well, our first purpose as humans—*all* humans—is to worship God. That's what He wants from us and the reason He created us in the first place. But the second purpose is we're here to help others—like Leeann and Alonzo. Like you and Gina and the kids. People who find themselves scared now, with no place to go, who want to get away from the world, who want to survive in this time."

Ben was quiet, so Reg continued. "You know all the stuff that's happening now with the economy, with the government and all? Well, the Bible speaks of it and Christians call it 'the end times'."

Ben's eyes rounded as he looked at Reg. "What? No." He shook his head in denial. "There's no way a book written so long ago could have predicted this, like Nostradamus or some crap like that."

Reg snorted again and laughed. "Yep, that's exactly what I'm saying. Considering God has always been here and always will be here, I guess it's safe to say that He knows what's happening and what's gonna happen. And Nikki and I have had a lot of 'end time' dreams and even Anna has had some. So, we've been doing a lot of studying about it, and yeah, all this is in the Bible. Not the exact wording that Greece's economy would collapse and then everything would topple after it, but the warnings are there, especially regarding what's to come. World domination by one man—the antichrist—in particular. One world government, one world religion and one type of currency. We're already getting to that point now.

"But there's a lot of hope, too. We also know that this ain't the end. No matter how bad things might get, there's hope for the future… hope for mankind." He didn't add that that hope only extended to those who put themselves under God's protective wings.

He looked at his friend. "If you'd like, you and Gina—and the kids, of course—are welcome to join us for the study we're doing about this. We usually have it on Wednesday nights, force of habit from when we were going to church, I guess, but we can do it any time you'd like. Or every night, for that matter."

Ben was quiet for so long that Reg was afraid he wasn't going to answer. Finally, he said, "Guess that'd be okay. Not like we have somewhere to be anyway," he quipped and both men laughed.

"Great. Well, why don't we start tomorrow night? We'll see if we can get Nikki's kids to join in too."

He sadly added, "Looks like that boy of hers could use all the hope he can get."

chapter 9

WITHIN a month, their little family that had started at three had suddenly exploded to forty-nine.

A week after Leeann and Alonzo had arrived, a young couple with three small children and two tiny Chihuahuas came walking onto the ranch, presumably from Mexico. None of them spoke English, but thankfully Ben could speak Spanish, so they were able to find out that the family had walked north nearly one hundred miles in the hopes that the United States' economy was better off than Mexico's.

The couple was very disheartened to find out that not only was the U.S. *not* better off than Mexico financially, it was, in fact, worse. But their fears were relieved—and tears stopped—when Reg told them they were welcome to stay at the ranch. The young father, Tomás, then told them a story that had everyone reeling when Ben translated. Even Ben looked a little shell-shocked by it.

"About a month ago, my wife had a dream where a man came to her and told her that we needed to move north, to America. She said he glowed, like he had a light inside of him, and she was sure it was Gabriel, the angel. She told the man that we had no more money, not even enough to buy milk for the children. And we had no visas to go to the United States. The man told her not to worry, that the way would be provided."

Tomás had paused then, visibly trying to get his emotions under control. Several moments passed and finally he composed himself enough to continue.

Wiping his cheeks, he chokingly laughed. "Forgive me… this is very emotional for me, as you can see. I am still shaking my head in disbelief." He did shake his head then.

"After the dream—the very next day—a lady came to our little village in a big automobile—the kind you see the police driving."

Ben interjected his own thought then to help with his translation. "I think he means an SUV."

At everyone's nod, Tomás continued. "This lady, she seemed to have much wealth, something not seen in our little village, except for maybe the cartel. She drove right up to our hut and knocked on the door. Esperanza opened the door, and the lady handed her an envelope. 'Here,' she said, 'this is for you. I cannot explain, but the Lord, He told me to give this to you.'"

Again, Tomás shook his head and swallowed several times. "The lady, she just left in her big automobile without saying anything else, except 'God bless you and your family.' Esperanza called to me to come and see. Inside the envelope was money—so much that we almost could not count it. We cried and thanked the Lord and knew then that Esperanza's dream was real. The Lord was providing for us."

Again, Tomás paused to collect himself. Reg noticed Ben looked slightly dazed and he almost laughed at the man's expression. *Witnessing God's miracles, eh, buddy?* The atheist certainly couldn't argue with yet another personal testimony.

Ben shook himself when he realized Tomás had continued his story and hurried to catch up with the translation.

"After we gave thanks to our Father for providing, we hurried to the next village to buy food from the little store there. The owner, he told us we were lucky that we came to him when we did, because he was going to close his store the very next day to move to his daughter's city. He was selling all of his goods for very cheap. He said he was shocked when no one had come to buy his things and so he packed everything in boxes to give to the poor. Instead, he gave all the food to us. Then, because we had the money to spend, we bought the man's truck and drove to the north. We did not know where we would go, but the angel said north, so that is what we did. We still worried over not having our visas, but we decided to not go to a city with a checkpoint and instead to cross the border like the illegals. But then we saw this place and knew we had come to where the Lord wanted us."

Everyone was silent for a few minutes, and Reg was sure even Ben was beginning to realize that the Lord really did provide for His people. Then a question came to mind and Reg asked Ben to translate for him.

"You said you bought a truck and drove it here, so what happened to it?"

Tomás waved toward the south and Ben translated once more. "It is still in Mexico, at the border fence. We need to get the food from it."

Reg went to get the ranch truck so that he, Ben, Alonzo and Garrett could go to the fence with Tomás to get the supplies. Gina and Nikki played with the children and tried to converse with Esperanza, even though they didn't speak Spanish and she only spoke a little English. But the language barrier was crossed when they all laughed at the eighty-pound Golden Retriever cowering from the aggressive barking Chihuahuas.

Thankfully, the Villareal family had a tent among their possessions, so the guys helped them set it up near the ranch house and Nikki made sure the couple had plenty of bedding and knew to come inside the house whenever they wanted and most certainly when they needed to use the kitchen and restroom.

A few days later, another young Mexican couple with a baby showed up looking for work in exchange for room and board. Reg and Nikki hurried to make room for the small family in the house until something more permanent could be arranged.

"Shoulda let me build those cabins," Reg had muttered to Nikki under his breath as he helped her move some furniture around in the living room.

"Remember what I said then—if the Lord sends them, the Lord will provide the room."

Sure enough, He did just that. Just two days later a caravan of RVs showed up, RVs were pulling yet another camper trailer behind them.

The huge caravan surprisingly only consisted of three older couples—all professing Christians from San Antonio—who said they'd escaped the city late one night after curfew, when they'd avoided all roads and instead had actually managed to drive the RVs cross country without mishap, over mesquite, tumbleweeds and who knew what else.

The retired couples had been well-off financially before the collapse, and "something" had told them to purchase the RVs and trailers back before the economy went south. They'd then converted all of them to solar power, filled the gas tanks and stocked the cupboards, then waited for the Lord to tell them what to do next.

When Reg asked them how they even found the ranch, they said that one night after they'd escaped, during a campfire prayer vigil they'd asked the Lord where they should go. One of the gentlemen said he felt like he was being told "south," while another lady said she heard very clearly "west." That started a mild argument until they all laughingly agreed to head in a southwesterly direction. Taking back roads to avoid the patrols, they decided to go as far as the fuel would allow or to the Mexican fence, whichever came first. And so, they ended up at the gate to the ranch.

Since they now had so much extra room, they moved the Villareals out of their tent and into one of the travel trailers, alongside the Mendezes, the couple with the baby. Since neither couple spoke English, Reg figured they'd feel more comfortable near each other.

The remaining trailer and three extra RVs, along with the tent, were moved into one of the barns "for the future," as Reg put it. That future turned out to be less than a month, when yet another group escaping a violent city showed up looking for sanctuary.

The ranch was now home to twenty-four adults and twenty-five kids, eighteen of which were under the age of ten. Plus, an assortment of pets: dogs, cats, a potbellied pig and even an iguana. And, surprisingly, all the animals got along together. Reg had somewhat jokingly remarked that it must be the Lord's doing, like with Noah's ark—lions lying peacefully with lambs.

Anna and Garrett, being that they were the oldest of the children, self-imposed themselves to be in charge of the young brood. They led the kids in games and even some schooling, in which the teens worked to teach the younger kids to read and do basic math. Most of the kids had some of those skills, and they in turned helped the younger ones. Even though some of the kids didn't speak English, the adults were amazed—and thankful—that the children all worked together so well, even teaching each other their own languages.

For the most part, the adults worked together just fine too. The men seemed to gravitate toward the fields, while the women took on the more domestic chores such as cleaning, cooking and the storing of food. Laundry was a constant chore, since the limited power from solar electricity wasn't enough to run a washer or dryer, so the residents resorted to washing their clothes with the old hand-crank washing tub Nikki had found in the ranch house attic. She and the other ladies had joked about going back in time and tossing women's lib out with the chamber pot.

Since he was the only adult who was fluently bilingual, Ben started teaching Spanish to the English speakers and English to the others. For an hour each evening after dinner he worked with the entire group. The adults struggled to learn, but the kids picked up the other language much more quickly, especially since they had a head-start on the learning from their schooling time each morning.

While Nikki had at one time worried about not having enough food for just she, Reg and Anna, the Lord had proven that He could more than provide for whoever He sent their way. In addition to the food they had already managed to store and grow on the ranch, those who had arrived had all brought additional provisions, many toting along enough food for a dozen people, plenty to last for months. And the truck the Villareal's had brought was filled with enough packaged food and dry goods to supply the entire ranch for a long time.

Even Leeann had emptied her cupboards when Alonzo had come to help her pack and had brought boxes of dry and canned goods. Even though the girl had refused to come to the ranch at the first sign of trouble, she had at least heeded her mother's warning about preparing for any disaster and had stocked up quite a bit, especially thanks to her college's student food donation program. Despite Leeann's protests, her neighbor—a woman who was dependent on "the system"—had even given Leeann a lot of her own food, declaring that she'd get "new stuff" from the government.

In addition to all the canned and dry goods now stacked to the roof in the storage shed Reg had built, the fields continued to produce more than enough varieties of grains and the garden was burdened with vegetables. Even the fruit trees were so heavy with their fruit that the men had to prop branches up with boards to keep them from breaking in half while the fruit ripened.

While everyone, including the youngest child, worked in some capacity or another, it soon became evident who was good at what, who wasn't good at what, and who really excelled in certain areas.

Before the economy collapsed, Esperanza Villareal had worked for the Coahuila governor's mansion in the kitchens and was skilled in cooking for large groups, so she put herself in charge of breakfast and dinner and recruited several others to help. Soon mealtimes were running as smoothly as any military mess line.

Charlene Freeman, one of the members from the group of Christians who had escaped San Antonio, was a nurse who also had an interest in natural healing. She had even trained as a homeopath after completing nursing school, although she never worked in the field. Having someone on hand who could at least stitch up a wound without sweating bullets relieved a huge burden from Nikki's shoulders.

Charlene's husband, Frank, and Tom Lee, one of the others who'd traveled with the San Antonio group, had volunteered hundreds of man hours with Samaritan's Purse, working in third world countries and devastated areas and knew how to quickly build a house from the ground up using scrap materials, so Reg put them to the task of converting an old barn into apartments.

Roberto Mendez, while only in his late twenties, had been a master carpenter in Mexico and Reg was more than happy to relinquish all woodworking to the young man. Using old wood from the sides of yet another barn that was no longer needed, the first thing Roberto made was a huge dining table that would seat all twenty-four adults. The group had been eating in shifts and Nikki had complained that she wished they could eat their two daily community meals together, but there just wasn't any room. The finished table was so large that they had to put it outside, next to the ranch house.

The kids were content to eat on blankets laid out on the grass, but Roberto hurried to also create four picnic tables for them, large enough to seat eight kids each, which he placed around the adults' table.

Nikki cried the first time they were all able to eat together, and she had asked if she could say the blessing for that meal, with Ben translating for the Spanish-speakers.

It took several minutes to compose herself and get her voice to where it didn't sound like she was gurgling. Finally, she began.

"Lord, You have been so generous to us throughout this difficult time. We all have stories of miracles, of Your protection and provision for those You've brought here, and we are so very grateful to You for all You have done for us. We praise You and thank You for bringing us together and for letting us share in Your bounty. Amen."

Reg noticed that even Ben, who was normally antagonistic toward anything he deemed "religious," said "Amen" at the end of the prayer. Reg smiled slightly, knowing the Lord was working hard to bring Ben to Him.

Reg lamented to Nikki later that same night about the one thing that was missing from their lives, the same thing the couple had missed the most when they'd first arrived at the ranch—the lack of church.

They were both feeling pulled—no, more like convicted—to do something about it, but neither knew what. They talked about it while lying in bed.

Reg was staring up at the ceiling when Nikki rolled toward him and propped her head on her elbow. "The first church, the one you read about in Acts, wasn't at all like what we've got today—or used to have, before the collapse. It was a lot less restrictive. They sang a lot of songs, took turns reading Scripture, and whoever had a burden to share could speak. And they ate together. There isn't any reason why we couldn't do something like that."

Reg thought about it for a minute. "Yeah, I suppose so. But getting everyone to attend might be kinda hard. Of course, the Lees, Freemans and McCarthys will be there—they've all been talking about missing church. But what about the Mendezes and Villareals?

They only just started learning English."

Nikki pursed her lips. "But if we just sort of include the service with a meal, then we'd get everyone to show up, at least for a little while. And as for the others, Ben can translate. I think he actually likes doing that, honestly."

Reg huffed out a laugh. "Yeah, I think it makes him feel superior to us."

Nikki whacked his arm with the back of her hand. "Behave," she admonished with a grin. "But I think you're right about that, actually. Only this time, think about it—he'll be translating God's Word. I'm going to have to try hard not to laugh when mister potty mouth atheist has to repeat Scripture."

He laughed. "Yeah, that will be good. Wish we still had our cells—I'd like to record that."

Nikki grinned. "And we can start with doing this maybe like on Wednesday, so it's not so obvious what we're up to. Sort of sneak in a church service on them through the back door."

Reg laughed. "We can call it Covert Church."

Nikki grinned back at him. "Covert Converts."

"We'll be eating, so we could call it Meal 'n Heal."

"Kneeling Meal."

"Good News, Good Chews."

Nikki rolled her eyes. "Ugh. How about Eating Meeting."

Reg raised an eyebrow at her. "And you said 'ugh' to mine…"

She laughed. "Okay, then, how about we don't call it anything?"

"Sounds like a good idea," he answered with a laugh. "And I think we should mix it up, too, so that it's never the same day or same meal. Like Wednesday dinner first, then maybe Friday breakfast, et cetera."

She nodded in agreement and laughed again. "Yeah, that way the heathens can't avoid God, not if they want to eat."

Reg talked to the other Christian men about what they were planning on doing and they were all not only in agreement, they were thrilled. In fact, Steve McCarthy volunteered to lead the meeting, sheepishly admitting that he'd been an associate pastor at their church in San Antonio.

"I hadn't said anything to y'all, cuz I honestly hadn't been feeling too godly until just recently," he'd confessed to Reg as his dark eyes teared up.

"My faith took a real nosedive just before the collapse, to the point where I had taken myself off all leadership in the church and was… well, I was doing some pretty awful stuff. Audrey was even on the verge of taking the kids and leaving me." His voice caught and he cleared his throat.

"But then when everything hit the fan, well, the Lord proved to me over and over how much He loves us and is in control, no matter what's happening in the world. And then the way He provided for us when we most needed it, how He was answering our prayers when we'd barely finished asking, the way He protected us until we got here, and just the fact that we knew to come *here*, where it was safe and full of other Christians—well, I don't need any more convincing."

He took a deep breath, seeming to mentally gird his loins. "Now I'm ready for whatever He wants, whatever He wills. And I'm feeling led to lead, so if y'all want, I'd like to be the pastor of this here group."

The other men were very much in agreement, and all exchanged "bro hugs" with Steve, one-armed with a fist pounding each other on the back.

"You're an answer to prayer," Reg told him. "Nikki especially is going to be so relieved that we'll have a man of God to lead us."

Steve put his hand on Reg's shoulder and squeezed lightly. "*You're* a man of God too, my friend," he'd admonished. "I see you as a warrior for Him and I feel like He's got some pretty big things in store for you."

The group of four Christian couples managed to pull off a pseudo "church" service the next day at dinner. Nikki had talked Esperanza into serving cold cut sandwiches and salads, things that didn't need to be kept warm, not telling her the reason was because they were planning on having songs and Scripture readings before eating.

Once they were all seated, Steve stood up and turned to Ben. "Would you translate for me, please?"

At Ben's hesitant—and somewhat suspicious—nod, Steve

started. "Folks, before we eat I'd like to share something with you from the Lord's Word, the Bible."

He paused to let Ben catch up in translating, then continued. "This is from Revelation, chapter twenty-one, starting with verse three: 'And I heard a loud voice from the throne saying, "Behold, the dwelling place of God is with man. He will dwell with them, and they will be His people, and God Himself will be with them as their God. He will wipe away every tear from their eyes, and death shall be no more, neither shall there be mourning, nor crying, nor pain anymore, for the former things have passed away."'"

Many in the group responded to the reading with an "Amen," although just as many were uncomfortably quiet. Reg and Nikki watched the group carefully, almost smiling at how more than a few looked a little shocked by what was transpiring.

Steve continued then. "I don't know about you folks, but these verses give me a lot of hope in a time when there isn't much reason to have hope. Things have gotten really rough here on earth the past few months—people are near starvation, barely surviving, many are dying. The criminals have become even more vicious in their attempts to rob and steal, and those who had never broken a law in their life are now turning to crime in order to survive. And those who are put in place to keep the peace are doing anything but. They're even worse than the criminals in a lot of cases."

He turned back to look at Nikki and Reg, smiling. "Thanks to these nice folks here, we don't have to worry about such things.

We're safe here and we have our needs met. But even so, we still have mourning and pain; bitter tears come in the night when we think about what we may have lost, or about loved ones who are still out there struggling to survive this crazy time."

Nikki placed her hand atop Reg's and squeezed, knowing he was thinking about his kids then, her eyes misting over when she noticed his own were shining overly bright with unshed tears.

Steve cleared his throat and stared at the table, obviously also trying to compose himself. Nikki wondered who he might be thinking of, what loved one of his was still "out there" trying to survive.

He finally continued after a few moments. "But these verses tell of a day in the near future when God Himself will wipe away our tears and give us comfort... and *dwell* with us."

Tapping his Bible, his voice became more urgent. "And this will be forevermore—no more will death come knocking at the door, wanting to steal away one of our beloved. No more will we have to suffer with physical pain from these frail, easily broken bodies. No more will we have the torment of past wrongs, childhood trauma, hurting hearts and the like. Not a single tear will fall in heaven. We won't even be able to remember those things. "

Another murmur of "amens" went through the group, although many were silent and still looked a little uncomfortable, obviously caught unaware by the seemingly impromptu sermon that was sprung upon them. Nikki prayed silently and fervently that any who didn't know the Lord would have their heart softened in this moment to accept Him.

Steve paused, looking around at the group, his voice rising in volume. "This is what gives me the hope I have for the future, the comfort I have that tells me that no matter what may come my way, even if soldiers come down that road and declare they're going to end my earthly existence, *no matter what happens*, I know without a doubt where I'm going to be in the end, and for all eternity—I'm going to be right in God's arms."

"Amens" again filtered through the group, and Nikki noticed there were more voices added to the chorus this time.

Steve closed his Bible and held it against his chest as he again addressed the group. "I know many of you already are Christians and understand what I'm talking about. But a lot of you aren't and maybe you *want* to know what this hope is all about, to know without a doubt that you'll be okay in the end, that your eternity is secure, and your home will be in heaven. If you want that today, then please raise your hand."

Nikki kept her eyes closed and prayed harder, barely noticing as Reg turned his hand over so that they could lock their fingers together, knowing he was praying too. *Father, please reach each and every person's heart here. Break through those barriers that the enemy has erected. Let Your love touch all of us and make Yourself known. Save us, Father, make us all Your children today.*

Steve's voice broke through her prayers when she heard him

excitedly announce, "Amen! Praise God!" She opened her eyes and looked around in astonishment.

Nearly every single person had their hand raised, including every single one of the children. Those who were already saved were laughing and clapping, a look of sheer joy on their tear-stained faces as they witnessed a miracle—the miracle of salvation.

chapter 10

AFTER what later became affectionately known as "Pentecost Wednesday," the group, in unspoken agreement, continued to have worship time with each dinner. It had become a time that everyone looked forward to greatly, a time of praise and singing, storytelling, miracle sharing, Scripture reading.

Although Steve was now considered the group's spiritual leader and pastor, everyone was encouraged to participate in the worship time, whether it was just to share a dream or vision, to ask for a prayer request, or to lead the group in a song. No one was exempted or stopped from sharing whatever was on their heart, for the group felt that the Lord was truly leading them, and they tried to keep the heart of the first church, the church described in the Book of Acts, in mind.

Even the youngest children had their chance to share when Anna and Garrett led them in singing "Shout To The Lord" one evening. Not only was it extremely cute, the performance was also very uplifting.

The only thing that was unchanging in every evening meeting and meal was the offering of the Lord's Supper. Steve had explained to the group that it was the only ceremony the Lord had commanded be observed to remember Him.

"He never told us to celebrate His birth. He never told us to celebrate His resurrection. The *only* thing Jesus told us to honor was His sacrifice for us, and if I have anything to say about it, that's exactly what we're going to do. He said, 'Do this often in remembrance of Me,' so I think we should have the Lord's Supper before every meal."

Everyone had agreed, and so every night before the evening meal the group broke bread and passed a glass of wine to share in an offer of worship.

The Saturday following "Pentecost Wednesday" had been a day for baptisms. Steve asked Reg to help him, and the two waded out into the pond as one by one the new believers committed the first act of obedience to the Lord.

Anna stood next to Nikki with the other believers who'd already been saved and baptized before "Pentecost Wednesday," and reminded her mother of the dream she'd had—where Reg and another man she didn't recognize at the time had stood in the pond while a line of people waited to be dunked. Both mother and daughter had tears in their eyes as they realized Anna's dream was coming true right before their eyes.

But the very best moment of the day for Nikki was when Alonzo walked into the pond. He'd been saved and baptized as a young teen but had backslidden so far that he'd decided he needed a complete recommitment, "A good dunk to wash away all the junk," he'd laughingly joked.

Nikki had tears of joy streaming down her face as she watched her oldest get right with the Lord once again, a thing she had prayed so hard for, but admittedly had had little faith in seeing happen. She'd silently asked the Lord to forgive her for lacking that faith in His abilities to bring His prodigals home.

Over the past month since Alonzo had arrived at the ranch with his sister, he'd struggled greatly. Nikki knew he was still on drugs from the very first, from the moment he got out of his old truck, and she thought he was an old drug addict and not her own son. The tell-tale twitching tics continued to plague her son for several weeks.

But everyone knew the day his drug supply had run dry. That was the day he'd crashed and fell hard, both physically and emotionally.

The physical withdrawals seemed to be the worst, at least a first. Al was so wracked with cramps he doubled over and vomited so much that his mouth became so dry he could hardly speak. Nikki was sure he was getting dehydrated. By the second day, he'd started having seizures.

But then the emotional withdrawals started, and it was so bad that those near the young man cringed and looked for excuses to leave. In almost the blink of an eye, Al had become so depressed that he desperately begged and screamed for a gun or a knife so that he could end his own life.

It was then that Reg, who'd been unfailingly with Nikki at Alonzo's bedside, had sought out Steve. One of the ministries the man said he'd worked with previously in San Angelo involved drug recovery. Reg didn't know if Steve would be able to help with the withdrawals, but he thought he might be able to at least talk Alonzo through the depression, if only to encourage him to hang on through the rough part.

Steve and several of the other men were out in the south pasture corn field, hoeing the rows that had collapsed due to recent rains. When Reg told Steve what was going on, he had asked the other men to join him, and they all headed to the ranch house.

On the way up the hill, Steve explained to Reg that he believed a lot of addictions—especially in those like Alonzo who hadn't grown up in an addictive environment—were caused by actual demons. Reg had raised an eyebrow at that, and Steve had quickly explained his position.

"I know it sounds farfetched, but the Bible talks about demons, doesn't it? And demon possession. So, what makes us think that demons have decided to leave us alone and go away just because we live in an 'advanced culture'? They *haven't* gone away—not yet anyway, not until the end when they're all going to be sent to the fiery pit permanently."

He shook his head. "No, they're still here, still wreaking havoc the way they always have. They're just more sophisticated with their attacks. And we just don't hear about it much anymore. For one thing, there are a whole heck of a lot more people nowadays, but the number of demons is the same as it's always been. Also, we don't want to even try to understand that there's a spiritual realm we're supposed to be fighting against, good versus evil. But it's possible that we explain the unexplainable by diagnosing mental illness or addiction, instead of considering the possibility that a person might be led around by the nose by an evil force."

Reg remained quiet, trying to absorb what Steve was saying. It was difficult to believe, but then Reg had reminded himself that he never believed in miracles either, not until he'd experienced them firsthand. He knew there were a lot of things about the spiritual world that he didn't have the first clue about.

Despite Reg's lack of response, Steve continued. "So, whenever an unlikely person has an addiction or unexplainable behavior—like in Alonzo's case, where he didn't grow up in an addictive household and Nikki said he was saved as a teen—then I look for those evil forces at the helm. At least I don't discount the fact that they might have a hand in guiding the ship."

The men arrived at the ranch house and Reg led them into the back bedroom where Alonzo continued to writhe in pain on the bed while Nikki mopped at his forehead with a washcloth. Watching his movements as he thrashed back and forth and mumbled incoherently, it was almost easy to believe he might actually be possessed. It reminded Reg of a scene from one of the horror movies he used to love watching before getting saved.

Reg stepped up to his wife and laid his hand on her slumped shoulder. She looked exhausted. "How's he doing?"

Nikki sighed as she dipped the washcloth in a bowl on the

nightstand. "Kinda out of it and still in pain. But it's more than that… it's like…" She shrugged almost sheepishly, as if admitting to an embarrassing secret and then darted her eyes to the other men who were trying to be as unobtrusive as five men can be while crowding around a bed in a small room.

"It's almost like he's fighting demons," she whispered to Reg.

Reg shot a glance to Steve, who stood closest to them. Steve grimaced and shook his head, an "I told you so" look on his face.

The pastor stepped up then. "He might very well be doing exactly that," he told Nikki, smiling at the way her hazel eyes rounded.

"Seriously?" she asked incredulously.

Steve shrugged and gave her the same explanation he'd given to Reg on the way to the house. Nikki nodded then.

"Yeah, you're absolutely right. Jesus spoke of demons and Scripture is full of stories about them. Nothing in the Word says they just went away, so yeah, it makes sense that they'd still be around to torment us."

She paused as she wiped her son's brow again. "But I thought demons couldn't bother someone who's saved."

Steve shook his head. "No, they can't *possess* someone who's saved, who has the Holy Spirit living in them. But they can certainly bother the heck out of us, and that they certainly do. They hound those who might be up to good, who are doing God's will, more than anyone else. Why would they bother the lost—those who already belong to the devil?"

Sighing as he watched her mop Alonzo's forehead, Steve continued. "And honestly, I don't believe the 'once saved, always saved' philosophy. I think we make the choice to leave God and His grace—and His salvation—when we choose to backslide and fall back into sin. So, it *is* possible your son could have a demon possessing him."

Nikki cringed at that, but Steve smiled reassuringly and patted her shoulder. "Either way, we're gonna pray for him."

She returned his smile, albeit feebly. "Thank you."

Nikki turned back to mop Alonzo's brow once again while the men, in seemingly unspoken agreement, gathered around and laid their hands on him. The thought of a demon possessing her son, of actually *being* there and feeling her touch was almost more than she could bear. She wanted to scream at him—her—it—to "get out and stay out!"

There was a moment of silence after Steve asked each man to pray for personal protection and forgiveness of each of their sins before they prayed for Alonzo. During the quiet time, Nikki drew the washcloth over her son's forehead and down his cheek to his scraggly beard and on down to his neck before dipping the cloth in cool water to perform the process again. Despite the ravages of drugs and homelessness, her son was still a handsome man with very masculine features, other than his lips, which were rather plump. She supposed a young woman would say they were "kissable."

She frowned at that thought: Not over the fact that her son might have appeal to a female, but rather that he'd wasted so much time in his addiction, time that might have been much better spent in a marriage and giving his mother grandbabies. She then shook her head. *No sense in crying over spilled milk and missed opportunities*, Jeanie, her favorite aunt, would have said. What's done was done and the past couldn't be changed.

Reg startled her out of her thoughts when he laid his hand on her shoulder while Steve began to lead them in prayer. He thanked the Father for His care and love for His children, even those who had chosen to leave the path He had set out for them, and then he began renouncing any evil beings who might be tormenting the young man and prayed for a quick recovery for him.

He then paused and others took their turns praying for Al. Most fervently, every one of the men prayed for the kid's salvation, for his return to the Lord. When it came time for her turn to pray, Nikki had the tears of a broken-hearted mama streaming down her face.

"Lord…" her voice cracked, and she swallowed several times to compose herself while Reg rubbed her back comfortingly.

After a minute, she continued, "Father God, you know my heart, You know how I've been praying for this boy's return to You. I've begged and pleaded with You for years. Now is the time, Father. Please heal my son, release him from the satanic forces that have a hold on him, rid him of the desire for drugs and the need to be high. But most of all, bring him back to You. He could be a great man of

God, Father, You most of all know that. He just needs another chance. Please give him that chance."

Their prayers were miraculously answered just an hour later when the fever suddenly left, the seizures stopped and Alonzo sat up in bed, grabbed Reg's hand and asked him to lead him in prayer for salvation once again.

An answer to prayer, a miracle healing, a salvation—all occurring within an hour—had the men who were present that day praising the Lord greatly.

But none sang the Lord's praises more loudly than Alonzo himself. When the prodigal son returned to his Father, he did so joyously and with no looking back.

A few days after the mass baptism, another vehicle came up the driveway, this time a large commercial-type truck. The sight of it immediately caused alarm among the ranch's residents. The women gathered children and headed to the nearest building while the men approached the vehicle cautiously. Ben led the group, their weapons drawn and trained on the driver's door.

Ben had self-appointed himself as head of ranch security, despite Reg's grumbling that he now had to return to being the ranch's butcher. Ben spent most of his days sitting on the highest knoll near the pond, watching the area for anyone approaching the ranch. He'd even gotten a team together, and now the ranch had round-the-clock protection.

So far, the protection hadn't been necessary, but everyone knew the day would soon come when they'd be forced to defend their new home. The group prayed every single day for the wisdom and courage needed to make the right choices when that time came.

Thankfully, that time wasn't now, as the group of men relaxed when Reg recognized the blonde headed driver and gave four short high-pitched whistles, the signal that there wasn't imminent danger, but to be cautious regardless.

It was Agent Henderson from Border Patrol, and he was alone. And badly beaten. Reg called to Frank Freeman, one of the men who'd joined Ben's security team, and told him to fetch his wife, who was the official healer for the group.

Frank ran off on his errand and Reg helped the young man out of the truck. "What in the Sam hill happened to you, son?" he asked incredulously as he all but carried the agent to one of the boulders that lined the top of the drive. He lowered him carefully to the rock.

The man grimaced as he sat and held his ribs, his voice breathless and obviously pained. "Got the crap beat out of me," he answered with a slight smile.

"Well, yeah, I can see that," Reg drawled sarcastically. "Who used you for a rugby ball?"

The agent panted a bit before answering. "Police... or military, whatever you want to call them. The Neos," he said as he motioned behind him toward the truck.

On the door was a red emblem that at first glance was rather

Celtic-looking… or maybe Middle Eastern. It looked like three swirls of fire that came together at the curve. Two of the swirls were on top like horns and the third was underneath. The design reminded him somewhat of the moon god symbol, the horns that adorned the top of some buildings he'd seen pictures of in Arabian countries.

Reg looked closer. Put together like they were, they looked like sixes. He shivered then. *Six-six-six, mark of the Beast. And Neo Geo— New World, as in New World Order.* Any doubts he might have had about being smack-dab in the end times left him then.

Turning back to the agent, Reg noticed him shifting his weight on the rock in an obvious attempt to get comfortable, but the wince he gave showed his failure. He took a few more shallow breaths before he continued.

His voice sounded strained. "They conscripted all weapons-trained DOD, DEA and Homeland Security agents. Most of the Border Patrol agents joined up without argument, because at least we would have a job and wouldn't starve to death."

He shifted once more and gasped a little. "At first I was happy to have that job. I was on security, just had to patrol the base's perimeter. Easy peasy. But then the new uniforms came in. One look at the logo and I knew there was no way I could… I just couldn't put it on. The hat, the sleeves, even the gloves, all had that *emblem*." He spat out the word with a vehemence that made Reg raise an eyebrow.

"Mark of the Beast, right? I know you saw it too when you looked at the door. I could see it on your face."

Reg nodded but didn't say anything. Another shiver ran up his spine.

The man sighed and then grimaced again. "I was one of the fortunate ones who was able to get away."

Charlene had walked up just as he made that last statement. "Boy, if you're one of the 'fortunate ones', I sure wouldn't want to see the less fortunate. You look like you fell out of the top of a sycamore and hit every branch on the way down."

Charlene Freeman was an ex-Army nurse who had served in battlefield M.A.S.H. units during both Gulf Wars and had then volunteered with Doctors Without Borders. She had traveled all over the world helping people with every disease and injury known to man. She had also seen her share of atrocities and knew just what her fellow man was capable of doing. That knowledge made her a bit gruff when dealing with people.

Reg introduced her to the young man. "This is Charlene Freeman. She's a tough ol' gal who happens to be a nurse. You'd best be listening to her, or you might end up in even worse shape," he teased.

Reg grunted then and grinned when Charlene poked her elbow into his ribs at his comment. Turning to the older woman who was standing at his side frowning with her arms crossed over her chest, he continued.

"And Charlene, this is Agent Henderson... well used to be, anyway."

"Just Jeff," the young man wheezed. Charlene nodded to him and, apparently deciding they were done with the formalities, moved forward to examine him.

Despite her bullish demeanor and mannish broad-shouldered figure that was only slightly softened by an overabundant chest, Charlene was very gentle when she prodded Jeff's torso and face, frowning and murmuring sympathies as she did.

Reg stood with his arms crossed over his chest as he watched her examination. It was the first time he'd seen her in action, and he was frankly surprised at how "grandmotherly" the ol' battle axe could be when she wanted to. He snorted as he thought back to just days before when he'd watched Charlene chase one of the teenagers through the east pasture with a stick, threatening to "tan his hide."

Carl, arguably the most rambunctious and obnoxious kid on the ranch, had hidden behind a mesquite bush while Charlene was stripping the bark to gather the gum that she used for making sore throat lozenges and salve for wounds. While she was concentrating on her task, Carl had shaken a twig in some dried leaves, the noise sounding just like a rattlesnake. Charlene *hated* snakes.

In her fear, she'd jumped back and tripped over a rock, falling hard on her backside. Once she realized her imminent demise wasn't looming, the old woman had jumped up and chased that boy clear through the ten-acre pasture and halfway to the pond before she finally gave up, yelling to Carl, "You better hope you don't get sick and need to see me, boy, or else you might just find yourself feeling a whole lot worse."

Reg—and most of the residents, except for maybe Carl—knew that was an empty threat. Charlene, despite her gruffness, would never hurt anyone, not even young boys who deserved it.

After a few moments, she straightened from her precursory inspection. "Well, without an x-ray I can't say for sure, but I'm willing to bet you've got at least six cracked ribs and one that feels broken clean through. I'm pretty sure that left eye socket is fractured too and you've most likely got a concussion."

She sighed. "There ain't a whole lot I can do for you with the limited supplies we have here. But I can at least wrap up those ribs to help you breathe better and give you a tea to help with the pain."

Charlene winked at Jeff then, surprising the heck out of Reg, who'd never seen her act anything but tough and rough.

"Good thing you're not with Border Patrol anymore, since one of the ingredients of my pain tea is marijuana."

The former agent laughed, then moaned as he held his ribs again. "At this point, I really don't care what you give me. Knock me over the head if you want. Anything to get some relief."

Charlene chuckled. "You've been knocked on the head enough, young man. What you need now is some TLC. I'll have the men fix you up a place to bed down and get some of the ladies to get you a plate of food. You'll need something in your stomach before you can have the tea."

She chuckled again. "And after drinking the tea, you'll be trying to eat a cow's butt through a fence, cuz you're gonna have the munchies."

With that, she walked off, leaving Reg and a few of the other men laughing as they watched over Jeff. One of the men had heard Charlene's comment about finding a place for him to sleep and had set off to do just that. Reg was always grateful for the group of people they had at the ranch, as everyone just met the needs of others, sometimes before those needs were even thought of.

"So, what's in the truck, or is it empty?" he asked Jeff as he crossed his arms over his chest. Some supplies would certainly be welcome, but at the very least the big panel truck would make decent living quarters. It seemed the group was going to continue to grow and finding a place for everyone to call home was going to become more of a challenge.

Jeff shrugged, then grimaced yet again. "Don't know. It was with a row of trucks just like it at the base. I heard someone say they were heading to the 'north quadrant,' but I'd never heard of it before, so I don't know where exactly that is. Anyway, when I was able to get away, I just jumped in the closest truck and took off. The dummies leave the keys in the ignitions of all the trucks, cuz they think no one can steal them from the base."

Reg frowned as he looked at the large trailer that had obviously been painted, as you could still see a moving company's logo bleeding through the gray color.

"You gotta key for the back?"

Jeff nodded. "Maybe. Check the key ring. I seriously jumped in the truck and drove straight here, so I haven't checked it out at all."

Reg smirked at the young man. "I doubt you jumped anywhere, in that condition."

He smirked back. "Yeah, I did. When you're literally running for your life, you don't think about pain, believe me."

Reg frowned and uncrossed his arms, his hands fisting at his sides. "That bad? They were really going to kill you?"

It was hard to believe that the government would stoop so low as to assassinate one of its former own. But then again, considering all the underhanded and even out-right illegal things that had gone on in the government over the past nine or so years, Reg knew anything was possible from that quarter. And now with the country—and the world, for that matter—in the current state it was in, there really was nothing to stop governments from becoming totalitarian regimes.

Jeff sighed heavily. "Yeah. Anyone who isn't for them is against them. If you refuse to join their evil forces, then they consider you a threat to national security and one that needs to be exterminated."

He took another slow, careful breath. "Our military, too... they're in the Neos' crosshairs. Remember all that talk about the government stockpiling ammo and weapons back before the collapse?" At Reg's nod, he continued.

"They're turning those weapons on our own military. It's crazy. There's even some terrorist groups that have joined them."

Reg couldn't keep the surprise from his voice or his face.

"You're kidding!"

Jeff shook his head. "'S'truth. They killed... what? Thousands? Of our people, and now the government is letting them join their ranks. Says a lot about the state of the U.S., doesn't it?"

Closing his eyes, Jeff swallowed hard. "It's really bad out there, I ain't kidding you."

Reg's frown deepened as he considered the ramifications of what the former agent was saying. Months ago, he'd told Nikki of his fears that the military would be hunted by the newly "reformed" government, but it was pretty upsetting to find out his prediction had come true. And now to find out that terrorists had joined them? He could only guess at what those who refused to join up with the Neos were going through.

They'd had a few reports from others in the group about some of the atrocities being committed in the name of "keeping the peace" and there were certainly more than a few stories of the horrors committed by the criminal element that seemed to largely be ignored by the "peacekeepers." From the newcomers to the ranch, they'd heard stories of billboard-sized television screens having been erected in the larger cities that constantly ran pro-Neo propaganda, making any opposed to the new government out to be the criminals, while ignoring the fact that theft, rapes and murders were becoming the norm. It was Orwell's "Big Brother" come to life.

Reg made a mental note to talk to Ben about adding extra security. While they certainly didn't want to turn anyone away who truly needed help and shelter, they also didn't need to allow troublemakers to come to the ranch. While it might be impossible to fight off an attack from the Neos, at least they could do their best to make sure they were protected from any others who were bent on taking what wasn't theirs and causing problems.

He left the young man on the rock and moved to the back of the truck, where he tried several keys until he found one that worked. After opening the latch, he cautiously pushed the sliding door up, standing to one side as he did, not knowing at all what he might find inside. For all he knew, it could have been a truck full of armed soldiers.

The sight that met Reg made him suck in a breath and call out for a few men to join him.

The truck was full of boxes, stacked floor to ceiling. All had the Neos' logo on them stamped in red. Reg climbed into the truck and moved to the closest stack, using his knife to cut the tape on the top box.

Inside was a variety of medical supplies—everything from wound tape to bottles of pills with generic labels. Several caught his eye that were marked "erythromycin." He turned then as some of the men walked up to the truck and asked Frank to get Charlene, knowing she'd be thrilled with the stash and might be able to use some of it to help Jeff.

Frank ran off to find his wife for the second time, while Reg climbed into the back of the truck and began pulling more boxes down and shoving them to the door. They were all unmarked and the men opened them one by one.

By the time all the boxes were opened, they had an abundance of medical supplies, canned food, dry goods, and even toilet paper and other hygiene products. The truck had obviously been a supply truck for FEMA, or whatever they were calling emergency government aid these days. Reg seriously doubted the supplies were going to help the public, though. Most likely they were going to be used to resupply a government facility somewhere, and for that he had no guilt in taking the supplies for what he considered to be the better good.

That was something he and Nikki had discussed over the past several months—was it morally okay to steal the things they truly needed now that the world was upside down? They both agreed that it wasn't, especially not when it came to individuals. But Reg thought that taking the enemy's supplies didn't fall into the immoral category, arguing that even God Himself had told the Israelites to take the "spoils" from wars.

It was a point they'd argued over until Reg had agreed that he'd trust the Lord to provide for their needs. But he knew if the time ever came where it was down to starvation or stealing, then he was heading to the nearest military base to stock up.

Now apparently the Lord was going to use the government to supply their needs without them having to resort to thievery. Yes, Jeff had stolen the truck, but until the moment he drove onto the ranch property, he wasn't one of their group. At least, that was how

Reg justified in his mind keeping the supplies. He was pretty sure Nikki might have something different to say about it, but there was no way they would be returning the truck to the Neos. Despite being dangerous, they really needed the supplies the truck contained.

And he was pretty sure that the time was right around the corner when any and all supplies, no matter how they were acquired, would be a desperately welcomed thing.

chapter 11

SUMMERS in Texas were miserable, energy-sucking affairs, and that year was no different. By early June, everyone on the ranch made sure most of their work was finished before nine in the morning and what was left to be done was completed late in the evening.

Since the ranch was run by solar electricity, only limited things could be powered and unfortunately air conditioners weren't on that list. While a lot of the buildings on the ranch now had solar power, the batteries just couldn't store enough electricity to power an A/C unit. With the ever-present humidity, this meant that being indoors was often more miserable than being outside where there was a chance for catching a breeze.

Most of the ranch inhabitants spent the heat of the day under the trees, begging the Lord for just such a breeze. Many headed to the pond to find some relief. Unfortunately, spending all day in the water under the blazing south Texas sun meant a whole lot of sunburns.

To combat the burns, Charlene mixed up a big batch of one part peppermint oil to two parts lavender oil and handed out little cheesecloth bags with used black tea leaves with instructions to put the bag in warm water and then gently dab it on the sunburn, allow it to dry, and to then apply the oil mixture.

These two treatments meant that, in most cases, a sunburn was gone within a day, leaving a nice suntan. Roberto had made the joking comment one night during their evening meal and worship time that "now all the gringos look Mexican."

"Let's just pray no one gets melanoma," Charlene remarked to Nikki and Gina one particularly hot day. "I'm not sure how to treat skin cancer."

The women were standing under a peach tree watching the kids swim in the pond while Jeff reclined against the tree trunk. The young man still wasn't completely healed from his beating despite three weeks' passage and Charlene watched over him like a hawk, knowing if she didn't, he'd be up trying to work and likely reinjure himself.

"Frankincense, clove and lavender oils," Jeff said. Charlene and Nikki both turned to look at him with a question in their eyes.

Jeff grinned back at them. "My mom," he explained, reminding Nikki of their conversation that seemed so long ago, back when he was still a Border Patrol agent, and her biggest worry was that the agency suspected she and Reg were growing marijuana.

"She cured my dad from two skin cancers that the doctors insisted needed surgery and radiation," he explained.

Nikki looked back to Charlene and Gina, explaining, "Jeff's mom is a naturopath doctor."

Charlene snorted. "Would be nice if she came here—any chance of that?" she asked the man over her shoulder.

Nikki saw the sad look that came over the young man's face,

although Charlene missed it since she stood with her back to him, arms crossed over her chest like a drill sergeant as she barked an order to some of the older kids to quit rough housing.

"No, I don't think so," he replied when Charlene finished her yelling. "My family is way up in northern Utah. I had mailed a letter to them right when all this started happening, before it got really bad, and told them where I'd head if and when I had to get outta Dodge. Since the Post Office was shut down shortly after that, I don't know if they ever got it."

Nikki smiled to herself at the thought that Jeff had planned on heading their way, even before things got really bad. She wondered who else might have the same idea and would be showing up at their doorstep.

She also was glad for the young man's foresight to mail an actual letter and not send an email or text, knowing that the government had been monitoring such things even before the collapse. It wouldn't do to have the Neos aware of them, knowing where they were and what they were doing. While wanting to just survive and live a peaceable life, the group was filled with those who came to them with horror stories of how the Neos were demanding that all citizens bend to their will.

In fact, Reg and some of the other men had been talking about conspiracies the other night and Nikki, Gina and a couple of the other wives had overhead the conversation. Their husbands were quietly discussing their fears of a government invasion of the ranch, and the need for a low profile. Jeff told the men that the Neos made regular reconnaissance flights over rural areas looking for places like their ranch, places that had become a sanctuary from the outside world. "They're especially interested in Christian compounds," he'd said.

What happened to those the Neos found wasn't clear, but Jeff said he was sure it wasn't good. It was then that Ben had mentioned the fact that they had very little by way of arms and ammunition, certainly not enough to defend themselves against an attack from the Neos.

The women had gone back to their respective homes with new fears, much worse than their prior worries of learning the art of soap making, assuring enough food was stored, and what to plant the next season. And they were all wishing they hadn't eavesdropped. Sometimes it's better not to know what evil might be coming down your road.

They had visitors show up the very next day, but it wasn't Jeff's family... it was Reg's. And coming along with his kids and grandson was his ex-wife, Brenda.

Reg was obviously relieved and excited to have his kids, and especially his grandson, safe and sound. Nikki knew it had been eating quietly at him, not knowing where they were, what they were doing, if they were safe or in harm's way. Having them show up at the ranch was an answer to many prayers they'd both been praying.

However, Reg was less than thrilled to have his ex there and that was putting it mildly. Thankfully, instead of being nasty or mean like Nikki was afraid he might be, he simply chose to ignore the woman as if she didn't even exist, like she wasn't standing right there next to his daughter. He just chatted with his kids and literally gave the woman the cold shoulder as he purposefully put his side to Brenda so he wouldn't have to look at her. It was obvious to Nikki what he was doing, and she assumed his ex-wife was no dummy and knew it too.

Nikki took a bit of pity on the woman and tried to put herself in her shoes. If she was being forced to rely on her ex-husband's hospitality, especially in light of the fact that he was now remarried, she knew how she'd feel. She'd be wondering if she'd be welcomed, or if she'd be flat-out turned away. Or worse, treated like some leper or pariah, scorned and abused... pretty much like the way Reg was treating the woman right now.

Nikki figured this was a chance to show Jesus, and she was going to take advantage of it.

"Hi, I'm Nikki, Reg's wife," she said as she stepped up to the woman with what she hoped was a warm smile. They'd never officially met but had seen each other once in a restaurant in San Angelo, when Brenda had sneered at them while they ate and was obviously making snide comments about them to her date.

"I'm glad you made it here safely," Nikki added, waiting for a response.

Now, normal people in Brenda's situation would have been

grateful to have been welcomed to a safe place, especially in light of what all they'd heard was going on "out there." It was a world gone mad, and Nikki knew that the ranch must seem like a haven, a sanctuary from all that craziness.

But Brenda didn't seem to have any gratefulness, or thankfulness. Instead, she seemed hostile, like she was being forced to do something she didn't want to. Nikki figured then that the kids had dragged their mother along with them, in an effort to get their mother to safety.

Brenda just stood there with her overly wide mouth pursed into a pout, making her look a bit like a surly child. But there was a look in her blue eyes that said, "Just step a little closer, I dare you." The look reminded Nikki of a snake about to strike.

Fighting back a shiver at that look, she forced herself to continue being pleasant. *A soft word turns away wrath,* she reminded herself. She then thought about another scripture and paraphrased it in her head. *If your enemy is hungry or thirsty, give to her and you'll heap burning coals on her head.* She got a little thrill as she imagined Brenda's flame-red hair actually being set on fire after Nikki dumped a shovelful of hot coals on it, and then immediately felt guilty for having such thoughts. *Geez, Nikki! Judgmental and vengeful much??*

Almost as if she could read her thoughts, the woman still hadn't said a word and just continued to glare at her with that hateful look on her chubby face. It was disconcerting, but Nikki literally shrugged it off and then turned to give Connie and Nathaniel a hug and Justin a tickle. She'd only met the kids a few times, but they'd treated her kindly and she thought maybe they genuinely liked her.

"I've been praying that you'd make it here safely!" Nikki exclaimed as she smiled at the kids. She ignored the disgusted-sounding snort their mother gave just then, wondering if it was in response to being at the ranch, or the fact that Nikki had been praying. *Probably both.*

Connie got a haunted look then. "Honestly, I wasn't sure we *were* going to make it," she said in a near whisper, which drew the attention of both her dad and brother, who'd been talking about the ranch. The latter wrapped his arm around his sister's shoulders in an obvious attempt to comfort her.

"Are things really that bad out there?" Nikki asked. She'd heard a few stories from some of the women, but strangely, most seemed reluctant to share their experiences of what happened before they came to the ranch. It was almost like they were afraid to speak of it, like talking about it out loud would somehow bring the evil to the ranch. She knew how they felt: the ranch was their haven, an oasis in the desert. No one wanted the peace to be tainted in any way, and talking about the evil running rampant in the world might just do that.

Connie nodded and swallowed, while her mother rolled her eyes in obvious disgust and finally decided to speak.

"Oh, for Pete's sake, don't be so dramatic. It isn't *that* bad, not as long as you do what they want and don't make waves."

Her daughter looked back at her mother with a look of disbelief mixed with horror. "I can't believe you said that, especially after the way Nate found you with all those soldiers—"

"That's enough," her mother hissed and shot a glance to Nikki, as if she were gauging her reaction. Nikki schooled her face into a neutral look, although she found herself immensely curious about what Connie had been about to say.

The girl frowned at her mother but remained silent. The moment suddenly became awkward, and Nikki decided to speak up.

"We'll have to put y'all together for a bit until we can get you your own places," she informed them, carefully looking at only Nathaniel and Connie as she spoke. She'd had enough of the glares Brenda was still sending her way and was afraid she might retaliate with one of her own if she dared to look back at the woman.

"We have some men who are great at building little houses, and real quick too, but we're starting to run out of wood," she added with a laugh as she pointed to the housing area near the Mexican border, several acres away from where they were standing. The neat row of little huts had grown to twenty and Frank and Tom were constantly working to make more.

The problem was, like she'd just told the kids, they'd nearly run out of wood. They'd run out of glass for windows several buildings ago, but Frank had made shutters for the newer huts and joked that he had found enough screen in the house attic to "cover all the windows at the Vatican." Since south Texas winters never got too cold, the screened window openings would have to do. At least they'd keep the bugs out and let the breeze in.

They'd converted one old barn that was still in decent shape into an apartment building for singles but used the wood from the other two barns that had been nearly falling down for furniture and huts for families.

Unfortunately, there were no more buildings they could cannibalize. The RVs and travel trailers were filled now and all but one of the huts was spoken for. Even the tents were being used voluntarily by some of the teen boys. The ranch was filled to capacity and Reg had joked about putting a "No Vacancy" sign on the gate.

The group had been praying about the situation at their nightly meal meetings, asking the Lord to continue to provide for their group, and to show them how to provide for any newcomers who might show up.

Sometimes the Lord answers prayers using the most unlikely sources. One of those times was at hand then, when Nathaniel—the young man known for riding with a rough biker gang and having a penchant for fighting and a reputation for involving himself in less-than-legal activities—spoke up.

"Hey, if you're out of wood, why don't you make adobe houses?"

His father looked at him like the kid had just solved world hunger. "Adobe? Well, hell—uh, sorry," he said to Nikki, who noticed that Brenda once again snorted.

"Why didn't we think of that?"

Nate crossed his arms over his chest while he gave his father a lopsided smirk which made Nikki realize he was the spitting image of his dad.

"Don't know, old man, maybe cuz you're *old* and your brain don't work so good no more?"

Nikki cringed at the put-down—and the use of bad grammar, which was also just like his dad—but reminded herself that was just how the father and son spoke to each other... a sort of joking insulting way. She didn't like it, or approve, but she knew they'd always been that way and sometimes a leopard couldn't change his spots.

Reg pleasantly surprised her when he didn't return his son's insult, but instead laughed and patted the young man's shoulder. "That's why I got you, son, to help your old man out."

Nate smirked again, his broad shoulders lifting in a shrug. He really was a handsome man, large and tall like his father, but with a more subtle version of his mother's flaming hair. Nate's was more a golden red than a pumpkin color like Brenda's and Connie's. Nikki noticed for the first time that he also had his father's hazel eyes.

"Before it all went to shi—" he stopped himself and glanced at Nikki, making an apology like his father had done just a few minutes before, "Sorry—uh, before the world fell apart, I was working for a contractor in Dallas who specialized in using natural resources, like solar and wind power. He built a lot of adobe houses, too, and had hired some men from Mexico who knew how to make the bricks. Since I was the new guy, he had me help them."

He shrugged again. "It's really simple, actually. Just gotta make sure you use sifted sand and straw."

Reg was suddenly very interested. "Do you think you can make them yourself?"

Again, Nate shrugged. "Yeah, sure. Don't see why not. Just need a frame for the bricks." He looked around at the landscape and smirked again. "Looks like you got plenty of sand."

Reg laughed and turned to lead his son away with his hand still on his shoulder. "Yeah, that we do. We got lots of screen to sift the sand too. Come on, I want you to talk to Frank and Tom, our builders, and tell them what you just told me."

Nikki watched them walk away in disbelief, a bit miffed that Reg would just leave her there with his hostile ex still glaring at her.

He seemed to read her mind, because he glanced back over his shoulder when they were just twenty feet away and said, "You okay, hon? We'll be right back…"

Well, now, that's just fine… not like I can admit to feeling just a wee bit stressed with having to stand here playing nice with Ms. Dagger Eyes, can I? Not with her shooting said daggers at me right now, waiting to hear what I say.

Nikki shook off her wayward thoughts and smiled and waved. "We're just fine, honey." *Check your pants, Nikki… they're on fire.*

"You boys just go take care of business and don't worry about us girls."

She noticed that Brenda gave another snort when she called Reg "honey." *Oh well, get over it. He's MY honey now, girlfriend.*

Turning back to the women, she noticed Justin was getting squirmy in his mother's arms, who looked hot and like she'd about had all she could take.

She smiled at Connie. "How 'bout I get one of the other kids to take him? This time of day most of them are at the big pond, but we've got a smaller pond just for the little ones and we have several older kids watching over them, so there's no need to worry. There's always a mom or two up there also."

At the same time that Connie answered, "Yeah, that'd be great," Brenda was saying in a hateful voice, "No, he's fine."

Ignoring the cantankerous woman, Nikki held out her hands to Justin, who promptly leaned to the side and practically threw himself at her. Laughing, Nikki set him on the ground and took his hand. As she led him away, she told him that he needed to "get ready to get muddy," to which he squealed in delight.

Behind her, she could hear Brenda mutter something about "trusting that woman." Nikki didn't turn back but smiled a bit vengefully when she heard Connie answer in a terse voice, "She's great, Mom, and *I* trust her."

After delivering Justin to Gina's daughter, Britney, Nikki took her time walking back to where Connie and Brenda waited. She noticed that Reg and Nate were still gone and shook her head. When it came to chatting, her husband could out-talk a gaggle of Baptist wives at an ice cream social.

Sighing, she mentally girded her loins and approached the women. Pointedly speaking directly to Brenda, who still had the look of a junkyard dog about to bite her hand through the fence, she said, "Let me show y'all to the cottage we have available." It wasn't really a cottage, but she figured if she called it a "hut" that might set the woman off. *Beggars can't be choosers.*

She turned and started walking toward the row of homes Frank and Tom had built. Well, they had led the team that built them, anyway. And the group thanked the Lord for that team. Without them, many of the residents would still be living in tents, or even out in the open. But with Frank and Tom's experience working with Samaritan's Purse to build easy and affordable homes in third world countries, the homes had been built quickly and with just a few mishaps.

One of those mishaps happened early on when they were subjected to a Texas-sized deluge. Several of the huts' roofs had leaked, forcing the men to rethink the materials they used in the construction. Tom suggested a thatch roof like they'd done in Zimbabwe, using woven grasses. But Reg had pointed out that they didn't have any tall straw they could use for that and all the wheat and whatnot that they'd grown was for their own food supply and the stalks were given to the livestock for bedding and feed.

Frank then suggested using sod like cottages in Ireland and Scotland. He said that obviously those places had a lot more rain than south Texas, and "if the grass could hold up to the rain there, it certainly should here." The team agreed it might be a good idea and headed up to the pond where wild grass grew in abundance, where they then cut strips of sod and laid it on one of the roofs for testing.

After weeks of slow, steady drizzles every other day or so, the hut was dry inside with no sign of leaks and the roof was not only still green, but the grass was actually growing. Since it was a success, the men had reroofed all the huts with the grass.

It had become a big joke among the group who were now calling the houses "chia huts." Some of the roofs even had a few flowers sprouting here and there. Nikki thought they were so cute that she'd begged Reg to sod the ranch house. She still hadn't been able to talk him into that just yet.

But apparently Brenda didn't think the huts were cute. She'd made several snide comments about the "slum shacks" and asked how they mowed the roof, or if they "threw a sheep up there to graze." Connie apparently had enough of it and snapped at her mother, telling her she needed to be thankful for what they had and that they were now safe. Nikki silently cheered the girl.

That woman needs a good lesson in humility and gratitude, she thought to herself. But then she supposed she was expecting Godly things out of a worldly person, and she knew that was about the same thing as expecting a dog to purr.

She thought then of their nightly meeting meals and started praying for the Lord to start softening Brenda, Connie and Nate to accept Him. She also added a prayer for herself.

Lord, I know it doesn't take a single drop more of Your blood to save someone like Brenda than it did to save me, and I have to ask You for help in remembering that. I'm feeling less than charitable toward her now, so I really need You to keep Your hand on me to keep me from tearing into her. Keep me on a short leash, Lord. And muzzle my mouth.

chapter 12

B Y THE time mid-summer had passed, the fields were filled from fence to fence with all manners of growing food, the gardens were overflowing with vegetables, the cattle herd had increased to fifty-three head, and every single lamb had survived—which Reg said was unheard of for sheep, who were notorious for losing lambs for no reason—increasing the fold to twenty-two. Even three of the horses had foaled. Life at the ranch wasn't just about surviving—it had become a lesson in God's blessings.

Pastor Steve talked about that very thing at dinner a week after Reg's kids and ex had arrived. They still had their meals outside, especially now that the group had grown so large, but had moved away from the ranch house and to the pond where there was more room. Roberto had made two more huge tables to fit them all, plus a huge buffet table where the food could be served cafeteria style. Frank and Tom had also led their team in erecting a gazebo type structure for the eating area to keep them out of the weather.

Before the meal, Steve stood before the crowd on the platform the construction team had made for that purpose.

"Jesus said that He came to give us life and to give it more abundantly," he reminded them before saying the blessing for the meal.

He stopped then and chuckled, shaking his head. "Well, the

Lord has certainly given us an abundant life here. We have more than we need, much more than we could have hoped for in these difficult times. Heck, we even have solar power and indoor plumbing. No outhouses for us, thank the Lord—and Reg."

A lot of the group laughed at that, and Nikki smiled when she noticed Reg's face turned red.

Steve waited until the chuckling stopped before continuing. "But despite our physical needs being met, our spiritual needs have also been met. We have a group here that is growing... not only in number, but also in faith. Yes, we have more people arriving at the ranch nearly every day—our numbers are now more than seventy!—but with those arriving here for safety and sanctuary, we also have experienced an amazing amount of souls being saved."

He paused again, and Nikki covertly glanced at Brenda, trying to gauge her reaction to Pastor Steve's words. She looked bored and was rolling her eyes periodically.

Brenda had continued to be antagonistic to nearly everyone—at least towards the women, that is. The men were another story and that was a big problem. The woman had been openly and brazenly flirtatious with them, to the point that the wives were coming to Nikki with their complaints, and she wasn't sure what to do about it.

It was that place between the proverbial hard place and rock—the woman needed to be talked to, but Nikki was pretty sure she wasn't the one to do it. Even though she and Reg were the unspoken leaders of the group, talking to her husband's ex-wife about her bad and intolerable behavior was sure to make waves of tsunami proportions.

Nikki sighed and tried to concentrate once more on what Steve was saying. When he started asking the Lord to bless the meal, Nikki said her own prayer for guidance and divine intervention in the Brenda situation.

Gina and Ben always sat with Reg and Nikki for meals. It wasn't something they had ever talked about or planned, but it just seemed the natural thing to do, since they had been eating every meal together since the Thompsons had come to the ranch. In fact, their table always seemed to consist primarily of the "originals," those who had been the first to arrive at the ranch—the Thompsons, Lees, Freemans, McCarthys and Jeff. Even though the Villareals and Mendezes had arrived before the others, because of the language barrier the Spanish-speakers tended to sit together, although with Ben's Spanish lessons, that barrier was thankfully getting smaller and easier to cross.

This night, Gina had made it a point to sit next to Nikki and when the men were engaged in their own conversation regarding Jeff taking over the security team, she leaned over and spoke to Nikki quietly.

"Look at them," Gina said as she nodded toward Anna and Garrett, who were sitting as close together as they could, their heads touching as they talked. Garrett had his hand over Anna's while he rubbed her wrist with his thumb.

"We better get busy with the wedding plans."

It was amazing how well the two got along now that they'd decided they didn't hate each other. They were nearly inseparable, and Steve had mentioned one night after watching Garrett threateningly stare down one of the other teen boys who had dared sit next to Anna that "maybe we ought to think about a wedding… quick." He'd said it half-jokingly, making both kids' father growl at him, but it had gotten the mothers to thinking—and talking.

The next afternoon, Gina had laid it on the line with Nikki while they sliced cucumbers for pickling. "Seriously, what's to stop them from getting married? I mean, yeah, she's only sixteen and he's seventeen, but it's not like they've got to quit school and get jobs, ya know? We don't have to follow the old rules any more about marriageable ages. People a hundred years ago—who lived like we're living now, by the way… well, minus the solar-powered fridges, coffee pots and, thank the blessed Lord, hair dryers—got married that young. Who's to say it's wrong?"

Nikki had reluctantly agreed, adding, "Yeah, it might be worth encouraging them in that direction, since I'm afraid they're going to be getting into trouble with the Lord soon. Better to be married than falling into sin."

She'd sighed then. "But we gotta convince their daddies first." Reg might only be stepdad to Anna, but he was just as fierce a papa bear as any other.

Gina laughed. "Leave the convincing to me."

Nikki laughed with her friend. If anyone could convince those two stubborn mules of anything, it was that outspoken little woman.

And now the same outspoken woman was once again speaking her mind. "We gotta do something about that she-devil," she stated after turning back to Nikki, dismissing the subject of the teens. There was no need to explain who the "she-devil" was.

Nikki sighed heavily and nodded her head. "I know. I'm just not sure what to do. I'd talk to her, but she wouldn't listen to me. I'm pretty sure she'd do the exact opposite of whatever I said, just to spite me."

Gina snorted. "You want me to channel some Puerto Rican and kick her butt?"

Nikki laughed. "I thought you were Mexican."

Her friend shrugged. "Yeah, I am, but I'm sure I can get some J-Lo going through my blood. Enough to take care of that snotty gringa, anyway."

The two shared another laugh, drawing the attention of their husbands. Reg was looking at her with a raised eyebrow. Nikki gave him a toothy fake smile, then turned back to Gina.

"I guess I could ask Reg to talk to her. I mean, after all, they have history." It wasn't something she wanted to ask of him, especially since he was so antagonistic toward his ex. But there was also the consideration that the woman couldn't be trusted not to throw herself at him, ex or not. Gina seemed to read her mind.

"You'd trust them together?" She waved her hand before Nikki could voice the protest forming on her lips.

"I didn't mean it like that. Of course, you trust Reg, and you should. But that woman—I wouldn't trust her in a room full of World War Two vets in wheelchairs on oxygen. She's like a cat in heat. Any male will do."

Nikki laughed again. "Yeah, I know. She was like that when she was married to Reg, too. I think she's got some sort of problem, like an addiction to sex." She had been trying to convince herself of that theory, mostly so she'd be more understanding of the woman and less homicidal.

Gina snorted again. "Well, I'll tell you *one* thing: She's gonna have some major problems—mostly broken bones—if she tries anything with Ben. She's already approached him at least once and was flirting with him, but I came up and glared her off." She snorted and tossed her thick dark brown hair over her shoulder.

"That hootchie is lucky that's *all* I did."

Another sigh escaped Nikki's lips before she answered. "I've had at least four other women come to me with the same complaint. Brenda actually tried to feel Tom up yesterday. *Tom*, of all people. He's what? Like seventy? Rebecca was ready to tear the woman's hair out."

Gina shook her head. "I bet. I would've, for sure. But then I'm less Christian than y'all are."

Nikki rolled her eyes at her friend. "That's the dumbest thing I've ever heard. How can you be 'less Christian' than us? What makes us 'more Christian'?"

Gina shrugged her shoulders. "Well, I'm still new at this. Y'all have been Christians a lot longer than me. I still have a lot of rough edges."

Nikki laughed again. "We all have rough edges, hon. Just when I think the Lord has one of mine smoothed out, I get another crack that needs filling and sanding. It's an unending process."

She sighed heavily once more. "Which makes me think we're all going about this situation with Brenda the wrong way. Only the Lord can truly change someone, so we need to be praying for Him to work on that Jezebel."

Gina nodded. "Yeah, true. I know once I accepted Him, I didn't want to do a lot of the stuff I'd been doing. Even my cussing has stopped, for the most part. Ben's too."

Nikki laughed. "And if the Good Lord can do that for *Ben*, He can fix anything and anybody!"

The ladies shared a laugh, then Nikki said, "Okay, so let's get the women together and we'll have a prayer vigil. Maybe I can get Reg to talk to Brenda at the same time we're praying."

To say that Reg was not happy with Nikki's request to speak with his ex about her behavior was like saying the Atlantic was a merely a pool of water.

He'd all but shouted at Nikki when she'd approached him about it. "She wouldn't behave herself when we were married no matter how much I begged, threatened or bribed her. So, what makes you think that she'll listen to me now?"

He shook his head in denial. "It'll be even worse now that she's got it in her head that I abandoned her and the kids. You know how she's been since the divorce."

Nikki felt for him, she really did. She imagined herself trying to reason with her ex, Matt, who was a male version of Brenda. But something had to be done and Reg was likely the only person to reach the woman.

She laid her hand on his arm. "I know, honey, believe me, I know. But just think about what kind of a witness you'll be now, how much you can shine Jesus to her. She needs Him as much as you did when you and I met. Having you go to her humbly and gently might just be what reaches her."

He snorted. "I doubt anything can reach the spawn of Satan."

Nikki grimaced and chuckled at the same time. A totally human and perverse part of her secretly rejoiced that her husband felt that way about his ex. But she pushed those evil thoughts back into the closet where they belonged and slammed the door shut. *Shame on you, Nicole Jeannette! That sure isn't how YOU shine Jesus, is it?*

Instead of voicing those awful thoughts, she tried a soothing tone. "Now, honey, you know that God can do all things. It's His *will* that we all come to Him, to get saved. Even Brenda," she added with a grin. "This just might be her day, you never know. And all us women plan to be praying for that very thing to happen when you go meet her."

They were both quiet a moment as they contemplated their thoughts. Then Nikki added, "I'd offer to go with you, but that woman spits venom at me like a rattler with a knot in her tail every time I'm within ten feet. Maybe Steve or Frank could go with you."

Her husband sighed heavily and ran a hand down his face, looking older and more tired in that moment of resignation to a duty he truly didn't want.

"Nah, I wouldn't want to subject either of them to her mouth. She can cuss worse than a sailor on shore leave in Bangkok."

Nikki smirked. "Well, I doubt either of them will hear anything they haven't before."

He smirked back. "Yeah, but it's not the words I'm worried about—it's the thought behind them. She'll spew all my dirty laundry, hers, and who knows who else's."

"Again, I doubt Steve and Frank have been angelic altar boys all their life. Heck, Frank was in the Army for both Gulf Wars. But if you're not comfortable with them, how about Ben?"

Almost as soon as she said his name, she was shaking her head. There was no way Gina would want Ben around that woman, not after the way she threw herself at him, even if he were "chaperoned." Reg seemed to agree, as he also shook his head.

"Not a good idea. Gina already wants that redhead on a platter as it is."

He sighed again. "I'll just go talk to her by myself, but I'm going to make darned sure there are witnesses within sight. I can just see her claiming I attacked her or some garbage like that."

Reg approached Brenda outside the row of huts early the next morning and asked if he could speak to her in private. He should have known by the knowing smirk she gave him when she agreed that trouble was brewing.

He led them to one of the dining tables under the gazebo near the ranch house, well within sight of at least a dozen people who were finishing up their daily chores before the day got too hot to be outside. He wasn't taking any chances with his vengeful, vindictive and conniving ex-wife.

After she settled her rather large frame onto the bench and Reg sat down directly across from her, he said a quick silent prayer for the right words and began.

He sighed first. "Look, this isn't easy for me, but as leader of this group, it's necessary—"

"Why would they make *you* leader?" she interrupted snidely.

Reg ignored her. He wasn't going to be baited into one of her argument traps. "I've talked to at least ten women and maybe even more men who have complained that you're propositioning the men."

She started to open her mouth in protest, but Reg shook his head and hurriedly continued.

"That isn't done here. We're almost all Christians and are trying to live within God's boundaries, His commandments. And despite that, most of the guys you've approached are married."

Brenda shrugged. "So? I've learned that doesn't stop most men. And those few that are stopped are just more of a challenge."

Reg shook his head and fought back the desire to wrap his hands around the woman's neck. "Well, like I said, here at the ranch, we're Christians and trying to be better than that."

She smirked again, an ugly look that Reg literally cringed at. For the hundredth time, he wondered what he'd ever seen in her.

"And I'm supposed to believe you're some sort of godly man, now? Sure."

She then leaned forward so that her low-cut blouse strained against her more than ample chest. Reg knew she was trying to get him to look at her cleavage. There was no way he was going to fall for that trick and kept his eyes firmly on her face, giving her what he hoped was a hard look.

"I can't say that I'm a godly man, but I sure am trying," he answered. "I fail miserably most of the time, but I know I'm forgiven for it, and for all the stuff I did in the past. I'm just—"

"You're full of it, is what you are," she harumphed.

Brenda waved her hand in the air to encompass the ranch. "Do all these people know what kind of man you *really* are, Reg? Do they know about all the stuff you did, that *we did*, when we were together?"

She smirked again and Reg found himself really fighting against wanting to slap her. He'd never hit a woman in his life and could never justify doing so. He was having the darnedest time remembering that fact now.

"I bet they'd be real shocked to know the real Reg Erskine, the one who used to be into all sorts of kinky sex. Maybe they *should* know the real you, the one they call the leader of this group of misfits."

His back teeth felt like they were going to crack under the pressure he was putting on them while flexing his jaw. The woman had always known just how to push his buttons and apparently she still knew exactly which ones to push. He said another prayer while he took deep breaths in an effort to calm himself.

Lord, I really need Your help now. This woman has always known exactly how to cut me the deepest and I don't want to react to her insults now. Please help me. Give me Your words to speak to her.

Suddenly he was reminded of the temptations Jesus went through. Brenda's comments sounded suspiciously like the devil's did when he was trying to get Jesus to deny His Father.

"Get behind me, Satan," he muttered under his breath.

"What?"

He shook his head. "Nothing. Look, I'm well aware of what I did in the past and how depraved I could be. But since I accepted Jesus, I know I've been forgiven for all that and I now try to live right in His eyes. It ain't easy, but I try. No one is perfect in God's eyes, and some of us are worse than others, but it don't take any more of Jesus' blood to save a bad person than it takes to save a good one."

The hateful look on her face had softened a bit, but she still looked skeptical, almost a confused look. She was frowning slightly, her eyes crinkling at the corners. Reg stared into those blue eyes, remembering a time when he'd loved the color, back when they were first married and all the cheating, lies and hatred that would later haunt him weren't even in the equation.

"He wants to save you too, Brennie," he added, using the nickname he'd given her when they were dating. He hadn't called her that in years and she looked startled.

But then made a sound of derision. "Yeah, right. Jesus don't care 'bout me. Maybe you think He forgives you and you've talked yourself into thinking He cares about you, but He don't. If He even exists, that is."

It was Reg's turn to make the sound. "Oh, He exists alright. I'm sure of that. I've seen more miracles since I gave my life to Him than I can even count. And every day I hear more and more stories of the way He cares about His children—about us."

Brenda rolled her eyes, while Reg shrugged. "But I can see by the look on your face that you're not gonna take my word for it. Go ask any of the others here, those who are Christians, about the miracles they've experienced. That'll convince you."

He turned on the bench so he was straddling the seat and nodded to the ranch in general, where people could be seen lolling about in the heat of the day, most of the work having already been completed.

"This ranch is full of those stories. Seriously, you ought to try talking to a few of them—*the women*," he stressed. "Leave the men alone, and I mean it. That takes us back to what I started to say here—you can't be flirting with the men around here. This group ain't gonna put up with it. Even the single men."

At her protest, he put up his hand. "Now, I ain't saying you can't have a relationship on down the road, but it's gonna be done the right way, God's way. We don't do casual sex here. Ain't gonna happen."

Her smile turned coy, almost predatory in nature. The look was worse than the smirk she'd given him before and he felt his skin crawl, knowing what she was up to, knowing exactly what she was capable of.

"Casual sex used to be our specialty, Reggie," she cooed as she leaned even farther over the table, her breasts nearly spilling out of the top of her blouse. Laying her hand on his forearm, she gently ran her fingers up and down, giving him goosebumps. She felt them, and apparently thought it was a sign of attraction, judging from the knowing smile she gave him. Reg wanted to yell at her that the raised flesh was a sign of revulsion, not attraction, but he managed to hold his tongue. Barely. He jerked his arm away from her ministrations.

Brenda dipped her head and looked at him from under her lashes. "We sure could have a good time in bed, couldn't we? Even just the two of us. It was always more fun with others joining in, but even by ourselves, we never failed to rock each other's world."

But for you, "others" were always the preference, with or without me there...

He swallowed against the argument that wanted to spill from his lips. Instead, he thankfully heard himself saying, "I'm happily married now. *Very* happily married. Nikki and I have a great relationship, one that you and I never had, because we have Jesus. I would never cheat on my wife. Not now," he amended.

The woman made that sound again, although he could see the hurt in her eyes. She wasn't used to being rejected. Even now, being past middle age and despite the several dozen extra pounds she carried, men wanted her. They always had. Reg had always suspected that there was something about Brenda that called to the male psyche, some voice that said, "I'm available for anything, anytime, any perversion you can think of." He could certainly attest to the fact of that truth.

She shrugged. "Yeah, well, no big loss. You never could please me anyway."

Reg stared at her and bit back the words he wanted to say at her contradiction. Just minutes before, she'd been talking about how they could "rock each other's world." Now, because of his rejection, she claimed he couldn't please her. He knew she was speaking out of angry hurt, trying to push buttons in order to retaliate, and so he was easily able to ignore the insult.

"This isn't about us," he gently told her, noting the shock in her eyes when he didn't take the bait to fight with her. She quickly covered the shock with a scowl.

"I was asked by the women—*and men*—of the group to talk to you, to ask you to stop trying to seduce the men. Like I said, it isn't acceptable, not here."

She stared at him for a minute, then smirked again. "Okay, so the men are off limits—"

"And the women," he gritted out through his teeth. Twenty-plus years of marriage let him know exactly what she was thinking. The woman sitting before him didn't care who she took to her bed and had no qualms about using either sex to fulfill her desires.

As he watched her roll her eyes and huff, for the thousandth time Reg wondered what had happened in Brenda's life to cause her to be the way she was. Her brother, Sam, too, had his share of problems. By the age of twenty, he'd been in prison twice and had never been able to hold a job. Last Reg had heard, he was doing five to ten in the state pen for grand theft auto.

If there was abuse in their childhood, some sort of explanation for their behavior, Brenda had never spoken of it. Her mother had been a single mom who worked hard to raise two kids by herself, their dad being a deadbeat who couldn't stay out of prison. The kids were often left in the care of their grandmother who was a strong Southern Baptist and strict with her beliefs.

Before being saved, Reg had always assumed that the kids had simply rebelled against that strict upbringing. Or maybe their wild behavior was caused by the inconsistency of living with rigid grandma during the week and then weekends with mom, who was a pot-smoking truck driver who liked to live a bit on the wild side. Maybe the back-and-forth caused some sort of rift. Then again, it could just be bad genes from the dad's side of the family.

But now that he knew the truth, Reg summed up the behavior as just sin. He knew that Brenda had chosen a sinful life, like most everyone else in the world. And while her choices may have seemed over-the-top in the sin department to most "normal" people, Reg knew that in God's eyes they were no different than gossiping or lying. Sin was sin, and Brenda was no less worthy to receive His forgiveness than the godliest person who ever lived.

Saying another quick prayer for the right words, Reg decided he'd try again to get through to her.

"Look, you of all people know how I was before. I was just as capable of finding some kinky sex game to play as the next pervert and drinking and fighting were my two favorite pastimes. So, I'm definitely not pointing fingers at you, because it's not up to me to judge. But the Lord *does* judge us. At the end of all this we have to stand before Him and give an accounting for all we did... or didn't do. And there's a price to be paid for those decisions."

He shook his head slowly. "When we commit a sin—any sin, no matter how big we humans may think it is, or how insignificant—then we've put ourselves in a place where we deserve punishment. Just like if we'd committed a crime. And God is the judge, jury, and executioner, but His judgment is eternal damnation, in Hell. Eternal, as in forever and ever.

"And no, don't be thinking Hell is some big party for sinners," he quickly added, guessing what she might be thinking. "The Bible says it's a place of utter darkness and torment. And just think: All those demons who hate us, who despise God's creation, are going to spend an eternity torturing those unfortunate souls who are there."

They sat in silence for a few minutes, the distant sounds of children laughing and playing in direct contrast to the seriousness of their conversation. Reg hoped that Brenda would realize just how serious he was being.

"But think again about standing on trial before God. The devil—the enemy of all mankind—is the prosecutor, and he's airing all your dirty laundry there before all creation, literally. And the sad thing is, you know you're guilty of everything he's accusing you of and you ain't got no leg to stand on, no argument to give. It's hopeless, you realize, and you're doomed. The verdict is guilty no matter how you slice it.

"But then in walks Jesus—God's own Son and your defense attorney. He walks right up to His Father, and He says, 'Yes, she's guilty, Your Honor, but I'll take her punishment.'"

Reg stopped for a minute, because just the thought of what Jesus had done for him made him choke up. His voice was watery when he continued.

"He loves us that much, Brennie. He already paid the price for every sin we've ever committed, and for every sin we'll ever commit, when He hung on that cross. And what really gets to me is the thought that He would have done it just for me, if I were the only one to ever accept that amazing gift of forgiveness. And He would have done it just for you, too."

Brenda snorted again, although Reg could tell some of the wind had gone out of her sails. "So, what's all this I hear about God being a loving God? If He loves us so much, why does He judge us and send us to Hell?"

Reg shook his head and picked at a spot on the table with his fingernail. "He doesn't send us to Hell; we send ourselves there by choosing to deny the only way out of the punishment. It's like being in that courtroom and having Jesus say He'll take the punishment for us, and we say, 'No thanks, I don't really know this guy, so I'll take the punishment myself.' Someone has to pay the price, and if we're not willing to accept Jesus' offer, then we send ourselves to Hell."

She started to speak again, but he held up his hand. "And before you say it, God didn't create Hell for man. He created it for Satan and his demons when they chose to defy God and leave heaven. So, if we choose to follow Satan—and we're either for God or we're against Him, meaning we're on Satan's side—then that's where we'll end up."

Brenda was quiet and Reg let her think on what all he'd said. He then reached over and placed his hand over hers, praying she wouldn't think it was an offer for anything more than comfort.

"Me of all people should be looking at an eternity of burning in Hell, you know that. But I'm not going to, hon."

He gave her hand a light squeeze. "I'm telling you the truth—when you accept Jesus as your Lord and Savior, all that guilt and shame just leaves, because you know that He loves you unconditionally and wants you to spend eternity with Him, in heaven. And because of that unconditional love, He forgives you for everything and anything you've done. It's an amazing, indescribable feeling to be free of all of that garbage."

She was quiet again for a long while. Reg kept silent too, knowing she was thinking about what he'd said and during that quiet time, he prayed for the Holy Spirit to work on softening her heart.

After many long minutes filled with only the sound of the children and birds chirping in the trees, she finally spoke in a quiet voice.

"So, what do I have to do to get what you have?"

chapter 13

B Y EARLY fall, the group had grown to one hundred and twelve people.

With that number of people depending on the ranch for support, the task to provide for the needs was daunting, even for just the basic necessities like food and shelter. But everyone worked and everyone was willing to go the extra mile to make sure all were provided for. If someone had need of clothes, then clothes were either donated, or one of the women who knew how to sew would make them. If a larger shelter was needed—as in the case of a new baby being born, which had happened twice so far—then the men got right on it and built a new hut or added on to an existing one. The group truly had the attitude of the first church spoken of in the book of Acts… when there was a need, it was met, no questions asked.

Nikki and Reg were constantly busy trying to solve problems, making sure needs were met and that the ranch's stored provisions were at the level they needed to be. The day-to-day stress of running of the ranch had started to take its toll on both their health and their marriage.

Reg had trouble sleeping, lying awake long into the night trying to solve all the problems he'd faced that day and anticipating the new problems that might creep up the following day. He was always exhausted and subsequently cranky.

Nikki had developed a cough that no amount of doctoring from Charlene had been able to fix. She, too, had trouble sleeping due to it. Thanks to the lack of sleep and sheer physical and mental exhaustion, the couple who had always been known and admired for their happy marriage had started snapping at each other.

Gina, being the most outspoken of the originals, was the first to say something, although many others had noticed the trouble in paradise.

She and Ben approached Nikki and Reg after dinner one night, stopping them from helping clear the table by asking to speak to them. Gina almost laughed when she saw the wariness that came over both of them when they assumed yet another problem needed solving.

Gina got right to the point. "So, you two think you're so amazingly perfect that you have to do everything around here by yourselves?"

That caught them both off-guard. "What?" Nikki asked in a shocked voice, the question echoed by Reg.

"You're both running yourselves into the ground," Ben explained. "It's hard to watch. You both look like you haven't slept in weeks, Nikki sounds like an emphysemic and you're constantly biting each other's heads off. Everyone has noticed, too."

Reg got his back up with Ben's comment. "Well, there's a lot to do around here and *someone* has to make the decisions. Since we seem to be in charge, it comes down to us. What do you want us to do?

Tell everyone to go blow and figure it out for themselves?"

Gina rolled her eyes and crossed her arms over her chest. "No, of course someone has to be in charge, and the two of you are the obvious choice for that, since you were the ones who started all this. But don't you remember the story of Moses when his father-in-law came to Moses when he was in the same condition with trying to do everything by himself? His father-in-law gave him the advice to *delegate*—oooh, there's a dirty word—some responsibility. That's all we're saying. Del-e-gate. Don't try to do everything yourselves. You've got people who can help, you know."

Reg looked like she'd just suggested he cut off his manly parts and fry them up for supper. Gina laughed and said so. "For Pete's sake, Reg, it's okay. Ben isn't less of a man since he decided to let Jeff run the security team cuz he wanted to go back to work in the slaughter house, you know. It's not a reflection on your manhood to say that you could use some help."

Ben cringed at her comments and looked askance at her, trying to give his overly vocal wife a silent warning that he himself knew was useless. He looked exacerbated and if Nikki hadn't been so afraid of having another coughing fit, she would have laughed at the look.

Ben held a hand up to his wife who was about to start in again. "What we're trying to say is that you're not alone in this, bro. We all have a stake in making this place run smoothly. We're just suggesting that while you might be the chief, you need some captains to help out. If you keep up the pace you two have been going at, you're going to drop dead in a month and then where will all of us be?"

Reg laughed at that comment, but secretly he knew it was true. At the rate they were going, either they were going to have nervous breakdowns, or end up sleeping in separate places. Or both.

He looked at Nikki who stood next to him with her shoulders slumped and looking like she was about to fall over. He noticed for the first time just how haggard she looked. Dark circles lined her eyes and she'd lost quite a bit of weight. She now looked a lot older than her forty-eight years.

The poor woman had had her hands full with trying to organize the food storage and distribution, which was a full-time job in itself. But she was also helping Garrett and Anna keep track of the younger kids' schooling, plus she made sure everyone had what they needed to make their living quarters comfortable and more like a home, and on top of that, she also dealt with the day-to-day problems and complaints of the women.

He, too, had worn himself into the ground working the fields, harvesting, planting, planning for the next season's crops, and trying to make sure everyone had at least minimal solar power and running water, which involved constant repairs. He also had the added responsibility of solving the everyday problems of the men.

Sighing, he knew they had to let go of some of that responsibility. It was just too much for only two people. Both he and Nikki were the type to just handle everything themselves, with the attitude that if they wanted it done right, they'd do it themselves. But it was time to change that attitude and let others step up to the plate.

He clasped Ben's shoulder. "You're right. We've been heading toward a cliff we're sure to fall off of. So, other than the two of you, who do you think should be 'captains'?"

Ben laughed. "Whoa. Hold your horses, there. Who said we wanted to be in charge of anything?"

Reg smirked at him. "Who said you had a choice? You've been voluntold."

Ben and Gina both laughed at that. She spoke before her husband could, placing her hand on his back to keep him silent as she laughingly replied, "We'd love to help out in whatever way we can."

Ben chuckled and shook his head while he looked down at the ground. "Yeah, whatever you need us to do. But as for others, I think we need to think in terms of departments, like food should be Esperanza's baby, medical Charlene's, housing Frank or Tom— probably Tom, since Frank is a little gruff for most people to go to with problems. Of course, any spiritual problems should be given to Steve."

Nikki piped up then. "Most of those 'departments' are too broad, though. Like food—Esperanza can be in charge of dinner preparation, which she already is, and Ben in charge of butchering, but someone needs to be on top of storage, and maybe another for distribution. And someone else needs to be in charge of clean-up after the dinners. Oh, and someone needs to be in charge of making the pets' food. Esperanza's been doing that by herself too."

Reg nodded. "Yeah, she's another one who's been running herself ragged. And we need to think about housing too—Tom can be in charge of the building portion and making sure we have enough space for everyone, but when it comes to furnishing the places, we need to put Roberto in charge of that."

"And then there's the distribution of linens and things for the house. I know a lot of people have come with their own stuff, but not everyone," Gina added.

Ben laughed and held up his hand. "We need to sit down and make a plan, apparently. Let's head to the ranch house and get this down on paper. Then we can talk to the others and then have Steve make the announcement tomorrow night during worship."

After they made the organizational chart of divisions and leaders and got everyone to volunteer for the division they felt called to work in, the ranch ran so smoothly that problems were kept to a bare minimum and Reg and Nikki were able to get their health and happiness back.

Since people got to choose the areas they worked in, for the most part everyone else was happy too. Laughter and singing were often heard throughout the ranch as the daily chores were being completed. Children who had finished their schoolwork and the few chores they were given played chase, hide-n-seek, and various other games that children throughout the centuries have played. And, surprisingly, not a single one of them complained about the lack of electronics.

Even the teenagers eventually quit complaining about being disconnected from the rest of the world. Instead, they would get together and just talk like the adults did. Sometimes they would play board games, or a cut-throat game of Charades. A few knew how to play instruments and taught some of the others how to play and now they had a very nice band and entertained the entire ranch with their music.

Gina remarked one evening after meal service about how much happier everyone seemed to be in "these times," despite the harder work and lack of some of the items American's had once considered "the finer things."

Nikki and Brenda agreed. Since Brenda had given her heart to Jesus after Reg's talk, she'd had a complete change of attitude and a radical about-face in demeanor. No longer was she flirtatious and provocative, making lewd proposals to any man who gave her any attention at all; instead, she had become respectful yet distant with them, but was friendly and helpful with the women. She'd actually become a very good friend to Nikki and Gina.

Nikki thought about how Brenda's kids had fit right in, too. Both Nate and Connie had both had dedicated themselves wholeheartedly in seeing that the ranch succeeded and that everyone was happy and comfortable. No need was too great or too small for them to jump right in and help. Steve had commented that although the young adults hadn't yet accepted Jesus, they sure were acting more like Christians than a lot of people who'd sat in church all their lives.

Tom had put Nate in charge of making the adobe bricks the ranch now used to build houses and Nate had asked Alonzo to join the team, since the two young men got along so well together, which had been a surprise to both Nikki and Reg. Alonzo had always been a city boy and Nathaniel was country through and through, but the two stepbrothers became fast friends as soon as Al got his drug habit kicked and was thinking straight.

Nikki smiled as she thought about how well her son was doing. He'd made a complete turn-about—thanks to the Lord, of course—and had even given a sermon a few times at the evening meal. He'd also become very close to Anita, one of the young Mexican girls who'd come to the ranch with her family. Steve had predicted a wedding in the near future and Nikki was thrilled at the prospect of more grandkids being added to their family.

Al loved working on the construction team, too, and had found his niche there. He'd always been creative and enjoyed working with his hands, so it was a perfect fit for him, since Tom, Frank and Nate gave him free reign on designing the huts. Instead of the usual square or rectangles, the newer huts had more flare, some with rounded alcoves, others with decorative parapets.

Since mud was in abundance and they were no longer forced to build tiny huts out of wood scraps, they'd replaced all the huts with houses, some even three bedrooms in size. Set on natural rock foundations, the men used the wood taken from deconstructing the huts for flooring and the leftovers Roberto used for creating furniture. A lot of people had remarked that the houses were nicer than what they'd lived in before coming to the ranch. And those who'd been living in RVs now had real houses and the RVs and trailers had been dismantled for their useful parts.

Grass was still the preferred roofing method and so the "chia hut" name stuck, regardless that the huts were now nice-sized homes. Nikki had finally been able to talk Reg into putting grass on the ranch house roof too. When she'd first wanted it just for the whimsical look, Reg had balked, but he soon realized that the sod was actually a very good insulator and it made sense to use in the hot Texas sun. When Reg had finally given in to Nikki's desire, Tom then made the decision to have all the ranch building roofs sodded.

The group realized that that decision turned out to be from the Lord, when one day the security team alerted Jeff to the fact that a military-type airplane was in the area and seemed to be doing reconnaissance. Jeff sounded the alarm—a hundred-year-old dinner bell on the ranch house—and when everyone came running, he told them all to go inside and stay inside until he rang the bell again, and then to meet back at the ranch house.

Shortly after everyone had run indoors, the plane flew directly over the ranch. It didn't even make a second pass. After waiting an hour to make sure it didn't return with reinforcements, Jeff again rang the bell. Once the group was reassembled at the ranch house, he stepped up on the porch and announced, "Apparently our chia ranch is safe from eyes in sky. Thanks to the grass roofs, I think it's pretty much invisible to those flying over!"

After cheering, most of the crowd started praising God. But even those who weren't yet saved knew that they'd somehow been protected, maybe even on a divine level. Regardless of the individual beliefs of the residents, every single person knew that they'd dodged a very real bullet.

But once the crowd dispersed, Jeff walked up to Ben and Reg with a serious expression on his young face.

"You know, the roofs aren't gonna protect us from a serious recon. If they decide to use infrared on us, they'll find us. There's no way to hide then."

Ben nodded. "Yeah. We just have to hope they don't have a reason to look closer."

Another bullet was dodged a few days later when a group of men came rushing up from the fields yelling for Charlene. Albert, one of the older men, had been bitten by a rattlesnake while hoeing a row of corn.

Charlene and her helpers, Julie and Rayanne, ran to the field where Albert was lying, writhing in pain. One of the men had already removed his boot and Charlene whipped out her six-inch knife to cut his jeans up the inside seam.

The rattler had bitten the man just below his knee, less than an eighth of an inch above the top of his boot. Some of the other men whistled and Ben, who, along with many others, had run up when they heard the commotion, gave voice to what many were thinking.

"What are the odds the danged thing would miss the boot?"

Charlene straightened and looked back at the group, a grim look on her face. "It was obviously a wet strike, judging from the pain he's in and it's already swelling."

One of the women asked, "What's a wet strike?"

It was Reg who answered. "Most of the time a rattler bites without injecting venom—a dry strike, one that hurts but doesn't really do much to you. But a wet strike is where the venom is injected and it's usually fa—" He let his voice trail off, not wanting to finish the word. *Fatal.*

The ranch didn't have antivenom, nor the capabilities of setting up anything fancy like dialysis or even the much simpler IV. There wasn't a thing that could be done for the man, and from the looks on the faces of the group, they all knew it.

It was Albert's wife Emily, who broke the silence. She was an old Texas farm-gal who could give Charlene a run for her money in the gruffness department. And the two women were fast friends.

Charlene grabbed Emily's hand when she stepped up to the group, giving it a slight squeeze in support. Her friend gave her a grateful smile before asking in a slightly acerbic voice, "Well, are we all gonna stand around gawking at my husband while he tries to curl up like an armadillo and die, or are we gonna lay hands on him and pray?"

That jolted the group into action and within seconds several dozen people were on their knees with a hand on Albert, praying vehemently.

One woman prayed, "Lord, just as you healed Paul from the deadly asp, we ask that you heal Albert the same way."

Another cried out, "The Israelites just had to look at the serpent on the pole to be spared, Lord. Instead, we're looking to You to spare Albert."

A man prayed, "You're still a God of miracles, heavenly Father. We know You can heal this man and we're asking it in Your Son's Name."

The prayers went on for about half an hour, until Albert suddenly stopped writhing and took a deep, gasping breath. Everyone went silent and looked at him expectantly.

"Anybody get the plate of the truck that hit me?" he joked in a raspy voice, much to the delight of the others.

Emily scooped her husband up to her chest tightly, crying and admonishing him at the same time.

"You old fool, you coulda died! You think you're just gonna leave me like that and get away with it? You're lucky the Lord spared you, or else I woulda been hot on your trail to heaven to whip your behind for leaving me!"

"Darlin', I love you too, but the Lord didn't spare me just so's you could smother me to death," Albert mumbled against his wife's chest. More laughter followed as Emily loosened her hold.

Again, the Lord chose to answer their prayers, and in yet another miraculous way.

Reg at one time had jokingly predicted that he and Nikki "might just end up with the entire military at their doorstep," since it was suspected the Neos might want to do away with the U.S. armed forces in favor of establishing their own military force.

He had no idea that prediction would come real close to coming true. Just weeks after the recon plane had flown over the ranch, an assortment of military-type trucks and jeeps—curiously interspersed with civilian vehicles—had come up the road to the ranch. The security team spotted them from afar and had rung the bell, but there wasn't much the ranch could do about a ground assault. For the most part, they were at the mercy of whomever—or whatever—came onto the property.

Reg, Ben and Jeff, along with many of the other men, walked out to meet the convoy where the top of the drive ended at a line of boulders. All the men were filled with trepidation and nervously shifted from foot to foot. The women and teenagers kept the younger children indoors and out of sight, most praying vehemently for protection.

When the first truck—a large military carrier, the type with a canvas cover over the back—stopped, the driver's door opened, and a man climbed down. The first thing Reg noticed was that the man wasn't wearing a uniform, just worn jeans, running shoes and a gray t-shirt with "ARMY" in big black letters on the chest.

He held up his hand in a wave and walked toward the men. "'Afternoon," he said by way of greeting. "I'm Don Martinez." He then shook hands with the men, who introduced themselves, then Don waved to the rest of his group behind him. A few more men were stepping out of various vehicles, all also dressed in civilian clothes. Reg thought they looked like they were wary, unsure of their welcome, certainly not approaching them like soldiers on a mission would. He relaxed slightly when he realized they likely weren't being invaded, at least not hostilely.

Don didn't say anything else until the rest of the group completed their introductions, and then in a very weary voice, he said, "We're sure hoping you can help us out." He sounded bone-tired, and Reg felt sudden compassion for the man. He was obviously feeling the stress of a difficult situation.

Clearing his throat, Don addressed the group of men in general. "We're all Army—well, ex-Army, I guess, now that the Neos took over—and we're in need of a place to stay for a bit. We're on our way to central Mexico, but one of our ladies remembered this place from back when she was a kid and was friends with the… Perkins? Pickens? She thought maybe it would be a good place to rest and recuperate before we attempt to cross the border."

Reg stepped forward. "The Pickens still own the place, and yes, of course, you're welcome to stay as long as you need."

Looking back at the caravan, he asked, "Do you have tents or something? I'm not sure how much space we have available."

Don nodded once, then clarified with a half-smile, "Like I said, we're ex-Army, so most of us are acquainted with sleeping on the hard ground. If you can find a place for our wives and kids, though, that'd be great."

A young woman stepped up then, her short-cropped blonde hair sticking up in all directions. Reg thought she looked a little like a hedgehog, and when she spoke, he thought she might be just as prickly.

Her voice was filled with disdain when she put her two cents in. "Not *all* of the ladies need pampering," she said with a smirk at Don, then stuck her hand out to shake the men's' hands. "Lieutenant Anderson—" she interrupted herself with a grimace.

"Heck, sorry, I'm so used to saying that, but now I guess rank doesn't matter. Angela, Angela Anderson," she amended with a grin.

At the woman's words, Reg noticed Don's face tighten and he almost, but not quite, rolled his eyes with what looked like disgust and frustration. Reg inwardly laughed. The lieutenant was likely one of those people who came out of college with their precious degree in hand, promptly joining the military to become an instant officer with little to no training, skipping over the non-commissioned promotions that were based on performance, just because she had a piece of paper that said "graduate." The "regular" soldiers had resented their type for decades.

Reg shook the woman's hand, then turned back to Don, effectively telling the woman that he considered Don to be in charge of the group, not her. While Reg certainly didn't have a problem with women in leadership positions, he did have a problem with those who threw their rank or title around, regardless of their sex.

"Yeah, I'm sure we can find a place for them." He paused and turned a worried glance back toward the convoy.

"Well, how many are we talking exactly?"

I-Insist-On-Being-In-Charge *Lieutenant* Anderson piped up. "There are twelve kids and seven women—well, women who feel the need to sleep indoors."

Reg turned back to Don again, refusing to give the woman the attention she obviously thought she deserved. "That ain't a problem, especially if the kids are old enough to be away from their mamas overnight. On Saturdays, weather permitting, our kids all get together for a camp-out under the stars… and don't worry, it's adult supervised."

He smiled slyly then. "In fact, if y'all are gonna be sleeping outside anyway, you can take on the babysitting duty."

Don laughed and shrugged, looking around the ranch, and obviously not seeing any children about, Reg knew he was assuming there weren't too many. "Sure, why not—how many are we talking exactly?" He grinned when he threw Reg's words back at him.

Reg grinned back. He liked this guy already. "As of right now, with your twelve, we've got seventy-three."

Don's eyes nearly popped out of his head and then he and the others laughed. "Holy moly. That's a gaggle of young un's. I may have bit off more than I can chew."

Reg laughed. "Yeah, believe me, even you soldiers would have a time of it trying to run herd on them. Actually, though, they're all good kids and mostly well-behaved, respectful. But you wouldn't be alone. We try to make sure there's at least one adult for every five kids, so you'd have help."

Don shook his head and laughed again. Before he could answer, *Lieutenant Loony Toons*, as Reg was now privately thinking of her, opened her mouth. Obviously, she didn't like being left out of the loop.

"Well, *I'll* run it by the rest of the group and see what they say. I don't make decisions without discussion." She paused and laughed with what Reg was sure was supposed to sound like self-deprecation. It fell far short of that and everyone around them knew it, judging by the looks they had on their faces.

"At least I don't anymore."

Reg had to fight his own expression. The woman was just so full of herself. Nikki and Gina—the latter, especially—were sure to fall into immediate dislike with her. Thankfully since Gina had gotten saved, the Lord had tamed the little Mexican firecracker quite a bit.

Brenda, too. The woman had an arrest record as long as her arm for various types of assault, although she was never charged with anything thanks to her past penchant for doing whatever it took to get out of trouble.

But, wow, did the Lord ever change her. Reg was continually stunned by the change in his ex. The woman who had been an enemy had now actually become a friend. He no longer had to worry that she might attack anyone, even snippy former Army officers who wanted the world to bow in adoration at their feet.

But he could tell this particular officer was going to antagonize nearly everyone to their breaking points. And he knew from experience that everyone had a breaking point—even devout Christians intent on following the Lord. Heck, even Jesus Himself had reached that point when He turned over the money-changers' tables in the temple. Sometimes you had to stand up for what was right, and sometimes you had to turn the other cheek.

Unfortunately, though, in "turning the other cheek," most of the ranch residents would let the lieutenant get away with an awful lot of bullying before someone snapped and did something they might later regret.

The only person he could think of that Anderson wasn't going to get away with bullying at all was Charlene. He grinned then when he thought of the two of them together. That old battle ax, who had been an Army lieutenant herself, would put the young whelp in her place, pronto.

After getting the military group settled with the men and their older kids in tents and sleeping bags outside, and the women and really young children in the ranch house living room, Reg had delighted in reminding Nikki of his teasing comment to her over a year before regarding the military camping out in that very spot.

Nikki and Gina invited the group to have supper with the rest of the ranch residents. At first, they'd declined, stating they had brought their own food and didn't want to be a bother, but when the women insisted, they relented.

Although still somewhat wary, the women were a little more open and friendly than the men. Nikki made mention of that to Gina, who theorized that the group was probably a bit on edge because they were worrying that the Neos might be somehow tracking them. It was a logical fear, since they'd stolen the trucks and jeeps they had been driving directly from a Neos' base.

Suzanne, Don's wife, told Nikki that her husband and the others in their group had been stationed at the base that was now the Neos' Texas headquarters. After the collapse came, most of the military personnel soon realized that they were going to be "written off" as unnecessary by the new regime and had scattered.

Their little group had come together to form a sort of commune in a large farmhouse outside of Killeen in the hopes of supporting one another and finding safety in numbers. So, when things really started going south and the Neos actually started hunting former military members, Don had rallied their little group. They formed a plan to sneak onto the base in order to procure supplies so they could head to Mexico and leave behind the madness that was consuming the United States.

Suzanne and several other spouses had protested the plan, not only because of the obvious danger involved, but also because many were morally against using thievery to meet a need. The problem was, since they were ex-military and basically being hunted, they weren't able to buy any supplies at all, not even food. The meager stockpile the families had managed to accrue was almost gone and things were looking very bleak. Faced with the very real possibility of their children starving, Suzanne and the others had finally come to terms with Don's plan.

Once on the base they'd gotten caught, and like Jeff months before, had run for the motor pool, taking the first vehicles they could find. Suzanne said Don thought the vehicles they'd taken hadn't been commissioned for use by the Neos yet, as their evil-looking logo hadn't been imprinted on the doors yet.

Nikki hoped she was right.

That night, the pre-meal meeting was being led by Jeff. The group often took turns speaking their mind about something the Lord had laid on their hearts. They tried to keep to the pattern set by the "early church," where no one person always took the lead.

"Man is he on fire," Gina whispered to Nikki, who nodded. By the looks of wonder on their faces, it was obvious the entire group was in shock while watching the excited young man who was normally soft-spoken and a bit shy.

Jeff had once admitted to Reg that being introverted was why he had been drawn to Border Patrol—long hours of alone time while on patrol without having too much human interaction, which had always made him a bit uncomfortable.

But that night he was giving every televangelist who'd ever given God's teaching on television a run for their money, preaching like the hounds of Hell were on his heels and his only hope for salvation was to speak the word of the Lord. *If only we all had that mindset,* Nikki thought.

Jeff had announced when he first began speaking that he titled his sermon "Smoking or Non-Smoking." He had everyone laughing with his description of a restaurant and the various patrons. While it was humorous, it certainly drew the message home of where you wanted to spend eternity.

He really laid it on the line about what Hell was truly like based on what the Bible said. Nikki had chills as she listened to the young man preach from the heart about the horrors of that dark place. She doubted anyone would willingly choose Hell as their destination after Jeff's apt description.

And sure enough, when Pastor Steve took over after Jeff was through and gave an invitation for any who wanted to accept the Lord, many of the newcomers did so. Most surprising of those going forward, though, was "Lieutenant Loony Toons."

Nikki smiled through her tears as she realized that everyone who had come to the ranch had been saved in one way or another—not only from the horrors of the current world, but many had also been saved from the horrors of an eternity without Jesus.

She sighed in pleasure, knowing that they had their own piece of heaven here on earth.

chapter 14

HELL LAID siege on heaven.

A week after the military refugees had shown up—and had been encouraged to stay at the ranch—another convoy made its way slowly up the drive. This time, however, the Neos' logo was clearly seen on the vehicles' doors and once again, everyone scrambled to their pre-assigned places.

The security team had sounded the alarm as soon as they saw the convoy coming down the dirt road leading to the ranch, but it was a futile ploy. Everyone knew there wasn't much they could do against a ground attack, especially not against an organized military unit armed to the hilt, as the convoy appeared to be. Some of the vehicles were even equipped with mounted guns on the hoods, and it was obvious that the soldiers would be well-armed, which was confirmed when the convoy got close enough to see soldiers hanging off the sides of the trucks with automatic rifles over their shoulders and side arms on their hips.

Jeff reminded them they would just have to play it cool and see what came of the visit. Hopefully, nothing bad.

But everyone knew it could be bad... very bad. The stories Don and his group had told of the Neos' strong-arm tactics were enough to scare even the bravest. Stories of brutal torture, executions without trial, kidnappings, rapes, holding children hostage until the parents bent to the Neos' will, and whisperings of Nazi-esque "medical experiments" on unwilling subjects filled the minds of everyone watching the group of vehicles approach.

Jeff had told the men to take whatever defensive position they could. Afraid that the buildings might be searched, the women gathered the children near the back of the pond, hiding in the wooded thicket.

Reg had ordered Don and his group to stay in the hidden cellar under the ranch house. He couldn't take any chances that they'd be taken by force to suffer who-knew-what horrors for desertion and evasion of the Neos.

Don had at first argued that he and his people wanted to help defend the ranch, but when Reg reminded him that *all* their families were at risk if the Neos discovered they were harboring the ex-Army group, he'd capitulated and headed underground.

Trying to appear interested and unafraid, Reg, Ben and Jeff approached the convoy unarmed, while the rest of the men positioned themselves in various hiding places to watch the interaction, armed and waiting, willing to do anything they could to protect their families. Everyone was so tense, Reg was worried one of the men might accidentally and inadvertently fire at the soldiers, the result being complete annihilation of the ranch.

Reg watched as the vehicles pulled to a stop and the men who had been hanging on the sides of the trucks stepped off, weapons in hand while scanning the area. Unlike the week before when Don and his group arrived at the ranch, the soldiers exiting the vehicles didn't give the impression of being friendly. Just the opposite. Animosity and arrogance rolled off them, their demeanor offensive and threatening. "Oppressive" was the description that came to Reg's mind.

The men, who had stopped a few yards away from the first truck in the long convoy line, waited to be approached first so they didn't get shot for being too aggressive. Reg felt a trickle of sweat roll down his spine and his cheek jumped in a nervous twitch. Fighting back the urge to roll his head to crack his neck, he tried to appear unaffected by the arrival of the group, knowing Jeff and Ben were doing the same beside him. They didn't want to appear like they were afraid or were hiding anything, no matter how contrary the truth might be.

While the soldiers continued to scan the area, weapons in hand, a man who was obviously in charge exited a jeep a few vehicles back in line and strode toward them. His uniform was a dark gray in contrast to the rest of the soldiers' black and he was followed by two large men carrying automatic rifles, obviously having been given the duty of bodyguard.

Medium build, medium height, mousy brown hair and muddy brown eyes, there wasn't anything descriptive about the man in charge to draw attention to him. Nothing at all, except for a feeling of evil that seemed to cloud the air around him, almost suffocating in its intensity. Reg fought the need to shudder and take a step back. He sensed Jeff and Ben were having the same feeling. *So, this is what they talk about when the Holy Spirit wars with evil…*

His beady eyes shifted around the area, barely glancing at the trio of men, who waited patiently for him to state his business.

"Colonel Olson," the man finally barked around an unlit cigar stuck in the side of his mouth. He didn't wait for introductions, making it clear he didn't care who he was talking to… or at, as was the case now.

The colonel propped his hands on his hips, puffed out his narrow chest and continued to look around while chewing on his cigar. Reg got a sense that the man had watched a few too many WWII movies and was trying to emulate General Patton or Winston Churchill.

He snorted. "Seems you've got Neos' property somewhere here on your little ranch," he said without preamble as his eyes continued to search the area with disdain etched on his features. Reg noticed the smaller man still hadn't looked him or the others in the eye. Either he was intimidated by them—which wasn't likely, considering the battalion he had backing him up—or he was just so arrogant that he didn't feel they were worthy of his attention. Most likely the latter. *Napoleon complex to the max.*

Reg not only didn't like the guy, but the ingrained "alpha male," as Nikki called it, physically wanted to harm him. He fantasized tying him into a pretzel and booting him over the Mexican border fence, yelling "goalll!" while running around with his arms raised. *Or then there's the idea of hanging him from a sycamore by his tongue and letting the kids use him for a piñata.*

The old feeling of violent aggression surprised him with its suddenness and intensity. He'd fought hard to change his ways over the past couple of years since accepting the Lord, but every once in a while the "old man" would creep out and shock him. This time, he attributed it to a feeling of protectiveness for his family, coupled with an overwhelming realization of real helplessness.

And knowing that they were all truly helpless when it came to fighting a battle against the Neos, that it would be useless—not to mention flat-out stupid—to take on the group who was now in charge of "keeping the peace" for what was left of the U.S.A, he forced the "old Reg" back into the closet where he'd locked him when he got right with the Lord.

He then reminded himself that, as long as they were living the way they were supposed to, asking for forgiveness when they failed and trying hard not to get to the point where they had to ask for that forgiveness in the first place, then the Lord wouldn't let anything happen that wasn't in His plan. Reg knew he had to rely on that knowledge and just trust and have faith. It sure wasn't easy to do, not for a man who was a warrior at heart.

But with a stubborn streak that wasn't willing to fully let go of the warrior inside, Reg spread his legs and crossed his arms across his chest in the time-honored male aggressive posture and stared down at the much smaller man.

"What property?" he growled.

The colonel finally looked at Reg and smirked, his lip curling at the corner into a snarl. The man obviously wasn't the least bit intimidated, knowing he had a virtual army on his side.

"Stupid doesn't suit you, cowboy," he growled back. "We have GPS trackers on all our vehicles and since a whole convoy of them went missing a week ago, we lit them up and traced them here."

Reg stifled an expletive as he realized Don and his group had inadvertently put them in the current situation. Reg didn't hold it against them, though; they were just seeking sanctuary themselves and had no way of knowing the vehicles were able to be tracked and that they were going to be putting the ranch in danger. Besides, it was he himself who had insisted Don and the group stay at the ranch instead of heading to Mexico like they'd planned. He was just as much to blame.

Reg couldn't exactly lie to the colonel; the lie would quickly be exposed when they searched the place and discovered the vehicles parked on the property. But he didn't want to just roll over and give up, either, so he did the next best thing.

Shrugging nonchalantly, as if he didn't have a thing to hide and their very lives weren't possibly at stake, he said, "You're welcome to look."

Again, the colonel's lip curled into a snarl. "I frankly don't need your permission," he arrogantly announced, then turned and raised his arm to make a circular motion above his head. Soldiers immediately poured from the vehicles and proceeded to scatter in different directions, each holding their rifle in front of them like a shield. The colonel stalked off without so much as a glance over his shoulder, effectively dismissing the group.

Ben's voice was low as he asked the question they all were thinking. "What do we do now?"

Reg mumbled back, "Pray."

He didn't wait to take his own advice. *Lord, please help us. We were sure we were working in Your will when we started this sanctuary, YOUR sanctuary. But now we're being threatened, and I feel like David standing against Goliath, only I'm sorry to admit I don't have the faith of David to know You're going to slay this giant for me. So, please, Father, give me the faith I need to stand firm and know that You're in control no matter what. Show us what we should do.*

A sudden feeling of calm and peace filled him so suddenly that it brought tears to his eyes. He heard a voice, almost a whisper, deep in his soul.

Wait on Me.

Such a quick answer to prayer was startling. He grinned and looked to the heavens, saying "Thanks Dad!"

He then grinned at Jeff and Ben. "God's got this. We just need to trust Him."

The Neos spent over two hours searching the ranch for the missing vehicles. Reg knew where they were; they were parked down by the border fence, out in the open for all to see. Jeff had had Don's group park them end to end along the fence, hoping the dark green color of the vehicles would look like bushes to any aircraft flying over. That plan might have worked for an aerial recon, but there was no way to miss them if you were walking within a hundred yards of them.

For some reason, though, the soldiers couldn't find the vehicles. While they were searching, the ranch men had been fervently praying for a miracle and, apparently, they were granted one.

Colonel Olson came stomping back up the drive, his cigar clamped tightly between clenched teeth. Reg, Jeff, and Ben stood silently, hands at their sides, trying to look non-threatening.

"This isn't over," the man gritted out to Reg while he glared at him with narrowed eyes. "I know those vehicles are here somewhere, and now this—" he waved at the ranch in general "—little farm of yours is on our radar. So, fair warning: We're watching you."

With that, he turned and stomped off toward his jeep, climbing into the passenger seat and barking out orders to "head back to headquarters."

The colonel's parting words of warning sent a shiver down Reg's spine, but that feeling was pushed aside when a jubilant group suddenly emerged from their respective look-out places and surrounded him, Ben, and Jeff, shouting praises to the Lord and hugging each other.

Nikki pushed her way through the throng and threw her arms around her husband. He wrapped his around her in turn, leaning down to kiss the top of her head, breathing in her warm, womanly scent.

Thank You, Father, for protecting us and defeating our "giant" today.

But despite the obvious miracle they'd just been granted, he couldn't help the lingering feeling of apprehension as he thought about those parting words, *"we're watching you."*

Being watched by a paramilitary organization that had been given carte blanche to "handle" citizens in any way it saw fit. How much worse could it be than that?

chapter 15

T
HE NEXT day Ben and Emilio—one of the young men who had recently come up to the ranch from Mexico— went missing for most of the day. Gina was nearly frantic with worry and Nikki spent most of the day alternating between comforting her and praying with her.

The two ladies had become fast prayer partners for everything from the simplest of needs, to those more urgent, like the day before and the terrifying visit from the Neos. They were often found holding hands, heads bowed and seeking the Lord.

After the Neos had left the previous afternoon, Nikki and Gina had told their husbands that they'd been praying the soldiers wouldn't find the missing truck or anything that might cause the ranch trouble. They'd begged the Lord to blind their eyes as when He Himself walked through the mob who wanted to cause Him harm. The group had laughed about the fact that that was exactly what He had done.

And now they were praying for the safe return of Ben and Emilio. Gina had added the prayer that she'd have patience not to choke her husband when he did turn up.

When the two wayward men finally returned near dinner time, causing everyone to come running to greet them with relieved shouts, Nikki nearly had to restrain her friend from killing her husband, remarking to Gina that giving her patience was apparently one prayer the Lord wasn't going to grant. Nikki was thankful Emilio was single. She didn't think she'd have the strength to keep two psychotic women in line.

After being bombarded with a multitude of questions regarding where they had been, Ben finally put his hands up.

"We went to Mexico to see Emilio's uncle."

Apparently, Gina didn't like that answer, as her face turned so red Nikki was afraid the woman's skin was going to melt right off the bones.

She poked Ben in the chest. Hard. "So, you two just thought you could take off to Mexico for the day without telling anyone? Not even your wife?" She yelled so loudly that several of the children, who were watching the exchange in fascination, put their hands up to cover their ears.

Ben put his hands up again in what he obviously hoped was a placating gesture. "Now honey, it's not like we were hanging out at the cantina drinking cervezas. We were on a mission for the ranch. But if we'd told anyone what we were going to do, y'all would have just tried to stop us."

He shrugged. "It was better for us to just go take care of business ourselves and get back as soon as we could. We didn't think it would take so long." At that, he glanced at Emilio.

The young man looked embarrassed and hung his head. It was such humbling gesture on such a huge man.

When Emilio had first come to the ranch, everyone had been a little afraid of him. He was so big that he could have made up an entire defensive line for a pro football team by himself. Even Reg looked small when he stood next to the man.

His deep voice was soft while he spoke to Gina in broken English. Nikki could swear his amber colored eyes were a little misty. *Gentle giant...* it was no wonder the kids all adored Emilio.

"I am sorry for your worry, Señora Gina. I think we come back to el rancho before breakfast. I did not know it would be so much time."

Before Gina could wind up for another attack at Emilio's explanation, Reg stepped forward, placed a hand on Ben's shoulder and asked the obvious question.

"So, exactly what *were* you two doing?"

Ben grinned at his friend, but Nikki noticed he glanced worriedly at his wife while he answered.

"Um, well, we took the GPS trackers off the Neos' trucks and put them on the cartel's vehicles."

Several surprised exclamations came from the group. Gina stepped forward with her hands clenched, her face impossibly redder than before. Nikki was worried the woman's blood pressure might be high enough to cause an eruption of fire from her ears.

Reg took one look at his friend's wife and backed away with a look that made Nikki bark out a laugh. Ben's face was priceless, too—fear and worry etched his features. The two large men were both afraid of one tiny, albeit very angry, Latina.

Again, the fireball poked her husband in the chest—this time accenting each word with a stab of her index finger.

"You mean to tell me you not only went to Mexico, but you went to the CARTEL'S CAMP? Are you completely insane?"

"Now, honey—"

The incensed woman's fisted hands went to her hips, and she bobbled her head from side to side. "Don't you 'now honey' me, you... you... you JERK!" Nikki half expected her to say "here, hold my earrings" next as she went after her husband.

But instead, Gina turned and stormed off, but not before Nikki noticed the tears pooling in her friend's eyes. She then hurried after her.

Ben started to go after his wife too, but Reg stopped him. "Let her go; Nikki will calm her down. Better to let her blow off some of that steam now, or else she's likely to rip your spleen out with her teeth."

He chuckled at his own joke, then turned to Emilio. "At least you don't have to be afraid of Mighty Mouse," he teased, using his nickname for the little woman.

Reg was sure Emilio paled beneath his dark skin. "Oh no, I am very afraid of Señora Gina. She is like... like the, em, like the hurricane."

Reg grinned further. "You, the human bull, afraid of a little mouse? Just the sight of you would send most running and screaming."

But of course, that wasn't true once you got to know the kid. Once the residents of the ranch had gotten used to his lumbering size and really started interacting with Emilio, they knew he was harmless. The ladies called him "sweet," which always made him blush. And none of the kids—who were notoriously good judges of character—were afraid of him; in fact, the youngest in the group were climbing up "Mount Meelo" every chance they got. Nearly everyone poked fun at his size, and he took it with a good-natured attitude.

Reg sobered then. "But seriously, what *were* you two thinking? That was some dangerous sh—" he paused as he looked around at the smattering of children who had stayed behind when the rest of the group had wandered off back to whatever they'd been doing before the commotion.

"Uh, *stuff* you two pulled," he corrected with another lopsided grin.

Emilio grinned back. "Not so, señor. We had... em, ¿cómo se dice?"

"Permission." Ben supplied.

Emilio nodded. "Oh, sí, we had autorización, permission. The cartel es mi familia."

Reg's eyes widened in surprise. "Your family? The drug cartel is your *family*?" That was surprising, but then they really didn't know much about Emilio, except that he was a new believer—he'd told them he had gotten saved just before the Lord had told him to go to the ranch.

Emilio's face reddened as he nodded. "Sí, yes. Mi tío—em, my uncle, he is in charge, the boss, to La Hermandad."

Ben added, "Emilio knew his uncle would have no problem messing with the Neos, so we took the trackers off all the trucks and Benito—Emilio's uncle—let us put them on the cars he uses for drug running. Or used to use, anyway. Suppose there isn't much call for drugs now that people are all struggling just to buy food."

Emilio shook his head. "You would be, em—what is word—*surprised*, Ben," Emilio said. "The people, they have their wants, em, no, their…"

"Addictions?" Ben asked.

Emilio nodded. "Sí, sí, addictions. Men and the señoras, they trade even comidas, em, the food, they have for the drugs. Before I come here, I was very much busy to deliver drugs for mi tío."

He reddened further and hastily added, "But that was before el Señor—em, the Lord—before He save me. I was bad before, now—" he shrugged. "Now not so much."

Reg laughed and patted Emilio on the back. "That's all of us, mi amigo. Bad before, not so much now."

The other men joined in the laughter, then Reg asked, "So, your uncle has no problem with the Neos showing up at his door looking for their vehicles? That could cause them a lot of trouble."

Reg thought about what he'd just said. *What a strange world we live in now, when I'm worried that the U.S. government is going to harass the drug cartel.* It was amazing that they lived in a time when there was evil and then lesser evil. The good was harder and harder to come by and it was nearly impossible to figure out which side to take.

"Mi tío, he does not worry. He said, em, er…" Turning to Ben, he asked him to translate what his uncle had told them.

Ben laughed and gave a meaningful glance to the lingering children, who, for the most part, were occupying themselves with talk of a game of chase.

"Well, to put it in cleaner language, Benito said to bring the, um, *jerks*, on. He's not worried about the Neos at all. In fact, he's looking forward to the fight, a little payback. He said that he's had to deal with dirty agents from the DEA and Border Patrol looking for payouts for many years, and now that a lot of them are part of the Neos, he'd like to give them a taste of their own medicine. That's if they have the cojones to show up in Mexico. And don't worry about La Hermandad being able to fight the Neos—they're armed to the teeth and could hold their own even during a siege."

Ben shook his head. "Since the crash, the Mexican cartels have been pretty much in charge. They're like the Neos of Mexico, or something. And funny thing is, it seems the cartels are more humane than the Neos."

He paused for a moment and each man was silent with his own thoughts. Reg was silently thanking the Lord for sparing Nikki—and Anna—from witnessing any of the atrocities they'd heard the Neos were capable of.

Ben cleared his throat and continued. "After we installed the trackers, Benito took me to an underground bunker that would put NORAD to shame. The place is a mile long and probably half that wide with everything from a medical center to a cafeteria and enough room to house hundreds of families. And they've got it stocked with enough food and arms and ammunition to last a good year. Seriously, the place is ready for anything that might come their way."

Reg tried not to let his eyes bulge out at the information, but knew he'd failed. "Holy cow, what the heck are they planning for—Armageddon?"

Ben shrugged, but Emilio answered. "It was going to be a... a tunnel for the big trucks to bring the drugs here, to America. But mi tío, he did not finish the tunnel. The money go bad—" He shook his head.

"No, that is not it. Uh, the, err..."

"Economy?" Ben asked.

Emilio smiled and nodded once more. "Sí, the economy, when it go bad, Tío Benito say he make a, em, a shelter, like you do here at el rancho, señor. Last year he spend all his money from the drugs to buy food and make it a nice place. He say he will save people from muerte—death."

The men were quiet a moment and Reg reflected on his earlier thoughts about evil versus lesser evil, rethinking his position regarding Emilio's uncle. In his eyes, the man didn't deserve to be in the "evil" category at all, no matter what he did for a living.

He cleared his throat. "Well, Emilio, your Tío Benito sounds like a man I'd like to meet."

Emilio grinned at Reg. "He said the same of you, when Ben and I told him of your rancho and what you are doing here. He most liked that you are working for el Señor and saving your people, like Tío Benito is."

The young man shrugged. "Tío Benito said he promise he will pay you a visit very soon, señor."

Ben laughed. "The place isn't that far away, maybe a mile. So, I'd hold the man to that promise."

Reg wasn't sure he wanted the head of the cartel—who had always been associated with violence and human atrocities—to pay the ranch a visit, to see their way of life and their operation. But then he remembered his earlier thoughts of how Benito must have *some* semblance of humanity, if he were willing to do so much for his people. He also knew that the Lord Himself walked among the sinners, those considered the worst of the worst, the "least of these," because they were the people most in need of Him. In fact, the Lord disdained the religious, calling them hypocrites.

He'd just have to trust the Lord to send whoever *He* decided needed to come.

Nearly a month of peace followed all the upheaval and the ranch seemed to settle into a quiet rhythm of work and rest and worship.

Unfortunately, though, Don and his group had decided to move on. They were afraid that the Neos would be back looking for them, despite Ben's insistence that they'd gotten all the trackers off their vehicles. Don just didn't want to take the chance of endangering the ranch, nor his own group, if the Neos came back.

Surprisingly, though, Angela Anderson decided to stay on. She'd found a place for herself working with the farm team and was loving every minute of ranch living and she'd even joined the teen's band as a singer and had started a women's new believer Bible study. It was such a far-cry from the persona of "Lieutenant Loony Toons," that there was no doubt God's hand was on her.

Now that fall was in full swing at the ranch and the days cooled just a bit, by unspoken agreement the residents got all their chores done during the day so they'd have more time in the evenings for worship. After the miracle of Albert's healing and then the Lord's blinding of the Neos, the entire ranch knew the Lord's hand was truly with them and they wanted to spend as much time praising Him as possible. Even the unbelievers—or "not yet believers" as Pastor Steve preferred to call the hold-outs—joined in.

But the praising wasn't limited to just the worship time in the evenings. Even more than before, praise songs could be heard throughout the day, and "thank You, Lord!" rang out continuously.

The attitude of gratitude seemed to put everyone in a good mood and very few complaints were voiced. Work was happily completed, help was given before it was asked for, and even the teens didn't complain when they were asked to watch over the younger kids when a big project needed completing.

Injuries and sickness were at a bare minimum, to the point that Charlene and her assistants were able to start a "clinic" for preventative treatments. They partnered with Hector Herrera, formerly a dentist from Monterrey, Mexico, and, coupled with the supplies they'd acquired courtesy of the Neos, were able to do basic check-ups and well-child exams, rudimentary pre-cancer screenings, pre-natal care for the two pregnant women at the ranch and Hector even did teeth cleaning and tooth extractions when necessary, always with the admonition of, "I bet you wish you'd taken better care of your teeth now that we don't have Novocain available, eh?"

Those on the farming team had turned all the fields and had planted winter corn for grinding into meal and winter rye for the livestock to graze on. With the food canning and dehydrating completed for the season, those on the food storage team had started working on squeezing juice out of the sorghum stalks, then boiling and straining it before bottling the thick, sweet syrup.

Since there hadn't been any recent new additions to the ranch and every resident had a hut, the building team had decided to create a "walk-in refrigerator." During dinner one evening Esperanza commented that it would make her work much easier if she had a big commercial refrigerator like she'd had when she worked in the governor's mansion.

Joe Sangre, a Lipan Apache, had speculated on building one. He described how when he was a child his grandmother would use two clay pots—a smaller pot inside a larger one with wet straw in between—to keep food and drinks cold while they were working outside.

"I put one of those pot coolers together for a science fair project in eighth grade," he'd laughed. "I put off doing a project until the night before and just threw it together. Took first place. The teacher was most impressed that I knew so much about evaporation and cooling. Heck, I didn't know anything about it, just that it kept my Dr. Pepper cold when I was working."

Nate had talked to Joe further about it and the pair got together with Tom and Frank to work out a design for a double walled "refrigerator" using adobe bricks that had been baked. They hoped baking the bricks would make them more like pottery, harder and more water resistant. They would then pack straw in between the walls and add a drip system to keep the straw wet. A small door would be added for access to the inside.

It was times like that—where one person mentioned an idea or a problem and people just jumped up to help—that kept Reg and Nikki shaking their heads in wonder. And kept them praising the Lord for keeping things running so smoothly.

But true to human nature, they were starting to worry about when the other shoe was going to drop.

In mid-October, a large group of armed men was seen crossing the border fence, heading toward the south pasture. They weren't wearing uniforms and were on foot, but for obvious precautionary measures, Jeff rang the ranch bell and told the women to take the children to head inside until they knew what was going on.

The ranch men gathered together, each one displaying their own rifle, shotgun or handgun. They had quite an arsenal, thanks to the stockpile of the Neos' weapons they'd found in one of the boxes in the back of the truck Jeff had driven to the ranch.

While they all knew they couldn't defend themselves against an entire army, they certainly could against this group of twenty or so men approaching their home. Reg almost laughed when he saw that Ben was holding his butcher's meat cleaver.

Once the group was close enough to recognize, Emilio was the first to react. He raised his hands in the air, his fingers wide while holding his nine-millimeter with just his thumb.

"¡Espera un momento!"

Ben quickly translated, figuring Emilio was too rattled to speak English. "Wait a minute!"

The men relaxed marginally and waited until the others walked up to them. An older, distinguished-looking man separated himself from the group and approached Emilio, who explained to the ranch men over his shoulder, "It is Benito, mi tío. I think he is here to, em, visit the rancho."

Reg asked, not just a little sarcastically, "Does he always go visiting with a whole platoon?"

Benito, a tall, heavy-set, sixty-something man with a head of thick, wavy gray hair stepped forward and laughed as he extended his hand for Reg. His English was nearly impeccable.

"Sí, señor. I always travel with plenty of back up, most especially in these troubled times. Benito Guerrero."

Reg nodded as he returned the handshake. "Smart man. Reg Erskine."

He introduced Jeff, Ben and a few others who were at the front of their group while Benito did the same for his entourage and then Reg invited the men to the ranch house for a cool drink.

Once they were settled inside, Benito got right to the point as he circled the rim of his tea glass with a fingertip. "I have a problem, Reg, one that I am hoping you might help with."

Reg narrowed his eyes as he considered the fact that anyone who chose *not* to do a favor for the cartel most likely ended up in hot water—or in deep water attached to a concrete pedestal.

Benito laughed as if he could read his mind, but it was most likely at the expression on Reg's face. "Now do not start worrying that I'll cause you or your ranch any harm if you say no," he said.

"My days of such things are in the past where they belong. This is a new time we live in and killing each other over such trivial things when we have a greater enemy to fight would be suicide for my group and for myself."

He sobered further. "The enemy we share is a formidable foe, my friend. We must join together if we have any hope of surviving."

Ben cocked his head to the side as he studied the older man.

"Excuse me, Señor Guerrero—"

"Just Benito, please."

Ben smiled and nodded slightly. "Benito. You just said, *We have a greater enemy*'. I'm a bit confused."

Benito sighed, a weary sound. "It seems the Neos have joined forces with the Mexican government, or what is left of our government anyway. The Neos have begun infiltrating all areas of the police and military." He waved to encompass his men, a few sitting at the table with them, and the others settled in various chairs and sofas in the living room.

"We have had to go into hiding."

Emilio sucked in a breath. "But you said you were not worried about them, the Neos, when Ben and I, when we took the, uh, the trackers to you, Tío."

The man shook his head, suddenly looking much older than he had just moments before. He rubbed his hands over his face before answering while he gazed at his nephew.

"Just a month ago, I was not worried about them, hijo. Then three weeks ago I received word from my, em, my contacts in Saltillo that Presidente Marques has signed an agreement with the American president giving Marques... what is the English word... *immunity* from any Neos attack. In exchange, our military will be added to the Neos' forces."

Ben sat up a bit straighter and leaned forward. "You mean, Mexico and the U.S. have merged? Like an annexation?"

At Benito's nod, he asked, "But why would Mexico do that? The U.S. is in horrible shape right now. I mean, seriously, our economy is probably no worse than the rest of the world's, but the problem is that our country has always lived in the lap of luxury and the people—most of them anyway—have no clue how to survive. There's rioting, crime is up to unheard of levels, martial law is in place with strict curfews being enforced by a group no better than the Nazis. We have absolutely nothing to offer to your country. What the heck was Marques thinking?"

Benito closed his eyes and sighed wearily. "Apparently, he was thinking that merging with the Neos would give our corrupt military the power it needs to completely take over. Just like the Neos have in America."

Silence followed that statement as the ramifications sunk in. Reg had a sinking feeling that things were just about to go from bad to worse... much, much worse. With the backing of Mexico's military, the Neo Geo Task Force was going to become a superpower. He was sure the smaller Central American countries would be next to follow in joining their evil forces, and then South America. Soon, they would be unstoppable.

After a few moments, Benito looked up. "It seems that, thanks to the bad decision of our very stupid and gullible presidente, my country is now in the same boat as yours. And that boat is about to sink."

The men eventually came out of the house and Reg took Benito and his group on a tour of the ranch. Jeff had given the signal shortly after Benito's arrival that all was well, and the residents had returned to their chores, while children happily played, thankfully oblivious to the terrors of the world.

Benito was suitably impressed. "You have done something very remarkable here," he said to Reg, who shook his head in response.

"I can't take responsibility for this," he replied. "We all work together. My wife and I are just overseers. But the full credit for everything goes to the Lord."

The older man harrumphed, and Reg assumed he was going to argue that God had nothing to do with the ranch and Reg mentally started preparing his counter argument.

But Benito surprised him once more. "But the Lord, He gave you the ability to lead these people, Reg. Do not discount yourself."

For the head of a major drug cartel to even mention the Lord's name, much less acknowledge His power, was, in Reg's opinion, pretty amazing. But still—what kind of believer would lead a life of crime?

Benito seemed to read his mind when he chuckled. "I am just coming to understand the Lord, mi amigo. I am what you would call an infant in this."

By unspoken agreement, they walked ahead of the rest of the group as they moved toward the pond, each lost in their own thoughts. Reg was still amazed that he was walking beside a notorious cartel leader and talking about God. Things sure had changed. And now with the Neos coming into the picture, it looked like he would be seeing a lot more of Benito and his men.

And that reminded him of something. "Hey, you don't still have the Neo trackers on your vehicles, do you?"

Benito chuckled. "They are still on the vehicles, but the vehicles are no longer in my possession. I traded them for solar panels to my competitor, Rolando Ruiz. Now it is his problem to deal with. I am sure the Neos will not appreciate finding their trackers attached to drug running automobiles. And Rolando will not appreciate them trying to take the vehicles away."

Reg laughed. While Benito dealt mainly in the marijuana drug trade, Ruiz was known for dealing in the heavy stuff—heroin, meth and crack. And along with the heavy drug trade came unspeakable violence. Before the collapse, Reg remembered seeing the newscasts of the horrible methods Ruiz' gang used in dealing with their enemies. La Hermandad was never known for that level of violence.

Another question came to him then. "But if you sold your cars, how are you, um, doing business?" He knew buying new automobiles would be out of the question in the current economy.

It was Benito's turn to laugh. He shook his head. "I have no need for the cars. I have not sold the marijuana for a while, señor. It started to bother me when Mexico's economy fell nearly as badly as the United States'. It just seemed... *dishonorable* to continue to sell— or trade, rather—something that was not necessary when the people were starving. I wanted to do something better with my life, and for that I blame Emilio."

He chuckled at his own statement, but Reg was quiet, letting the man fish through his thoughts. Benito walked with his hands clasped behind his back, absentmindedly kicking at rocks that were in his path.

"I do not know if you are aware, but my sobrito—Emilio—he was my right-hand man, my second in command. There was nothing I could ask of him that he would not do. He has killed for me, señor, many times. There is much blood on his hands… and mine. I have much to answer for."

That surprised Reg greatly—the kind young man he knew seemed incapable of swatting at flies. But Reg knew from firsthand experience how the Lord excelled at changing the seemingly unchangeable. He never ceased to amaze.

Benito sighed heavily, supposedly at his confession. Then he continued.

"But one day a young American girl came to our villa where I had the headquarters for my, em, my operation. She said she was looking for work. Chrissy was a beautiful young girl, innocent. What I would call 'fresh'. She had a way about her, a look that I cannot describe. It is as if she were shining a light from inside, you know?"

He shook his head, as if his admission were unbelievable. "She was a Christian, and it did not take her long to convert my hardened nephew. Emilio fell head on his heels for her, and for Jesús. There was no getting him back after that."

Reg smiled at the misuse of the American expression but didn't correct the man, who continued his story.

"Chrissy said she was traveling with a preacher, a missionary, who had been killed just weeks before by some thieves when they were crossing Mexico, going back to the United States from Belize. She was looking for employment as a maid, which I gave to her. She said she had no way to return home, as the thieves stole all of their possessions, including her passport. I suspect they took much more from her than that, but she would not speak of it."

The older man sighed once more. "After working for just one month, she left us. Emilio was heartbroken, but she tried to explain to the boy that she had a duty to the Lord and could not be burdened in a relationship with a man. She was very strong in her faith. In fact, not only Emilio was saved because of her, eh, her—"

"Preaching? Witness?" Reg offered.

"Sí, but also much of my staff... the other maid, my cook, one of my drivers. Even a few of my—how do you say?—my banditos." Benito gave a sly grin at the last part.

Reg grinned back at his word choice. "Wow, that's pretty good. So, now you're surrounded by believers, huh?"

Benito shook his head, the look on his face a bit sad. "No, unfortunately for me, all those who accepted the Lord moved on to other places. Even Emilio, as you know."

He reached up and pulled a twig off a tree they were passing under, then proceeded to peel the tiny leaves off of it. His head was bowed as he continued in a soft voice.

"I think that the new Christians, they just could not handle being with the others—with me—who were doing so much wrong, so much sinning, as they say. I suspect that might be part of the reason that Chrissy left us so soon. Sadly, she saw much more than she should have in her time with me."

He shook his head as he dropped the twig. "But I do not want my nephew to know this. I am sure he will blame himself for not protecting her. In fact, she left us in the middle of the night with no word; I am sure that was so Emilio could not try to leave with her."

Benito's voice was soft when he added, "I hope she was able to get where she wanted to be. It was never safe for a pretty young girl to travel alone... especially in Mexico, and certainly not now in these evil days. I joked that I blamed Emilio for giving me the desire to want to do better with my life, but truly it was Chrissy who changed my way of thinking. She was—is—a good girl. I hope only the best has come to her, but that is probably a false hope in this time we live in."

The men were quiet as they reached the pond, both staring out over the water while considering the atrocities mankind was capable of committing upon its own. Benito sighed with a defeated sound, and Reg had the impression the man might be thinking about his own crimes. His next words confirmed that suspicion.

Benito's voice was thin, tired sounding. "While I am happy for my friends and family to have found some peace, my heart is heavy from missing them. But I cannot judge them for wanting to leave, nor blame them. But now I have a new look at life, one from a different place, and see the hurt that is caused when we do not respect life. That lack of respect turns us into something less than human. And those who are kinder, or maybe have the Lord with them, they do not want to be around such others, almost as if they cannot stand it. It as if there is an unseen war going on."

"Like angels versus demons," Reg added.

He nodded. "Sí, yes, exactly. We have committed so much evil that we have become the evil." He shook his head. "It is a very ugly place to be."

Reg nodded in agreement. "I may not have done all the things you have done—well, at least not on the same scale—but believe me, I have done my fair share of sinning. I still do. It's a daily battle to fight that old bad man in me."

He paused and glanced sideways at Benito, who continued to look out across the pond at the ducks playing on the water. The man obviously wasn't a believer, but he was showing signs of being convicted and Reg wanted to maybe water some seeds that had already been planted.

"If it weren't for meeting Nikki and her introducing me to the Lord, I'd still be wallowing in that cesspool I was in, looking for ways to fill the emptiness that was in me. Drinking, women, fighting— none of that filled it though. I found out from Nikki that it was a

God-shaped hole I was trying to fill, like a missing puzzle piece that only He fit into."

Reg laughed. "Life sure has changed since I made that decision."

Benito laughed with him. "Not knowing you before you found your God, I can still say that, looking around at what you've created here at your ranch, I must agree."

"Yeah, life is definitely different now," Reg agreed, "but I didn't create this." He waved back at the ranch.

"This was all the Lord's doing."

Benito chuckled. "Well, I am glad el Señor has done so much for you and your people. I only wish He would help us too, but I am afraid we have done too much bad, too much evil, to ever be in His good graces."

Reg shook his head and picked up a rock to skip across the pond. "Now you're sounding like I did back when I was arguing with Nikki that there was no way an old sinner like me could be forgiven for all that stuff I'd done. But ya know what? I was. I am. Forgiven by God Himself. He'll forgive you too. Just gotta ask."

He shook his head again as he found another flat rock to toss. "It's an amazing feeling, my friend, to know that you're not gonna have to answer for that stuff you did. Funny thing is that it sure makes you not want to do anything else bad."

Reg tossed the stone and watched as it hopped four times before sinking. "But like I said before, that old bad guy still manages to creep out of the closet and do stupid stuff. Sometimes it's a daily battle to keep him contained."

Benito laughed with Reg as he too picked up a flat stone to try his hand at skipping. He tossed it the men watched as it skipped five times. He grinned at Reg.

"I still have my talent, I see." He puffed his chest out in exaggerated pride and tapped it.

"I was the stone-skipping king as a boy in my village. No one could beat me."

Reg laughed and the two men continued to try to best each other for a while, the serious talk forgotten for a bit. The other men joined them when they realized the need for privacy was over and several of them took their turns at skipping stones and soon a contest was on.

Reg couldn't help but think how freeing it could be sometimes to just act like a kid. It was certainly easier to just play than it was to think about the troubles of the world and the worries of what was to come.

chapter 16

BENITO became a regular visitor to the ranch and soon was joining them at least twice a week for the dinner and worship time. He always came with an entourage, but he rotated who he brought so that all of his "staff" had a chance to join in. Since they hadn't seen the same people twice, it was obvious Benito employed quite a lot of people.

After a month of hearing the Word preached, Benito finally accepted the Lord and asked if Emilio could be the one to baptize him. So, on Christmas morning when the wind was blowing fiercely, and the sky gray with clouds, Benito and Emilio stood up to their hips shivering in the pond while Emilio repeated the words Pastor Steve had said to him just two months earlier when he himself had been baptized.

As he dunked his uncle, the former infamous drug cartel criminal, into the cold water, Emilio's deep voice rang out clearly and it was obvious that he had practiced the English words.

"By your confession of faith in Christ Jesus and the admission that He died for your sins, was buried and rose again in fulfillment of the Scriptures, I baptize you, Benito José Martín Ramires Guerrero, in the Name of the Father, and of the Son and of the Holy Spirit."

Not only had Benito gotten saved, but most of his people had too and the baptisms went on for nearly a half hour. Pastor Steve and Emilio had blue lips by the time they got out of the pond and into some warm, dry clothes.

Since it was Christmas and also a baptism day, Esperanza and her team had planned a huge midday meal instead of the usual dinner. The buffet table was loaded with a variety of meats: A stuffed wild turkey one of the women had gotten on a hunt; savory prime rib from a cow Ben had butchered; roasted lamb with rosemary; fried catfish some teens had caught in the ranch pond; hamburgers and homemade hotdogs. There were also some Mexican dishes: tamales, sopes, carne asada, menudo and posolé.

There was an abundance of vegetables too: Sweet potato casserole; garlic mashed potatoes; buttery roasted corn-on-the-cob; fried green beans; pickled vegetables—beets, okra, cauliflower, carrots and peppers; and, thanks to the greenhouse, they had an abundance of fresh lettuces mixed up into a huge salad.

A separate table had been placed next to the buffet table just for the desserts Esperanza's team had prepared: Pecan, pumpkin and cherry pies; chocolate cake; peach cobbler; apple dumplings; cookies of every imaginable kind; brownies and tarts; and all types of Christmas candies. It was a feast that proclaimed the Lord's goodness and abundant provision to all.

Benito's entire staff had come with him, which added sixty-two people to the ranch's group. Roberto had prepared for the extra people by fashioning a few more huge tables, but these were made so they folded for storage when not needed.

After everyone had eaten to their fill—and many had overeaten and were groaning—Pastor Steve climbed up on the platform and addressed the crowd.

"Judging by the groans coming from some of you, I should be preaching against gluttony," he quipped, drawing good-natured laughter.

"But I'm not preaching at all, lucky you. Frankly, I think I'd put us all to sleep, especially with our full guts. I wouldn't want any of you passing out, falling off your bench and rolling into the pond. We already had the baptisms for the day."

More laughter followed, and then Steve opened his Bible.

"Psalm ninety-six: 'Oh sing to the Lord a new song; sing to the Lord, all the earth! Sing to the Lord, bless His name; tell of His salvation from day to day.'

"'Declare His glory among the nations, His marvelous works among all the peoples! For great is the Lord, and greatly to be praised; He is to be feared above all gods.'

"'For all the gods of the peoples are worthless idols, but the Lord made the heavens. Splendor and majesty are before Him; strength and beauty are in His sanctuary.'

"'Ascribe to the Lord, O families of the peoples, ascribe to the Lord glory and strength! Ascribe to the Lord the glory due His name; bring an offering, and come into His courts!'

"'Worship the Lord in the splendor of holiness; tremble before Him, all the earth! Say among the nations, "The Lord reigns! Yes, the world is established; it shall never be moved; He will judge the peoples with equity.

"'Let the heavens be glad, and let the earth rejoice; let the sea roar, and all that fills it, let the field exult, and everything in it! Then shall all the trees of the forest sing for joy before the Lord, for He comes, for He comes to judge the earth.

"'He will judge the world in righteousness, and the peoples in His faithfulness.'"

Steve closed his Bible and hugged it to his chest. He grinned at the crowd.

"Now I know that isn't what some of you have been used to hearing for a Christmas sermon, and maybe not what our new brothers and sisters were expecting to hear." He shrugged.

"I know it's not the 'baby in the manger' story in the Book of Luke or the foretelling of the coming Savior from Isaiah. But hey, it's not up to me what the Lord wants y'all to hear. He tells me, I read it or speak it. And from this passage He wanted us to hear today, I'm guessing that He's telling us to hang on, He's coming soon, and that we're to rejoice and praise Him for all things."

Steve smiled at the crowd. "I think here lately we've been doing a pretty good job of that. I'm always hearing the Lord's Name being praised around the ranch as y'all do your chores. Even in the butcher room, we sing His praises."

He looked up at the sky and changed his voice to that of an overdone televangelist, over-accenting his vowels and adding extra syllables.

"Thaaank You, Lord-duh, that I didn't cut my precious finger off just nowww when that knife slipped. Esperanza doesn't like *man* mixed in with her stew meat and she miiight have cut off more than my fingerrr if I'd messed her order up-puh."

The crowd laughed and Esperanza shook her head at Steve, her face red as she grinned. Ben and the other butcher laughed good-naturedly.

Steve laughed at himself and shook his head. "Sorry for that, folks. It's just that, well, all the Lord's goodness and provision has made me a little silly. He just puts you in such a good mood, ya know? We have so much to be thankful for and so much to praise to give Him that it's hard to contain it!"

There were a lot of "amens" and "praise God!" coming from the crowd. Steve then asked if anyone had anything to share. A few teens raised their hands and headed to the platform with instruments in hand to lead the crowd in singing a few praise songs. A few more people shared some recent experiences of the Lord's provision and mercy.

Then Garrett hesitantly raised his hand and Steve called him up to the platform. Garrett grabbed Anna's hand and pulled her along with him. Nikki nudged Gina who sat next to her, and Gina waggled her eyebrows at her friend.

The boy's face was beet red as he stood next to Steve and faced the crowd. Anna elbowed him, which might have been sort of an encouraging gesture, had she not overdone it and caused him to wince and rub his ribs, drawing a laugh from everyone.

Gina muttered to Nikki, "He hates speaking in front of a crowd. I'm surprised he hasn't fainted... or puked."

"Give him time, he just got up there. Maybe we should warn Steve about the puking, though, especially after all the food Garrett just ate," Nikki muttered back and the ladies laughed, covering their mouths when their husbands, who were sitting in front of them, both turned in unison and glared, causing even more giggles.

Garrett cleared his throat a few times. Apparently, he had a death grip on Anna's hand, as she pulled it away from him with a grimace and then hooked her arm through his.

"You can do this," she encouraged him. He looked down at her and smiled. It was such a sweet look that it was obvious to everyone the young couple was certainly in love. Such a change from just the year before when they could barely stand to be in the same room.

"Um, Anna and I wanted to let everyone know that I, um, I, er..." He blew out a breath that puffed his cheeks and then took another deep breath.

"I asked her to marry me, and she said 'yes,'" he finished in such a rush that it almost sounded like one word. There was a pregnant pause as the people processed what he'd just said, and then everyone erupted with cheering and clapping.

Garrett and Anna looked at each other, grinning, and then Anna spoke up without taking her eyes off him.

"I know we're like young and all, but we love each other and...

well, who knows how long we have left here, you know, so, like, we just want to be together and all."

With that, they left the platform and were immediately surrounded by well-wishers.

Nikki rolled her misty eyes at her daughter's teen-speak, then Gina leaned into her side and muttered, "Finally. Took a whole month of hinting. I didn't think the boy was ever gonna get around to asking her." They high-fived each other.

Nikki suddenly felt like a naughty student caught in the act by a teacher, because their husbands had apparently heard what Gina said and both men turned around and were glaring at them once again.

It was Nikki's turn to speak through the side of her mouth. "Uh oh. The boys look a wee bit perturbed," she said with a fake look of horror.

Gina once again answered through the side of her mouth. "To say the least," she said before giving the men a huge fake smile.

"You two planned this?" Ben asked with a scowl.

"Who, us?" Nikki asked innocently as she laid her hand on her chest in mock shock.

She and Gina looked at each other and shook their heads. "No, no, we had nothing to do with this."

"Uh, huh," Reg responded with a whole lot of sarcasm. "If I didn't know better, I'd say y'all had *everything* to do with this."

The ladies both giggled and then Gina answered Reg.

"Well, with the way the two of them are attached at the hip all the time, it's better they get married than have sex out of wedlock, right? I mean, you're the one who made the ranch rule of no fooling around when you're not married, so this is a good thing. They're in love, they're hot-blooded teenagers, so why shouldn't they get married before they break the rules?"

Reg frowned. "I made that rule because *God* made that rule!"

Gina laughed and held up a hand. "I know, I know. Don't get your feathers all ruffled now, Foghorn. I was just pulling your chicken leg."

Reg's frown turned into a scowl. He hated when she called him "chicken legs," a nickname she had given him the first time she saw him in shorts when he went swimming in the pond. Reg was a huge man, but his legs weren't nearly as large as the rest of him. Nikki thought his legs were fine, sexy even—certainly *not* chicken legs. In other circumstances, Nikki would have vehemently defended her husband, but Reg always called Gina "Mighty Mouse" and patted her on the head, knowing she *hated* that. Nikki figured it was only fair that her friend had something to use to get back at him.

Ben still hadn't said anything, and Nikki knew he was steaming, as he was glaring daggers at his wife. He had said on numerous occasions that the kids were too young, that they shouldn't be spending so much time together. He argued with Gina frequently over the subject and Nikki knew he was now fit to be tied.

Nikki decided to jump in before he blew up at his wife. Although he'd made leaps and bounds in the short-temper department since getting saved, he still had his moments of nuclear explosions. And it looked like an ICBM was about to launch and the coordinates were set on his petite wife.

"Ben," she said and waited for him to tear his eyes away from Gina and look at her. "The kids *do* love each other. And did you hear what Anna said about not knowing how much time we have? She's right. The way the world is going, we could all be taken off this rock tomorrow. And we also don't know when the Lord is going to return and recreate all this," she said as she waved her hand around.

"The Bible says the new heaven and earth won't be anything like this and our relationships then will be entirely different. So, why not let them have a life together as husband and wife while they can?"

She grinned at him, noticing that he was looking less antagonistic. "Look at it this way: At least we don't have lawyers, so they can't ever get divorced."

That drew a reluctant laugh from him, and he nodded his head. "Yeah, it might be punishment enough for them to have to stay with each other."

Gina groaned, muttering something about "Mr. Positive Attitude," but she stood and walked to her husband, wrapping her arms around him. Ben didn't return the hug but remained ramrod stiff.

"It'll be okay, honey. At least we don't have to worry about them moving back in with us when they can't make it on their own. No one else wants to work with the little kids, so they'll always have a job," she quipped.

He finally returned the hug after a moment and placed his chin on her head. "Yeah, that's true. There isn't much failure possibility when you have complete job security."

He shrugged then. "I guess I'm just still hung up on the fact that they're too young."

Reg walked up to his friend and clapped him on the shoulder. "My thinking, too, but I guess that thought process doesn't hold water anymore. Before the collapse and all, yeah, they would have been too young. But now?" He shrugged himself. "The world is a different place."

Those words held a dozen meanings, and the group was quiet, deep in their own thoughts. Reg then suggested they pray for Anna and Garrett and their future—what there was of it.

Steve had called for everyone's attention and the crowd hushed from their talking and gave him their attention once again. Nikki was shocked to see Al and Anita standing next to the pastor, but she started grinning as she hoped she was going to hear yet more good news.

"Alonzo and Anita would like to make the announcement that they also want to get married," Steve announced with a grin.

Al and Anita's face were also red, but they smiled and thanked the well-wishers who shouted congratulations. Steve waited for the crowd to quiet before he picked Leeann out of the crowd.

"Leeann? That's two out of three siblings... wanna make it a

Trifecta?"

Leeann's face was even redder than her brother's when she shook her head vehemently and exclaimed, "Don't look at me!"

People were milling around, some picking at the food still on the tables before the cleanup team could put it away or give it to the pets, while others were just chatting with each other. Most of the children were running around the lawn of the ranch house, playing chase while a multitude of dogs chased them, barking happily.

Benito and his group were talking with Ben and Jeff when three loud, long blasts from an air horn caught their attention.

Jeff muttered, "That's the lookout... it's something serious judging from that signal." He then started to run toward the mesa where they always had a man stationed to watch the area, and shouted to Alan, one of his team members, giving the order to run to the ranch house and ring the bell.

Reg and Ben ran behind Alan so they could collect their weapons. Since it was Christmas, everyone had mistakenly thought that they were safe from anything bad and very few had carried a weapon with them. Reg and Ben were both mentally kicking themselves for that assumption.

Benito and a few of his group had run along with them on the jog to the ranch house.

"What's going on?" Benito asked as he ran alongside Reg.

"Don't know," Reg answered a bit breathlessly, while realizing he'd barely run a hundred yards. *Dang, I need to get some of this extra weight off.*

"We're getting our rifles just in case, though."

"Yes, we were headed that way too. We did not think we would need them today of all days," he said with a bit of disgust in his voice, speaking aloud Reg's earlier thoughts. Reg also noted wryly that the older man wasn't even winded, while he was practically gasping for air.

It seemed they'd run a mile when they finally reached the house and Reg grabbed a porch post, holding on to it while he gasped. Ben ran in to the house first, heading to the secret cellar where they kept their small armory.

Ben was already handing out weapons when Reg finally made it inside, gasping and panting. His chest was killing him, and he was dizzy. *That's it… nothing but salads for me for a month.*

Reg felt a hand on his shoulder, and he turned to see who it was, but the edges of his vision blackened, and he thought he might pass out. He fought against the feeling, and it eased a bit. He then realized Benito was standing behind him with a concerned look on his face.

"Are you all right, my friend? You look very white, even for a gringo."

Reg smirked halfheartedly at the offhanded insult. Not trusting his voice, he nodded at the man, then grabbed the rifle Ben handed up to him and passed it to Benito. He continued passing weapons back and when all of Benito's men had one in hand, he took a rifle for himself. By then his breathing was returning to normal and the dizziness and chest pain had eased a bit, but he now had an ache in his jaw and his shoulder was hurting for some reason.

"Let's go," Ben said as he climbed out of the cellar, then lowered the door and covered it with the rug. A couple of Benito's men stepped forward to help move the table back into place.

The group headed out of the house and ran back toward the top of the pond, the designated meeting place for the defense team, those who would help defend the ranch.

Months before, it had been decided that the elderly and infirm men among them would stay back to help the women defend the children in the case of an attack, and with the way he was feeling, Reg was starting to wonder if he should join them.

He was surprised to see Garrett standing with the group, holding a rifle. The teens, by unspoken agreement, had always stayed with the women to help occupy the younger children so they would hopefully stay quiet. Reg turned a questioning eye to Ben, who shrugged.

"I just told him if he wants to be a man and get married, then he needs to step up to the plate and defend his family."

That was a bit surprising, but Garrett had just turned eighteen and would have been old enough to serve in the military if the world were still going the way it had been just a few years earlier. Reg also knew that Garrett was an excellent shot, thanks to spending much of his young life at the shooting range with his then-cop father, so he was a welcome addition to the defense team.

Along with the rest of the men ready to defend their home were his own sons—Nathaniel and Alonzo. Both newly saved—or rededicated—and both trying to live their very best for the Lord. The young men were nearly inseparable, and Nathaniel had recently taken an interest in Lupe, one of the young ladies who had come to the ranch with her sister's family. He and Nikki had just been talking of the possibility of having yet another wedding if things got serious between the two. The thought of his son—who had been so troubled in the past, so antagonistic and hateful—finding peace and happiness, and most importantly, finding the Lord, was something Reg never thought he'd see in his lifetime.

And Al—the kid who'd come to the ranch addicted to meth, strung out and half-starved, but who had still somehow managed to get his sister out of a dangerous situation and drive back roads hundreds of miles to get to the ranch. What of him? He was now clean, healthy, happy, and fully rededicated to the Lord. He worked hard and was often seen studying his Bible. He'd even recently preached a sermon before dinner one evening. Nikki was hoping her son was maybe feeling led to be a pastor.

These young men had a future to look forward to. But what kind of future?

Not knowing what was coming their way was excruciating. The greatest fear was that the Neos now knew about the ranch, thanks to the visit from Colonel Olson and his group. So, many tragedies could happen this day—loss of lives, loss of futures, loss of freedom.

His chest was feeling tight again, so Reg tried to push the worries aside and waited for Jeff, who was trotting back from the lookout post.

Despite the distance he had to run—and up a hill nonetheless—the young man wasn't out of breath, a fact Reg was slightly irritated to note. The thought that he himself needed to get in better shape took a firmer hold in his mind. It wouldn't do Nikki any good to have him collapsing from a stroke or heart attack. He snorted when he thought about her saying she'd never forgive him if he died on her.

"There's an RV coming down the road, headed toward the ranch," Jeff explained.

The men all collectively relaxed, but then Jeff held up his hand and added, "They're coming fast, and it looks like the RV's been shot up. There's also a dust cloud coming up behind it, probably ten miles back. Could be another vehicle—or vehicles—chasing the RV. We have to expect the worst."

Instantly, everyone was back on alert and Alan ran back to the ranch house to ring the bell again—the second warning, the one telling the women to keep everyone out of sight and the kids quiet.

Reg explained the meaning of the bell ringing to Benito as they trotted to the end of the driveway to meet the RV. Benito apparently decided to stick with him, but ordered his men to spread out, to ask Jeff where they were needed.

"That is a very old-fashioned system, but effective," the older man nodded. "However, it is noisy. Have you thought of what you might do if you ever need to warn your people quietly?"

They hadn't thought about that, at least not to Reg's knowledge. He made a mental note to mention it to Jeff. Benito apparently guessed the answer from Reg's face, and he smirked.

"You need to think like that show *The Walking Dead*," he explained. "The zombies, they hear everything." Reg laughed a bit at the analogy, somewhat shocked that the man had watched the show.

They had reached the top of the drive when Reg realized he was gasping and had to slow to a walk. The tightness in his chest had again become painful, and it felt like his heart was in a vise. Assuming the worst, he said a quick prayer, asking the Lord to keep him upright and breathing.

The RV was already on the drive and coming at them fast—so fast Reg was afraid they weren't going to stop. But the driver slammed on the brakes a dozen yards away, dusting the men who waited for them with a cloud of Texas sand.

Before the men could even take a step toward the vehicle, the driver jumped up from the seat and ran back toward the side door, then threw it open and leapt out, ignoring the steps. Reg recognized her immediately. *Annie... no, Amy. That jerk's wife—Tiny's son, what's-his-name.*

He shook his thoughts away and stepped toward her, realizing she was covered in blood. Her white blouse looked like a prop from *Texas Chainsaw Massacre*.

"Amy?"

She was crying. "You gotta help me! Jerry's been shot and they killed *my baby!*" The last part was a wail as she collapsed to her knees.

Reg started forward to help her up, but stopped, surprised to see Benito had already moved toward her as soon as she fell. Chivalry was apparently not dead among former crime bosses.

Jeff motioned to a few men to follow him to the RV, weapons drawn and held close to their bodies. Benito was helping the woman off the ground and Reg moved forward to assist him.

"Are you hurt, señora?" Benito asked in a gentle voice as he led her to one of the smaller boulders that separated the drive from the path that led to the ranch house.

Reg helped Benito set the woman carefully on the boulder. She continued to cry, sobbing incoherent words.

Reg looked back to the RV, noticing that one of Jeff's men was leaning out of the door, motioning to some other men to come inside. He wondered what they'd discovered. From the looks of Amy's blood-stained clothes, something gruesome indeed.

"Can you tell us what happened, señora?" Benito asked her, again in a very gentle voice.

Amy sucked in a stuttering breath and choked out, "The s-soldiers... there was a r-r-road block... Jerry tried... he t-tried to s-s-stop them... but they took her and... and..."

She started sobbing again and surprisingly, Benito grabbed her into a big hug and tried to soothe her.

"Shh, shh, it will be all right, little one. It will be all right." He rubbed her arm with his hand and looked up at Reg, a grim look on his face. He mouthed the word "Neos" as he nodded toward the dust cloud that they could now see approaching the ranch. It looked like whatever was coming their way was bearing down on them—and fast.

A chill went up his spine then, a premonition of sorts, and all the worries he'd had before swamped over him. His already rapid heartbeat shot up and the pain that he'd been trying to ignore suddenly seemed unbearable. The edges of his vision were once again turning black, and Reg silently begged the Lord to not let him pass out—or away. Not just yet. He had a family to defend.

After a few deeps gulps of air, the black edges receded, and the pain lessened a bit. "Thank You, Father," he muttered.

"What?" Benito asked him as he continued to hold Amy, now rocking her like a child while the woman wept rivers of tears on his shirt.

He glanced at the man who had already become a very good friend. "Nothing. Just thanking God."

One of Benito's dark eyebrows shot up. "You might want to wait to thank Him, my friend. We have not survived this—" he looked down at Amy. "Em, we have not completed this latest task yet."

Reg nodded in understanding. "I know, but there is always something to be grateful for. That's something I've learned lately," he smiled down at Benito, who returned the smile.

"This is something I am looking forward to learning as well."

Amy seemed to come out of her sobbing stupor, at least briefly, as she sat up and pushed herself out of Benito's arms.

"They took my baby, my Becky," she stated matter-of-factly, suddenly so coherent that Reg was a bit worried over her mental state. But he knew he'd better use her sudden clarity to get the story out while he could.

"Who took her?"

She took a deep breath and then laid her head against Benito's chest. "The Neos," she whispered.

"There was a roadblock. They were checking for travel passes when we were trying to leave Del Rio. Jerry handed them ours, but they wanted to search the RV. When they yanked open the bathroom door, Becky was in there, um, using the facilities, and the soldier grabbed her. She yelled and whacked at him and that's when he started to drag her out of the RV."

She started sobbing again, but continued her story, her voice once more stuttering, broken, as Benito started rocking her once more.

"J-Jerry tried to s-stop them, tried to explain that she was just p-p-peeing, but they wouldn't l-listen. When he g-g-grabbed the arm of the s-soldier who had Becky, the man t-turned around and sh-shot him." The last part was just a whisper.

Amy softly cried against Benito while Reg asked, "And they

killed Becky?" He hated to ask the question, but he needed to know what happened. None of it made sense. The world had truly gone mad, and he again gave silent thanks that he and his family hadn't had to witness the insanity firsthand.

"No, they killed *Ronny*," she wailed and took great gulps of air.

"He j-jumped out of the RV, g-g-going after the s-soldier who had his s-s-sister and who had just sh-shot his daddy. The man t-turned and shot him in the head. He was just a b-baby and now my B-b-becky is gone too! What are those m-m-monsters going t-to d-do to her?"

Benito shushed her again and rocked her a bit harder as she clung to his arm and let her heart break all over his chest.

Reg racked his mind for memories of the boy from the time he and his family had come to the ranch—he'd been about fifteen then, so he would be sixteen or seventeen now—pimply-faced, a member of the entitlement generation and obviously spoiled, full of disdain and disgust at being forced to endure fresh air. In short, the type that Reg had never had patience for, and he remembered he had wanted badly to teach the kid some manners at the time of their visit.

Despite all that, though, the kid certainly didn't deserve to die, and absolutely not at the hands of some sadistic paramilitary organization.

Amy continued to sob in Benito's arms, who continued rocking her, a stricken look on his face. Reg wondered if the man might be thinking of some young men he himself had killed, or had ordered to be killed, and how their mothers might have grieved in the same way. Regret was a bitter pill to swallow.

But that regret could easily fester into self-condemnation and then spiral into self-loathing. He knew Benito had plenty to be sorry for, but as a new believer, he needed to be reminded he was forgiven.

"'If we confess our sins, He is faithful and just to forgive us our sins and to cleanse us from all unrighteousness'," Reg quoted.

Benito smiled with both relief and a hint of embarrassment. "You are reading my mind, my friend."

Reg snorted in response. "Only because I've been there, done that. I beat myself up quite a bit in the beginning of my own walk."

Benito just nodded and then glanced down at Amy. Reg knew what he wanted, and he walked over to gently take Amy's arm and pulled her away from her newfound comforter.

"C'mon, Amy. Let's get you to the house where you can be with the other women. And I need to get our medical people so they can take care of Jerry."

At that, she stiffened and looked up with him, her face red and swollen.

"Jerry?" Her red-rimmed eyes opened wide in shock, as if she were just remembering her injured husband. A look of guilt and shame crossed her face.

"I need to go to him!" She exclaimed as she twisted to release Reg's grasp on her arm. He had to tighten his hold, afraid he might be bruising her.

"No, now, there's nothing you can do. And you know how us men are—seeing you so upset will just make him want to try to fix things, and that's not gonna help nobody. Just come with me to the house and I'll get Charlene, who'll take good care of Jerry."

At that she relaxed a bit, sending one last indecisive look at the RV over her shoulder, but didn't give Reg any problems as they hurried up the hill. He himself glanced back and saw that Benito and some of the other men were forming a heavily armed human wall at the top of the driveway in anticipation of the new guests' arrival.

chapter 17

L IKE A sandstorm ominously sweeping across the desert, the dust cloud from the approaching threat swirled and wafted into the air dozens of feet above the road, making it visible for quite a distance. And the men could see that that distance was closing quickly.

Reg had taken Amy to Nikki and Gina, then told Charlene what happened, and she grabbed her medical bag. The two of them jogged down the hill toward the RV while Reg again tried to ignore the persistent pain in his chest and simultaneously prayed for divine healing.

He stopped at the rock where he'd laid his rifle while Charlene continued on to the RV. Grabbing his weapon, he pushed himself into the "wall" in between Benito and Ben.

A heavy sigh—more a burst of air—came from Ben. "Here we go," he muttered as a vehicle became visible at the bottom of the drive, what looked like a Hummer. But the dust cloud was too large to be coming from just one lone vehicle, and soon a dozen or so more could be seen flying up the road.

The Hummer slid to a stop next to the RV. Reg snorted to himself, thinking that if the ranch drive had been paved, there would be quite a few skid marks on it.

He didn't think the driver had even gotten the thing in park before the doors flew open and soldiers started exiting. The man riding "shotgun" was obviously in charge, as the others seemed to be waiting for his direction.

Reg was reminded of the day not too long ago when Colonel Olson and his group had shown up looking for the missing Neo vehicles, another day the ranch residents were tense with waiting and worrying... and, he hoped this time too, praying.

This wasn't Colonel Olson, though, and Reg thought that the man now approaching them made the overbearing Colonel look like Mister Rogers.

His dark gray uniform was nondescript; as far as Reg could tell, there weren't any markings to indicate rank. In fact, the only markings at all were the Neos' logo on the cuff of his shirt's right sleeve and also on the front of the cap that he wore. Reg again thought about the "mark of the Beast," and of the Scripture that speaks of the mark being placed on the right hand or the forehead. He started wondering then if maybe that mark wasn't something permanent like he'd thought, but the very thing he was staring at— just a simple symbol sewn onto cloth, benign, really, but showing allegiance to the Beast and dooming one's soul for all eternity just for the wearing of it.

The man was dark-skinned—most likely of Mid-Eastern descent—and had eyes the surprising color of topaz, which Reg could see even from the twenty or so feet of distance between them. They were striking against his dark skin, standing out like a neon sign against a black window. Most of his face was covered in a shaggy black beard, but even with that, Reg figured the man would be considered very good-looking by most standards.

But the look on his face took away any fuzzy feelings one might have had toward the soldier. The only term Reg could think of was "chilling." He seriously looked... evil. He stifled a shiver.

Reg had come across people since he'd been saved that gave him the "willies," that made the hair on the back of his neck stand up and his stomach feel fluttery. Nikki had said it was the Spirit warring with the evil within those people. But this was the first time he'd ever just looked at someone and knew without a doubt that they were evil through and through. *Possessed...*

He shuddered slightly and noticed that the men on each side of him seemed to be feeling the same. Benito whispered, "Dios mio," under his breath and Ben apparently decided comic relief was necessary when he muttered, "Oh, look, could it be *Satan?*" with the "Church Lady's" voice.

Reg had to fight back a grin. Leave it to Ben or his wife to find humor in the worst situations. It was usually a trait he appreciated, but right now he just wanted to concentrate on what was happening, while at the same time ignoring the pain which was getting worse by the minute.

The man had paused at the front of his Hummer and was looking back at the other vehicles, giving unspoken directions by making slashing motions with his hand. Men—but surprisingly, no women—silently jumped out of Hummers, jeeps, and out of the backs of trucks and scattered off. Their uniforms were black, also with the Neos' logo on the cuffs and center of their caps. Reg noticed quite a few of them also looked to be Mid-Eastern.

Jeff's words about the Neos from many months before when he'd first come to the ranch ran through his head: *some terrorist groups have joined them.* Looking at the armed, fierce-looking men who were jogging off in different directions, he shuddered.

If terrorists had joined up with the Neos, then there was no stopping them. They were trained to be killers from infancy.

The man in charge watched his men for a moment, then turned to some others and jerked his head toward the RV. Those men rushed to follow the silent orders as they moved toward the open side door.

Reg knew Charlene was in the RV trying to help Jerry and instinct won over common sense. He started toward the vehicle but was brought up suddenly when the dark man with the shining eyes yanked his side arm out of its holster and pointed it at Reg's head.

"Do not move," he practically growled in a thick accent.

Reg realized he was still holding his rifle and slowly lowered it to the ground in front of him, then held his hands up, never taking his eyes off the man holding the gun.

"I have a lady—a nurse—in there trying to take care of a man," he explained, not mentioning the fact that it was this man's soldiers who'd likely shot said man. "I just wanted to give her a hand."

The man's cheek twitched, making his eye squint. He was staring at their group with such blatant hatred that Reg figured if the Holy Spirit gave *them* the willies over this guy, then whatever evil possessed him was apparently doing the same thing on his end.

"I do not care about your wishes." He waved the gun at the line of men.

"Your little group of... protestors... also need to disarm themselves," he said. Reg's own cheek twitched at the obvious attempt to make them feel inferior.

It was Jeff who answered, and Reg was surprised at the vehemence in the young man's voice... and the bravery.

"We won't drop our weapons until you and your men do," he snarled.

A murmur of agreement moved down the line and Reg noticed a hint of uncertainty in the leader's eyes. It was so fleeting, though, that he wondered if he had imagined it.

Ben relieved the tension but shocked everyone when he started speaking to the man in a language they'd never heard. He asked a question and the man's eyes showed frank surprise before answering with a small smile. Then the ferocious mask fell back into place as he holstered his weapon, turning to watch as his men scurried about following his orders. He put his back to the ranch group as if to say, "You don't scare me." It was a proverbial slap in the face.

Reg turned to Ben, eyebrow raised, wanting an answer to how he spoke the man's language. The man knew what he was asking without words being spoken.

"The two tours in Iraq," he quietly explained. "I learned some Arabic and Farsi there." He shrugged. "Guess I have a knack for languages. Too bad the Army didn't pick up on that, cuz they might have given me a better MOS than combat recon."

Reg frowned at him, and Ben gave him a lopsided, somewhat apologetic grin.

"Sorry. I just asked him if they planned on killing us, because it was a holy day for us and it would give us honor to die today."

Reg's face must have showed the shock and horror at Ben's explanation, because he quickly muttered under his breath, "reverse psychology."

Fighting not to roll his eyes, Reg gritted out, "And the answer?"

Ben muttered again, *"It remains to be seen."*

The men who had entered the RV were now carrying a covered body—presumably Ronny's—and if the task hadn't been so heartrending, Reg might have smiled at the way Charlene was bossing the men around. And they surprisingly were following her orders.

He watched as the men carefully laid the body on the ground—most likely per Charlene's orders—between the Hummer and the RV, then entered the vehicle once more. They soon exited, carrying another covered body. *Jerry.* He felt an ache deep in his soul then for Amy—losing both children and her husband in one day was going to be unbearably devastating to the young woman.

The men then left the RV and moved in different directions, leaving Charlene alone, presumably to gather her things. *Guess they don't think she's a threat.* Reg almost laughed again when he thought that Charlene was the one out of all of them they should be most worried about.

It was Benito's turn to mutter under his breath, speaking his thoughts. "Poor woman to lose her child and her husband in one day."

"Both her kids," Reg corrected, since Becky was still unaccounted for. He started to wonder if the girl might be held in one of the vehicles parked on the road in front of them, since presumably this group of Neo soldiers was the same one who had stopped Jerry and Amy. Benito once again seemed to sense his thoughts.

"Do you think—" he began.

"Maybe. Think we can figure out a way to check?"

Even though their conversations were whispered so the as-yet-unnamed-leader wouldn't hear them, Garrett, who stood on Ben's other side, apparently had heard them and handed his rifle to his father. He stepped forward before anyone could stop him.

The men watched in horror as the teen raised his hands and approached the evil-looking leader. Reg put a hand on Ben's shoulder to stop him from going after his son.

"That won't help him now," he said quietly. Ben's shoulder was tense under Reg's hand.

"Excuse me... sir?" Garrett said in a soft voice, gaining the man's attention, who then trained those strange eyes on him, which were narrowed in suspicion.

He didn't speak, but Garrett stopped about ten feet away and continued. "Could I check on my mom? She's still in that RV. She's not very good with... with, uh, death."

The man curled his lip up in an approximation of a grin, although it was more of a sneer. Reg thought the man might be impressed with the kid's bravery, or maybe he was sneering at the thought of a woman being bothered by death. Reg knew his thoughts would have been considered profiling back when the world was concerned with being politically correct, but he also knew that the Middle Eastern culture thought that exact way about women in general... as weaker, ineffective.

When just moments before he'd denied Reg the same request, this time the man jerked his head toward the RV and Ben's shoulder then relaxed slightly under Reg's hand.

"Be quick," he warned as the teen ran off toward the vehicle.

Reg figured the man hadn't seen Charlene, or else he'd be questioning how a seventy-plus-year-old woman could have an eighteen-year-old son. The group watched as Garrett entered the RV. They then had to try to contain their expressions when a few minutes later, Charlene stealthily exited and moved down the row of the Neos' vehicles, looking in windows and into the beds of the trucks, lifting tarps and container lids.

That woman has no fear, Reg thought, mentally shaking his head at her actions. He didn't think Garrett had gone into the RV to ask

Charlene to look for the girl, but figured that the woman had probably asked Garrett what he was up to, then wouldn't let him go himself.

The men who were in a position to see what Charlene was doing collectively sucked in a breath when they saw a young soldier approach her at about the fifth truck back. He said something to her—probably asking what the heck she was doing—and Charlene subtlety moved so that she was behind the truck, thankfully out of sight of the leader, who continued to scan the area while keeping a peripheral view on Reg and the others.

Reg watched as the soldier's expression went from a gruff interrogator's to that of a chastised child. He noticed his shoulders slumping and could almost swear the soldier paled, although that would be difficult to determine from such a distance. But the man slowly lowered the rifle he held at his chest and was alternately shaking his head and then nodding. Reg could picture Charlene standing there, hands on hips, giving the young soldier a dress-down like he'd never had. Reg and the others fought not to laugh, most of them having been a victim of the woman's dress-downs themselves a time or two.

It was just a moment before the soldier turned and walked back the way he had come, looking like a chastised dog with his tail tucked between his legs. Charlene appeared from the back of the truck then and looked toward the ranch men. Reg swore she winked at him before continuing her search down the line.

Apparently, she found the girl in the next to the last vehicle, as the woman suddenly walked quickly back up the line with an extra pair of feet behind her. When they got to the RV Charlene tried to push the girl in the door, but Becky balked on the top step when she turned and saw the sheet-covered bodies lying on the ground. Reg was afraid she was going to cry out, and apparently so was Garrett, when his hand suddenly shot out of the RV door and covered the girl's mouth as he simultaneously jerked her into the vehicle with his other hand.

Thankfully, none of the soldiers seemed to notice anything unusual happening. After just a minute, Garrett exited the RV and loped toward the group. He glanced at the leader who was still standing in the same position.

Garrett addressed the man as he passed. "Thank you, sir. My mother is… uh, sick, in the bathroom. I'm sure she'll be better soon though."

The man gave a barely perceptible nod, a politeness which somewhat surprised Reg. The man so far had been fairly antagonistic, but Reg figured because Garrett was so young, maybe he didn't feel he was a threat.

A movement by the RV drew his attention. A soldier was standing near the door and was looking into the vehicle, saying something. The leader turned then and watched the interaction. Reg thought the man might be able to see into the RV from where he stood and he said a silent prayer asking the Lord to keep Becky out of sight, while at the same time knowing Charlene would have made sure she was.

In just a moment, Charlene stepped down from the RV and right into the personal space of the soldier. She stumbled—or rather, Reg thought she pretended to stumble—and slumped against the soldier, who was forced to drop his rifle to grab the woman. The leader apparently didn't like what he was seeing and started stomping their way while yelling something at the soldier in Arabic. Ben snorted beside him.

He muttered under his breath. "He told the kid to 'drop the old bag' and if he ever saw him release his weapon while they were in a hostile environment again, he would 'cut off his hands.' Never mind the fact that he's not holding a weapon himself. Hypocrite."

Reg whistled slightly through his teeth at the threat. He thought the evil-looking man would follow through with it, and apparently so did the soldier, as he hurried to comply with his leader's orders. Charlene didn't make it easy on the man, leaning heavily on him while he struggled to grab his rifle from where it hung from its strap on his shoulder. He managed to get it and snapped it to his chest just as the leader reached them.

Ben snarled and took a step forward when the leader nabbed Charlene by the arm and yanked her toward him. Reg grabbed him by the shoulder again.

"She's fine. You know she's a tough ol' gal. She sure is hamming it up though. I ain't gonna nominate her for no Emmy, that's for sure."

Ben relaxed a bit and said over his shoulder, "I know she's tough, but that jackass better not hurt her. She *is* an old woman, after all."

Charlene stumbled into the leader then, nearly knocking him to the ground. The man surprisingly didn't shove her away or drop her like he'd ordered his subordinate to do; instead, he led her to the wide bumper of the Hummer and set her down.

Reg let go of his friend's shoulder then and chuckled. "Better never let *her* hear you say she's old. She'd take a switch to your backside, for sure."

Garrett spoke up then. "Reg is right, dad. You know Charlene could kick all their butts and then would probably bandage them up when she was done." He laughed quietly.

"This faking sick was my idea, by the way—she was a little, uh, mad when I told her that I had told the guy in charge that she wasn't good with death. She started giving me a lecture about how many soldiers she'd seen die, but I stopped her when I told her I had to find Becky. Then she got all bossy and wouldn't let me go look for her."

Ben nodded. "Yeah, we figured as much. Is the girl okay?"

Garrett nodded. "She was better when Charlene told her that her daddy ain't dead."

Both men looked at the kid and Reg was sure they both wore the same shocked expression.

Garrett was watching as the leader turned and headed back toward them. He hurried to explain through the side of his mouth.

"He *is* bad off though and Charlene gave him some shot of something to knock him out. Said it slows the heart down to help him not bleed as much. She threw a sheet over him and told the soldiers he was dead, and they didn't even question her, cuz there was so much blood, I guess."

Ben chuckled. "Smart woman."

The angry man had returned to his spot in front of the line of ranch men. His own men were also returning, apparently having searched the ranch and not finding any sign of Amy. One of the soldiers—a blonde-haired, light-skinned, middle-aged man—spoke to his leader in Arabic. Reg wondered if it was a requirement for the Neo soldiers to learn the language.

Ben quietly translated what the soldier was saying. "His name is Alami."

"Salami?" Benito asked in surprise.

Ben chuckled and enunciated more carefully. "His. Name. Is. Alami. Commander Alami. Said they didn't find anyone else except a couple of old ladies playing cards."

Reg gave a barely perceptible nod, knowing that Nikki and Gina would have moved the younger women and children into the hidden cellar if they thought there was danger. He shuddered to think of how cramped they all would be in the small space. The kids were probably terrified too, and the ladies and teens most likely had their hands full trying to keep them quiet.

The "old ladies" they found were probably those who couldn't negotiate the ladder into the cellar. Or else—and most likely—it was Emily and Sandy, Charlene's friends who matched her for stubbornness and tenacity. Those two would have refused to cower and hide. Reg could almost hear Emily saying, "What are they gonna do to us? Kill us? Heck, we already got us one foot in the grave as it is."

The commander waved the soldier off and then turned to the group once more. "So, it seems that you are harboring a fugitive. Tell us where she is and I might let your—" he waved his hand with a dismissive gesture, "—little group here live."

Jeff spoke up before anyone else could. "There isn't anyone else here." He waved at the line of men, much as the man in front of them had.

"There's just us and the old ladies you found." He lied so smoothly that Reg was a bit shocked. The kid had always seemed so strait-laced.

The man snorted, obviously not believing them. "And where is the driver of the RV? The woman."

Jeff shrugged. "There wasn't anyone else." He nodded at the two "bodies" lying on the ground.

"Just the dead kid and the man, who I'm guessing died right after he parked the RV. If there was a woman with them, they must have dumped her off somewhere on the way here."

Commander Alami narrowed his eyes, and Reg could almost see the wheels turning in his head, trying to figure out the next move. He looked very intelligent, shrewd and calculating, and Reg thought he was someone they wouldn't want for an enemy. But that was exactly what he was.

He reminded Reg of one of those professional chess players, whose sharp eyes and even sharper mind calculated his opponent's every possible move and had already figured out his countermove before any decision had been made.

"Then perhaps she is hiding in the vehicle," he said, and Reg could sense Garrett stiffening, knowing that Becky was still in the RV.

"No one else was in there," he offered. "My mother would have said something."

The man narrowed his eyes at the teen and stepped closer. "And I am supposed to believe you?" He snorted, then turned to one of the soldiers standing at attention behind him and said something in Arabic.

Ben didn't translate this time, as Alami had moved close enough he would hear any whispering, but Ben stiffened and Reg knew it was an order to search the RV. Apparently, Charlene had also learned Arabic from her time in the Gulf Wars, as she immediately stood from the bumper of the Hummer and ran toward the RV, leaping in through the door before anyone spotted her. *Dang, that ol' gal can move!* Reg thought.

Garrett took a step forward and immediately Alami—who obviously had amazing peripheral vision, or hearing—whipped his head around while simultaneously unholstering his weapon. He trained it on the boy, aiming it right between his eyes. Garrett put his hands up and froze in place.

Apparently, the sight of your child being targeted by an evil-looking man brought out protective instincts in a parent, as Ben literally growled like a bear protecting its cub and charged the commander, who turned his weapon at the movement and fired.

All hell broke loose then as the Neo soldiers and the ranch men all started shouting and shooting while running for cover. Reg paused for a split second while his mind registered what was happening. Somewhere in the back of his mind, he thought it was amazing that time really did seem to slow when chaos erupted. He watched as the Neos ran to take cover behind their vehicles, while all his own men ran to the boulders at their back.

We're outmanned and outgunned, he thought as he watched the fighting. He knew that he was standing in the middle of the path of bullets flying, but for some reason he couldn't make himself move.

A movement in his peripheral vision made him turn to his left where Ben was holding his son upright. Both had blood all over them and Ben looked like he was about to stagger and lose his grip on Garrett. Reg then grabbed one of each of their arms and dragged them toward the largest boulder that lined the top of the drive.

Ben was shot, but he said it was just his shoulder.

"Help Garrett!" he yelled over the gunfire.

Garrett had blood oozing from his right side and Reg had very little medical knowledge to know if the wound was in an area with a vital organ. He yanked his jacket off and pressed it to the wound, knowing he had to at least stop the blood flow. Ben held his shoulder with his good hand while he watched in horror as his son's blood dripped onto the ground.

The gunfire was deafening, and Reg thought again how the ranch was seriously outgunned. It was a fact they had always known—that they really couldn't defend themselves against the Neos. If the Neos decided to attack, then they knew they would die.

Reg turned his face to the sky and fervently prayed that their men would be spared, that the ranch, and especially their wives and the children, would live through this. He begged God like he'd never begged Him for anything before.

It was a quick prayer, like the petitions that had been lifted up over countless centuries by those finding themselves in impossible life-threatening situations, but Reg felt suddenly calmer, and he thanked God in advance for saving them.

Ben scooted over to them and held Reg's jacket to Garrett's wound with his good hand.

"They need you!" Ben yelled as he nodded toward their friends who were frantically trying to hold off the Neos' attack. Since there wasn't anything else he could do for Garrett, Reg nodded. He was then wishing he had grabbed his rifle, which was still lying on the ground where he had laid it.

He looked around for a weapon, then had a bit of a tug-of-war with Garrett over the rifle he still gripped in his hands. The kid was bleeding profusely, but still refused to release his weapon. Reg was proud of his soon to be son-in-law. The boy had some grit.

He finally released the weapon and Reg got up on his knees to find a good position. It was then that he realized with a great deal of horror that Nikki, Gina and some of the other ladies were running down the hill toward them. Toward the mayhem and flying bullets, and, unless the Lord decided to save them, toward almost certain death.

He waved frantically at them, telling them to go back. There were about ten ladies in all, but they ignored him and continued running down the hill. He noted belatedly that they were all carrying rifles and shotguns and some of the ladies had paused mid-stride, dropping to one knee to shoot toward the Neo soldiers, while the others behind them fired over their heads. Somewhere in the back of his mind, Reg wondered where they'd learned that technique. It looked like something he'd seen in a Revolutionary War movie, something the British had done.

The ladies then spread out to take cover with the men behind the various boulders and Nikki and Gina dropped behind the boulder with their men. Gina surprised him by doing a quick triage of her husband and son, while berating them at the same time.

"What the heck do you think you're doing, getting shot like this?

Dang it, now I'm gonna have to scrub your clothes with baking soda, not to mention having to sew up bullet holes and you *know* how much I hate to sew!"

Reg figured the woman was making light of the situation to keep her men from worrying, or maybe she was doing it to placate herself. Either way, it did lighten the situation somewhat and Ben even managed a slight laugh. Reg was amazed at her strength. Her voice wasn't even wavering.

With Gina there to take care of the men, Reg moved to the side of the boulder and started shooting at the soldiers who were hugging the left side of the RV, aware that Nikki had moved to the opposite side of the boulder to do the same.

With every pull of the trigger, a bit of guilt went through him. He wasn't shooting at bullfrogs like he was fond of doing at the pond on warm summer evenings. And this wasn't a hunt for food, like shooting at cottontails or mule deer that would fill their bellies. No target practice here, with hay bales painted with a bright red bullseye.

These were human beings, living, breathing, God-created beings. Beings that had a chance to have their souls saved, to become one of God's very own. How many times had Nikki said those words to him when he'd griped about some jerk? "But honey, he could be one of God's kids, just like you or me and maybe he just doesn't know it yet."

Suddenly, a soft—yet imposing—voice filled his mind, bringing an overwhelming reassurance.

These are our enemies. They have doomed themselves by choosing to take the Beast's mark. They are never going to be Mine. Defend your family.

A feeling of determination filled him then and he prayed for a steady hand and a sure aim as he continued pulling the trigger, no longer seeing the men as humans, but rather just as moving targets.

Out of the corner of his eye he saw Charlene and Becky running toward them from the RV with their heads down. Charlene had the girl by the upper arm, and she was running them in a zigzag pattern. Reg almost smiled at the woman's tenacity while he increased his barrage, hoping to cover them until they could reach the boulder. He managed to hit two of the soldiers, but one of the soldiers that fell he knew he didn't shoot, and he realized then that Nikki was also giving Charlene and Becky cover. He wondered then how his soft-hearted wife who couldn't shoot a jackrabbit without crying felt about killing another human being and hoped the Lord had given her the same reassurance he'd just received.

They reached the rock safely and Charlene pulled the girl down next to Ben and Garrett. The woman then immediately assessed the men and started tearing Garrett's clothes to see his wound. Reg knew they were in the best hands they were going to be in for the moment, so he motioned to Nikki to tell her he was moving to the boulder next to them that Benito, Jeff and two of the ladies were behind. He ignored the frantic shaking of his wife's head. He needed to find a better angle, because they'd already shot all the soldiers on their side, but those who were hiding behind the line of vehicles were still a problem.

Benito saw what Reg was planning, so he started firing at the enemy nonstop. Reg realized then that the man had managed to get one of the semi-automatic rifles they had, and he was very grateful for that fact as he crouched down and ran toward the boulder.

Once he was safe, he looked back at Nikki, who had an irate look on her face that said, "just wait until I get you alone..." He grinned back at her, then twisted around and began shooting over the top of the rock.

Commander Alami was across from Reg, behind the Hummer he'd arrived in. The man suddenly moved to the other side and began shooting toward Nikki and the others. Reg saw red when he realized the man was shooting at his wife. He was terrified she was going to get hit, as she was the only one defending their position, since Charlene and Becky were unarmed and were both trying to bandage Garrett.

His heart racing at the thought of losing his wife, Reg stood then, hoping to draw the man's attention away from her. He fired at the commander, although he couldn't get a clear shot from his position. The bullets ricocheted off the side of the Hummer and hit the RV. Reg then realized he was in danger of hitting Jerry, who was still lying on the ground under the sheet where he'd been left between the two vehicles. If the man wasn't dead, Reg certainly didn't want to be the one responsible for finishing him off.

Alami saw Reg then and stepped away from the Hummer and

turned to fire back toward him. Reg ducked down behind the boulder once more and then gasped as a sudden pain in his chest nearly consumed him. It was much, much worse than what he'd been feeling before. He was vaguely aware of Benito and the others shouting with excitement and realized someone must have shot the commander.

Reg couldn't breathe because it felt like there was a truck parked on his chest. The edges of his vision were again turning black and now there were flashing spots added to the mix. He wanted desperately to help the others, needed to defend his family, the ranch, but for some reason he just couldn't move.

A voice was calling to him from somewhere in the distance. "Reg! Reg! What's wrong? Were you shot?" It was Nikki. She sounded like she was in a long tunnel, at the far end of it, and was yelling to him across the distance. Someone was shaking him and he forced his eyes open.

Nikki's face was inches from his own. There was a frantic worry in her hazel eyes that were filling with tears.

"Don't you dare leave me here!" She yelled and cried at the same time.

"I can't do this without you! Don't... don't..."

Reg reached up to touch her face, the face he adored, the face she lamented was wrinkled and weather-worn no matter how many times he'd told her she was the most beautiful woman he'd ever seen. He had to try to let her know everything would be okay, that he was fine and just needed to rest.

But he realized it was a good thing he was robbed of breath and incapable of speech. He didn't want his last words to the love of his life to be a lie.

And then the world went black.

epilogue

HE WAS standing beside a gently flowing brook, soft grass tickling his feet. His bare feet.

Since when do I walk around bare-footed?

It felt good though, somewhat freeing, and he walked a little way along the brook. The grass was so soft, like silk, and a green like he'd never seen. And the sky! Such a brilliant blue, like the ocean water near a white beach, but more… much more blue.

Blue? Green? But I'm colorblind. How can I know these colors?

He walked a little farther along the brook. There weren't any stickers or rocks, nothing to hurt his tender feet. Nikki had always teased him about being a tenderfoot, someone who wouldn't even walk barefoot in the house, not without at least socks on.

Nikki… my wife.

Where was she? He turned then, hoping to see her walking behind him. But there wasn't anyone there in the meadow where he stood. He felt confused, a little lost.

But then a soft voice called to him from near the brook and he turned to see who it was. A man—who hadn't been there just a moment before—was leaning against a tree, smiling at him. He knew immediately who it was.

Jesus… Yeshua… Savior… the Christ… Messiah.

The names of the Lord ran through his head then, all the names he'd ever heard, and some he never recalled hearing. He wondered what name was the proper one, what He would want to be called. But he knew that it didn't matter. He was Him... the Son of God.

"Lord," he whispered, "it's You."

His smile was gentle. "Yes."

A return smile crossed his face as he realized where he was, and Who he was with.

"So, I'm dead then? This is heaven?"

He waved around him, toward the meadow and the brook, the brilliant colors almost blinding him with their intensity. This had to be the ultimate paradise. It was so glorious.

The Lord smiled again, the look on His face amused but kind, and pushed away from the tree to walk alongside the brook, apparently knowing he'd follow. He did.

"No, it's not. This is... what you might call a hallway. A foyer."

"But I'm dead, right?"

He smiled once more. "You're mostly dead," He answered in a voice that sounded just like Miracle Max from *The Princess Bride*.

He laughed. The Lord had a sense of humor—he knew it! He'd always said that He *had* to have a sense of humor, because He'd created armadillos after all.

They walked along not speaking and he was struck by how quiet it was. Only the sound of the water trickling over the smooth stones lying along the bottom of the brook broke the silence.

The Lord was a tall, dark man—His height and build matched his own. Those pictures of the frail, pale, blue-eyed blonde Savior that graced so many churches and homes certainly hadn't gotten it right, not even close.

But somewhere in the back of his mind was the realization that he wasn't really in his body, that earthly container for his soul. Maybe souls—or whatever he was walking around as—weren't limited by height or weight. They might just all be the same size.

There was a question he had to ask, but he was a little afraid to voice it. Before he could work himself up to feel real fear, though, a feeling of calming peace washed over him. He opened his mouth. Or maybe he just thought the question. *Do souls even have mouths?*

"So... do I get to go to heaven?"

The Lord laughed again and actually turned to give him a playful little punch in the arm, like a friend would.

He is my Friend.

"Do you really think you'd be here walking with Me, talking with Me, if you didn't 'get to go to heaven'?"

The Lord—the Savior of the world—rolled His eyes. He laughed out loud at that. Nikki would love to see that.

Nikki...

"Lord, my wife... is she okay? I mean, I left her back there... the fighting..."

The Lord's face turned somber then. "Nikki is fine. The others too. I heard your prayers and answered them. Remember? 'Ask anything in My Name...' You asked, I delivered."

He said the last part in a voice that sounded like a bad television commercial on late-night TV, and he laughed.

"You're really funny, Lord."

The grin was back in place. "Thank you, thankyouverymuch. I'll be here all week."

They both laughed and he was struck by how much "pop culture" the Lord knew. Of course, He knew everything... He knew everything, and yet, here He was, walking and talking with him as a friend. *And heaven will be so much better...*

A nagging thought wouldn't let go of his mind, though, and he felt a question burning, begging to be asked.

"Lord? I don't mean to seem... ungrateful... I mean, I always wanted to end up with You, in heaven and all, but—"

He nodded as He interrupted. "I know. That's why you're just mostly dead. You feel drawn to go back because you haven't fulfilled your purpose in this final time. If it were your time to die, you wouldn't still be thinking of earthly things."

He felt almost guilty then, like he was a naughty child for clinging to the "former things."

"It's just that... Nikki... and the others... they sort of look to me—"

The Lord laughed and stopped then, putting His hand on his shoulder. "I know. Believe Me, I know. Remember?" He tapped His temple.

"I know everything," He said with another grin as He turned to continue walking alongside the brook.

They walked a short distance when He suddenly commanded, "Look down."

He complied and was startled once more to realize his feet were bare. He knew they were bare because of the feel of the grass, but to see them was somewhat shocking. But they didn't really look like his feet; where was the crooked toe from when the mule stepped on his foot? And the thickened and slightly yellow nails? These feet were too... *perfect*.

The Lord laughed. "I wasn't asking you to critique your pedicure," He quipped, reminding him that He knew every thought. "I wanted you to notice that you can *see* your feet. That's something you haven't been able to do in a long time."

He jumped when the Lord turned to pat his stomach. His flat stomach. *Weird*. "You're now in a perfected form, how you were designed to be." He chuckled then.

"Paul rightly said in his letter to the Corinthians that the body is a temple. But you, my friend, built a cathedral. When you go back, you need to knock off a few rooms in that building, all right?"

He laughed as he nodded his agreement and thought his face should be red with embarrassment, but somehow he also knew that this new form—this "perfected body" as the Lord called it—wouldn't show embarrassment. It seemed negative emotions had no place here.

They continued walking as the Lord continued. "Now you're going to go back because you have a purpose to fulfill. The time on earth is coming to an end and I have many, many of My own who are struggling to survive. Many won't. Many will be martyred, as you know. The famines, the plagues and pestilence, wars… those are coming soon. Millions will die.

"But those who believe in Me, those who will survive this time—and those who aren't Mine yet, but soon will be—they need someone to lead them, to protect them, help them survive. That is your purpose."

I felt shocked at that. *Me? Why me? I'm nobody.*

He interrupted my self-depreciation, His voice chiding, once again reminding me that He knew everything, including all thoughts.

"You're not 'nobody'. You're MY child, MY son. You're a prince, the son of the Most High King! You, and many others, have been chosen to be warriors for Me. Warriors for Christ. You will protect, you will fight, you will defend. The fighting is going to increase a hundredfold. The enemy will win many battles, but WE will win the war."

He grinned back at him then. "Haven't you read the book?"

The story continues...

excerpt from *Surviving the End,* Book 2 in *The End* Series:

NIKKI WASN'T in the tunnel, and she wasn't at the base of the hill. Reg gritted his teeth against the worry and tried to console himself with Ben's reassurance that she was most likely waiting for them in the bunker, ready to give them a piece of her mind for taking so long.

From the base of the hill where the tunnel exited into Mexico, it was quite a distance to the boulders that hid the entrance to Benito's bunker. Even though there were a fair number of sandy hills and sparse trees that offered cover, there was still the chance that they'd be spotted by any soldier on the ranch who happened to be looking south. But it was a chance they had to take. Reg made a mental note to make tunnel digging a priority in the coming weeks. They absolutely had to connect the ranch's tunnel to the bunker to avoid this type of situation.

When they reached the boulders hiding the bunker entrance, Ben pulled the heavy metal door open and Reg dragged Jeff inside. He was still unconscious, and Reg was starting to really worry about him. They needed to find Charlene or one of her helpers fast.

The bunker's west entrance had a flight of steps leading down into a narrow hallway. Unlike the tunnel from the ranch to Mexico, this tunnel-turned-bunker was completely concreted. Even the walls and ceiling were lined with concrete panels. While it was certainly safer than their tunnel that could only claim wooden beams across the dirt ceiling as a safety feature, the concrete was cold, both physically and psychologically.

"At least there's good lighting in here," Reg said with a huff as they both struggled to drag Jeff's limp body down the stairs and to the hallway that headed toward the rest of the complex.

"Yeah. Emilio said Benito had installed solar panels for lighting the tunnel when he was gonna use it for drug running. Then he added backup diesel generators he got from a military surplus auction after he decided to make the bunker."

They made it to the end of the hall and turned into a wider hall that had doors lining the length of it. Thankfully, they knew where the medical room was from previous visits. Reg was contemplating Ben's comments about the lighting as they made their way toward where they hoped Charlene, or at least Julie or Rayanne, would be.

"You know, I need to talk to Benito about the solar panels. I mean, wouldn't it be a little suspicious to have solar panels in the middle of nowhere? If I saw something like that, I'd sure be investigating what the heck was being powered."

Ben was quiet for a minute and paused outside the medical room door, which was closed. He stood with his hand on the knob and looked like he was thinking. Ben rarely made a comment he didn't think over a dozen times first. Gina always said he ran through every possible scenario and outcome in his head and had joked that it taught her to never ask him what he wanted for dinner.

"Yeah, I think you're right. If the Neos spot those panels, they're gonna investigate."

He turned the knob then and they entered the room, which was deserted. After hauling Jeff up onto one of the hospital beds, they pulled the sides up in case he rolled over and went in search of Charlene... and Nikki.

"She's probably in the cantina getting something to drink," Ben suggested when he sensed Reg's worry over his wife. Reg snorted at his perceptiveness.

"Hopefully."

She wasn't in the cantina, but Julie was and when they told her about Jeff, she ran off to find Charlene. Leeann, who had been sitting nearby at a table with Amy and Anna, gasped and jumped up when she overheard what they told Julie and she ran out of the cantina.

Ben watched her exit, then turned to Reg with a raised eyebrow. Reg shrugged. "Probably gonna have another wedding soon."

"Anybody see my wife?" Reg said in a loud voice. There were at least fifty people in the cantina. He figured they thought they were waiting out a "visit" from the Neos and weren't interested in settling down in the rooms they'd been assigned. He didn't really have the desire to tell them that they likely wouldn't be going back to the ranch—at least, not any time soon.

No one claimed to have seen her and Reg was starting to feel a bit of panic. He ran back out into the hall and headed toward the dorm room he and Nikki were assigned to. Taking a deep breath and saying a quick prayer before he opened the door, he was disappointed to find she wasn't in there either.

Their room was larger than most, as Benito insisted they have "luxury accommodations." He and Nikki had both argued against that, saying they were certainly not entitled to anything larger, but Benito had insisted. And since it was his facility and his generosity that they were there in the first place, they'd reluctantly agreed.

Even though it was larger, it still had just the bare necessities—a double bed, one night stand with a lamp and a wardrobe closet. None of the rooms had private restrooms, but there were two very large restrooms with showers close by. They'd already designated "men's" and "women's" facilities.

After checking the restroom by knocking on the door, then opening it a crack and yelling her name—and after apologizing profusely to Esperanza, who'd been in one of the toilet stalls at the time—Reg was in full-blown panic. He bumped into Gina and Ben, who'd filled his wife in on what was going on.

"She never showed up here," Gina said, her brown eyes filled with worry for her best friend. "I kept waiting for her, but she never came. I just assumed she was with you guys."

"She was," Reg groaned as he ran a hand down his face. "She insisted on helping us get Jeff back from the Neos, and the last we saw her, she was crawling through the connecting tunnel. I know she made it at least to the front porch, though, cuz she rang the bell."

His voice turned anguished. "Dear God, please don't let tell me she was captured!" The thought of his wife in the hands of those monsters—men who had well-deserved reputations for gang rape and horrifying torture—made him sick and his skin literally crawled with the panic he felt.

Surviving the End, Book 2 in The End Series, available on Amazon now!

More books from VJ Dunn!

Beginning the End Book 1 of The End Series

My name is Nikki. Just a country gal with no real mad skills. But after the global economic collapse, my husband Reg and I found ourselves leading a ragtag group of survivors, those who managed to escape the cities...and the Neos. The Neo Geo Task Force is the new government. The new world order. They were supposed to be the law of the land, the peacekeepers. They were anything but.

Surviving the End Book 2 of The End Series

This time, our present, was the end of the age. Or, at least the slippery downward slope heading toward the end. My name is Nikki and with my husband Reg we tried our best to protect our growing group of survivors. Everything that happened had been foretold in ancient texts, some written long before Christ walked the earth. But even knowing the prophesy didn't completely prepare us for just how difficult those times would be.

Embracing the End Book 3 of The End Series

While the rest of the world was celebrating the establishment of the "new world order," we were struggling just to eat. We fought to live, to exist. We never could have imagined just how bad things would get. But betrayal was our worst enemy. The Lord never left us, though. His promises kept us going, gave us direction. He led us and guided our steps, even when those steps took us right up to the Neos' doorstep. And then we were no longer fighting. We were storming the gates of Hell.

Conquering the End Book 4 of The End Series

The hunt continues. But now the entire world is after us. We are Followers of The Way—believers of the Christ. Our enemy, the Neos, have morphed into something even worse than the demon-possessed Satan minions they were. Now they rule the world and their quest is to annihilate anyone who stands in their way. Which means us. We know that Christ wins in the end; we just have to survive until then. We just hope the last day comes quickly, because the earth is going to Hell.

The Releasing Book 1 in the Reign of the Lion Series

The End Series continues with Allie and the Remnants in the Millennial Period. It's been nearly one thousand years since the Tribulation, and it's supposed to be a time of peace. But Allie is up to her eyeballs trying to deal with backtalking Remnants, arrogant angels, a joking Abba and an annoying growing affection for her right-hand man. And of course, there is the small fact that Lucifer is going to be unleashed on the world soon…

The Tempting Book 2 in the Reign of the Lion Series

While Satan oozes his fake charm to gather all those who might turn to the dark side, Allie has her hands full — an unruly team of Remnants, a man who keeps her teeth grinding and hormones raging, a pet bobcat who couldn't keep her nose out of Allie's business, angel warriors who insist on doing things their own way…and, oh yeah, that pesky angel rebellion to deal with.

The Gathering Book 3 in the Reign of the Lion Series

Never in a million years would Allie have ever guessed that she'd be part of Lucifer's tempting of those born in the Millennium. But after being captured by the gorgeous Prince of All Things Slimy, she was not only a part of it… she was the biggest tool in the evil dude's arsenal. By keeping her bound under the paralysis power Allie had come to despise, Lucifer assumed she was completely under his control. Powerless. Helpless. That was his biggest mistake yet.

The Consuming Book 4 in the Reign of the Lion Series

Allie isn't thrilled with her new assignment. It means putting herself in danger of being captured by Lucifer once again. But this time, she won't be a captive--she'll be an example. She'll do her best to follow Abba's wishes, but she knows it's not going to be easy. Witnessing to Lucifer's army is not exactly going to be a church picnic. To top it off, she has the upcoming war with said army on her mind. At best, they'll be able to win the army to Abba's side, to salvation. At worst? Allie's head will become Lucifer's new war helmet.

Mama's Heart Book 1 in The Tapestry Series

Misty is shocked to learn she's pregnant, and out of wedlock too. But all things work out, until a fateful day when her entire world is turned upside down. Misty becomes bitter, angry, and questions everything she ever knew about God. But a surprise visit from a stranger helps her put life into perspective and to see God's handiwork in weaving the tapestry of her life.

Unanswered Prayers Book 2 in The Tapestry Series

Steve Tyler is the typical mid-western kid...a little nerdy, very smart, with a great future. Through a series of life-changing events and "unanswered" prayers, Steve turns his back on God and turns to drugs for his comfort. Homeless, friendless and hopeless where every day is a struggle just to survive, Steve finds himself in such a deep valley that the only way up is by taking God's hand.

Here, Hold My Beer, Confessions of the Common Sense Challenged Male

Stories that will break your funny bone and keep you in stitches...and you won't have to go to the ER! Humor satire about the dumb things that guys will sometimes do. You know, those decisions that usually start with a trip to the liquor store and end up with a trip to the hospital. If you like to hear those "chill around the fire pit, guzzling six packs and spitting tobacco at the flames" kind of stories, this book is for you!

Road Trip Revival Series, Seniors Road Trip (and by "senior," we mean well-seasoned!) 8 Books completed.

When you lose everything you have... you might just gain the world. In the Road Trip Revival Series, Jean finds herself just a bit lost after the death of her husband. Suddenly alone—and lonely—she doesn't quite know where her place in the world is. But when she hears a pastor talk about a revival, something changes.

Now she's on a mission from God.

Follow VJ on Social Media:

Amazon as VJ Dunn

Facebook @vjdunnauthor

Instagram @authorvjdunn

Twitter @authorvjdunn

Website vjdunn.com

Made in the USA
Middletown, DE
09 September 2021